CW01669790

THE UPRISING

TWIN FLAMES (BOOK 2)

RACHEL HENKE

RED BALLOON PRESS

DEDICATION

For Eve - for always believing in me

TWIN FLAMES SERIES

Book 1: Twin Flames

Book 2: The Uprising

Book 3: The Runner

Book 4: The Covenant

"And when one of them meets with his other half, the actual half of himself, the pair are lost in an amazement of love and friendship and intimacy, and one will not be out of the other's sight even for a moment."

Plato

A NOTE TO MY DEAR READERS

I hope you enjoy this second novel in the Twin Flames series.

I used old style language sparingly to infuse the period flavour but keep it easy to read.

The Uprising is a work of fiction, but I spent considerable time on background reading and research to create an atmospheric and authentic backdrop for the multiple historical timelines. I also researched and talked to people who experienced the mind-blowing Twin Flame phenomenon in real life.

Creating this historical time travel series is the most challenging writing I've done, because there is a potential knock-on effect for every action in the interlinking timelines. I have done my best to make the story as believable as possible, within the fantastical time travel context. I don't, however, make any apologies for the intensity of Cara and George's Twin Flame love. *It's a wild thing!*

Our Red Balloon Press publishing team, made every effort to create a typo-free and beautiful book for your pleasure, but if the occasional error slipped through, please email me so we can fix it. I love hearing from readers and you can write to me anytime with your thoughts about the book at: Rachel@Rachelhenke.com

If you enjoy this novel, I'd appreciate you leaving a review on Amazon and recommending it to your friends. Independent authors thrive on good reviews and word of mouth because we don't have a big powerhouse publishing machine behind us. With your support, I will write many more novels.

With much love and gratitude,

Rachel

www.Rachelhenke.com

CHAPTER 1

York - Present day

Cara and George had lived together for the past year, ever since George gathered his nerve to knock on the cottage door after the timeline reset and he lost his old life.

That was the day their lives changed forever.

It had been a wonderful year. There was no more heart-wrenching double-life secrecy, which was a great relief.

They took their time to decompress and relax into the quiet, idyllic rhythm of their new life together after the stress of their intense on-off love affair and manic time travel adventures.

A few months later, they married, surrounded by an intimate circle of family and friends. Eddie Makepeace, the five-hundred-year time traveller, and Sylvia Skye, their trusted psychic advisor, were amongst the small number of guests.

The bride and groom exchanged their vows underneath a spring floral wedding canopy in the gardens of *Willow Manor*

Hotel. They both agreed there was no more perfect time or place for Cara to once again become Mrs Cavendish. Tears spilled down her cheeks when she looked into George's dark shining eyes. Her voice choked with emotion when she said, 'I do.'

After an elegant reception in the grand old hall, Cara and George said farewell, waved, and blew kisses before rattling away down the majestic, willow tree lined drive in George's olive-green sports car.

'I don't fancy rattling all the way to the airport with Eddie's tin cans in tow,' George said, and he pulled over by the gates and jumped out to remove them.

They spent a magical month in Corfu in a villa overlooking the sea and were enchanted by the soothing island lifestyle. As the month drew to a close, they grew edgy and apprehensive.

'I wish we could stay here forever,' said Cara, as they strolled hand in hand along the seashore, one afternoon. Their sun-bronzed toes left prints in the golden sand before shallow blue-green waves lapped and gurgled over their feet and erased any signs of life.

Upon their return to York, with serendipitous timing, George's position as a company director of an import-export company, in Seville, which he had inherited with his new life after the timeline reset, ended abruptly.

Cara and George, who were desperately sorry the honeymoon was over, holed up at Rose Cottage and continued to spend almost every moment in each other's company as they figured out what George would do next. Their relationship had been tested in extreme circumstances, and they had emerged stronger than ever, secure in their love.

Cara decided she was long overdue a sabbatical from her consultancy work and made a bold decision to take a year off to write a follow-up book to *The Rise and Fall of the Tudor Dynasty* and to prolong the blissful period.

On the warm, summer mornings, Cara settled down to write in the garden at the table with her laptop, in the shade of a yellow sun umbrella. George kept her topped up with freshly brewed coffee and wandered out to join her mid-morning and flop in a nearby sunchair. He was a comforting, yet unobtrusive presence, flicking through the pages of his newspaper or reading a book, as she tapped on her keyboard.

Occasionally she would look up from the screen and he would catch her eye and they'd share a look. Not everything had to be spoken aloud. The long, lazy summer days full of sunbathing, snoozing, love-making, and dining in the garden, followed by leisurely evening river walks, rolled by.

'If you'd told me last year that everything would work out for us perfectly like this, I would never have believed it,' said Cara.

They lay entwined in each other's arms, early one morning, cherishing the precious still moments before York stirred. The only sound they could hear was the gentle cooing of a wood pigeon in the old oak tree which towered above the bedroom window.

'Well, at the risk of sounding like a bit of a know-it-all, I did tell you it would work out,' said George.

Cara smiled and traced her fingers across his chest.

'But I never would have believed I was a time traveller,' he continued.

'I've grown used to it; although it's easier now we're together all the time. We're actually living a normal life.' Cara paused, and looked up at him, her smile coy. 'I know it sounds corny, but I still pinch myself.'

'Trust me, there's nothing normal about our life.' He kissed her nose. 'I'm so happy you married me here, too,' he said and then dropped a trail of featherlight kisses onto the sensitive skin behind her ear, and Cara shivered.

'Me too, darling—it was the most wonderful day of my life. Although, I would love you until the end of all timelines, married or not.'

George pulled her closer as the familiar fire of lust ignited between them.

'I love that you still believe in marriage, you old romantic,' she said.

'Less of the old.' He kissed her mouth, first gently and then with increasing urgency, crushing her lips as though he would devour her. She pushed into his warm chest and returned his kiss with equal passion. He pressed against her; his desire growing as he ached to satisfy his burning need, and they melted into each other's touch, becoming one.

Sex between them had always been explosive. There was no need for discussion; they were sexually compatible in a way neither of them had experienced before. Each intuitively understood exactly what the other needed to fulfil both their soul and their physical desires.

Cara had wondered whether this kind of contentment with another human being was possible; now she knew for certain it was.

Some couples were lucky in love, while others had to go through hell to be together.

Most never even suspected love like this existed.

Sylvia had explained that people rarely met their Twin Flame because they weren't on earth simultaneously. She said you were fortunate to meet someone from the same soul group, but it was unusual to meet *the one.*

As romantic as it sounded, Cara had learned the brutal way that the path to Twin Flame union, although breath taking, was not for the fainthearted. Twin Flames mirrored each other's soul. They were karmic teachers, and there was much to learn.

Cara was relieved they were now *in union,* as the mystics called it, and all of that dreadful heartache was behind them.

Wasn't it?

Willow Manor, York, 1536 - Tudorville

Cara blinked as she gazed out the window and admired the dense woody mass of willow trees that anointed the stream and snaked through the estate to the rear of the regal Tudor manor house. The autumn sunlight cast a glittery sheen onto the luminous green of the hedgerows and reflected off the gently bubbling water.

Here she was back in Tudorville with no warning. One minute she was quietly working at the kitchen table at Rose Cottage, salivating at the thought of George's delicious spaghetti, and the next, she was transported to her favourite room in the Cavendish family home, Willow Manor.

Cara's eyes moved away from the window and surveyed the library. Her gaze rested on the oak writing desk with the ornate dainty drawer handles. The delicately carved legs stood in one corner of the elegant room, next to a book-lined wall and overlooking the vast gardens.

Happy memories of writing her correspondence pirouetted through her mind, and she took several deep breaths. Despite her agitation at abruptly being pulled back in time, a sudden comforting wave of déjà vu washed over her. She adored Willow Manor, and besides, she would finally get to be with their children again. Nerves wrestled in the pit of her stomach as she wondered what they had been up to since she left.

She had hoped her time travelling days were over and her and George's karmic challenges resolved. She'd prayed that their Twin Flame mission was complete.

Well, so much for that. She would have to make the best of it. How wrong she had been. There'd been a phone call and then *whoosh,* the vortex swept her back five hundred years. Was it the call that reactivated her time travel? There had been an instant sense of *here we go again,* but that was it. She'd known in her bones she was about to go, and there had been no time for even a quick goodbye. She'd forgotten how unsettling and disorientating time travel was.

The library door swung open, interrupting her reverie, and George Cavendish entered in a flurry; the handsome features she adored composed into an uncharacteristically disgruntled expression. His furrowed brow framed his brown eyes, and Cara's heart leapt at the sight of him. She'd missed Tudorville George. She glimpsed an official-looking letter clasped between his fingers.

Cara stood and quickly covered the distance between them, launching herself into her beloved's arms. 'There you are. I've missed you.'

George embraced Cara with one arm. A look of amusement played over his face while he attempted to hold his wife steady, and the thick parchment of the letter flapped about over her shoulder. 'You're a funny one, my love. It can't be over ten minutes since I left you. You're acting as though you haven't seen me for a year.'

'Yes, I suppose I am. Silly me. What the devil is going on?' Cara said, almost too scared to ask, but determined to discover as much as possible about the current state of affairs in Tudorville.

'Well, I must say everything was splendid until this letter arrived, delivered by the king's own messenger, no less.'

Mention of the king was enough to turn her skin white and send icy shivers whistling down her spine.

'The king? What does he want of you now? Pray tell me all is well, and it's only an exchange of pleasantries.'

'Alas, it is not. I wish it were so, but we suspected it would only be a matter of time before one or both of us would be summoned back to court. We were discussing it only the other day, remember? Once a courtier, always a courtier... You know that.'

'Knowing it and accepting it are two completely different things. I had fervently hoped that it wouldn't be the case for us. I dared hope we might be free of the king and his circle of foul friends, forever. It would be too soon if I ever saw him again. He was going to have you killed.'

'There, there, don't fret, all is well. There's no need for us to get in a spin.'

Cara appreciated his calm solidity.

'Would you like the good or the bad news first?' he continued, still holding her close, his eyes twinkling.

'There is good news? In that case, let's hear the bad first, I think...and be done with it.'

'King Henry VIII has summoned me to court on what he calls a matter of critical importance to our country's safety—and I must leave immediately.'

'Oh lord, I feared as much. The king only ever wanted you at his side. I'm surprised he's got by without you until now.'

'Well, as you say, I almost lost my head. We both almost lost our heads to be precise, but six months have passed. I confess I too wondered whether we might never return to royal favour.'

'Did you hanker for it, my love? Do you miss being at court? Did you secretly yearn to be back in the political hotbed?'

'No, of course not. These past months have been heavenly; spending every possible moment with you and the children, instead of being called away on the Crown's business at a moment's notice. I could not wish for a greater blessing than being here with you at Willow Manor, and all the joy that comes with it.'

'I feel the same. Being together every day without the constant drama and intrigue of court has been a gift, indeed,' said Cara. She reached up to kiss him.

Cara admired his lips as he spoke; they were shapely—almost feminine in their fullness—but George was all man.

She wondered when her memory would update with the more recent Tudorville goings-on. She remembered little beyond their return to Willow Manor, following George's exoneration.

In their present-day discussions, they had considered the possibility of the resumption of time travel to Tudorville, and she had yearned to see their sweet children, Thomas and May, but they had hoped that George would be conscious of what was going on. She sighed. Judging by his responses so far, he wasn't.

As far-fetched as it seemed to her logical mind, she knew that a version of Cara and George would continue on as normal in the present day, oblivious to what was happening in Tudorville. If George's current awareness was anything to go by, she assumed he wouldn't even realise she'd gone, which evoked a bittersweet feeling in her chest. She sighed again, and tears filled her eyes.

It appeared George was suffering from total timeline amnesia. Cara would never forget her rite of passage into Tudorville when she met him, and her ability to time travel was unlocked. She'd found herself married to the dashing hero from the bookshop; locked up with him in Newgate Prison.

She studied George's eyes and roman nose and decided to test him, just in case he was playing her at her own game and putting on a front for her benefit. 'Have you seen Cornelius?' she asked, hoping that their agreed secret time travel coded question would jog George's memory or prompt him to be truthful. Perhaps he was in the same predicament as her.

He looked confused and responded, 'What an unusual question! If you must know, last time I saw that wily hound, he was in the kitchen using all of his persuasive powers to convince Cook that he is the rightful recipient of our breakfast leftovers.'

He does not know what I'm talking about. Damn it!

Cara contemplated her husband. A weariness permeated her soul as she considered how she would navigate the situation to avoid the inevitable complications of messing up the timelines. She didn't want to risk throwing them both into mortal danger again. So much was at stake, and the responsibility lay like an iron cape on her slim shoulders. She didn't want to go through all this on her own again. Should she confide in George this time? Would he even believe her, or would he think her quite deluded?

I can't believe I'm back in this impossible spot.

'Cara, Cara...where have you gone? You're miles away.'

'I'm sorry, my love. I am filled with dread at the prospect of you leaving and not knowing what the king has planned for you.'

'But you didn't hear the good news.'

'Oh yes, do tell,' she said, trying to keep the frustration out of her voice.

'The good news is that you shall join me very soon. Queen Jane requests your presence as her lady-in-waiting.'

'That's strange—she must surely recall how close I was to Queen Anne. I wonder why, of all the possible ladies, she would desire me at her side? Whatever do you make of it?'

'You're overthinking it, my love. The king and queen need to be surrounded by experienced and reliable courtiers, and the king has no doubt reflected on past events and realised we were not at all at fault in the Queen Anne conspiracy. Good, loyal courtiers are in short supply, as I'm certain he must appreciate. And besides, knowing him, he regrets ordering Anne's execution. It will trouble his soul.'

Cara nodded. 'Yes, that makes sense, although I shall be not a little nervous about joining the queen's ladies. In the meantime, I will miss you terribly when you leave, but at least I'll have time to prepare the children for our absence. Your sudden parting will be shock enough after we've had such a wondrous, prolonged period tucked away here.'

George pulled her towards him and held her tight for a minute before releasing her.

'Let's round up the children and Cornelius and go for a nice long walk.'

Arm in arm they strolled, keeping slightly behind the children who bounced about, throwing sticks for Cornelius, and chattering in high-pitched cheerful notes, not knowing their idyllic life was about to end.

CHAPTER 2

Willow Manor, York, 1536 - Tudorville

Cara and the children waved off George and his faithful servant, Swifty, as their horses carried them away down the long tree-lined drive. They waved until George's back was a distant dot between the rows of vibrant green willow trees, and then it turned the corner and he was out of sight.

A gloomy feeling descended over Cara; she was more worried than she let the children know.

'When will Father return?' asked May.

'I don't know. He could be away for some time. It depends on why the king wants him back at court.' Cara squeezed May's hand.

'But the king wanted to execute father and strip him of his title,' chimed in the little girl, mature beyond her years.

Cara's tender heart stirred as she looked at her daughter. 'I know, my love. But that's all behind us now. Our title wasn't removed, remember? We are still the Earl and Countess of Gloucester; that was all a terrible mistake.'

'When will you join Father?'

'I'll need to await word from court. I don't know yet when Queen Jane will require me to attend, but your father thinks it may be soon.'

'I wish you didn't ever have to leave,' said May, her pink bottom lip overlapped her top one, forming a sulky pout.

Cara turned to hug May, as much to fortify her own resolve as for her daughter's sake. Thomas stood ramrod straight, his small shoulders stiff, as he attempted to control his emotions and be the strong young man they had raised him to be. 'I will miss father a great deal,' he said, his youthful voice serious but thick with tears.

'We'll all be together again soon, my boy. In the meantime, we'll be depending on you to keep an eye on things here. Grandfather isn't getting any younger, and he needs your support. And yours too, May.'

'Yes, Mother, of course. May I return to the schoolroom, now? Tutor Edward awaits us,' said Thomas.

Cara touched his head to give him her blessing. She knew he didn't like her to see him near tears. They were all still haunted by George's not-too-long-since date with the hangman, when even Cara and the children had been thrown into the Tower for a brief spell.

Cara spent the morning in the library, attending to her correspondence and feeling wistful. She wondered what was happening in present-day York, and also what awaited George in London. Would he be welcomed as the long-lost devoted friend of the king, or would the bad blood linger? He would need to watch his back with Thomas Cromwell serving the king as Chief Minister and recently risen to even greater heights of formidable power.

George promised to write. Cara steeled herself for a long

wait. Now she was time travelling again, she must slow down and adjust to the natural pace of life at Willow Manor, or she would go mad with impatience. The thought of being anywhere for long without George, filled her with a dark dread that gripped her soul. She prayed they would be reunited soon.

After allowing her melancholic mood to consume her for a few minutes, Cara resolved to make the most of the tranquil period at Willow Manor, with the children, but despite her misgivings about royal life, as the days passed she longed for the new queen to summon her. She was acquainted with Jane Seymour from when they both served Anne Boleyn. Cara had been Anne's favourite lady-in-waiting but knew little about Jane; only that the sentiment in the country was she was a sweet girl and the king was thoroughly besotted. That was nothing new; Cara had witnessed a similar scenario before, when he had pledged eternal love to Anne.

Any plans could be dashed in a second if she lost her awareness of what was happening in Tudorville. She reminded herself to stay alert. She had learned that too much planning was pointless. Living-in-the-moment had been one of the guiding principles that had helped her stay sane when her life turned upside down in the present day and she began time travelling.

A week passed, and all Cara received was a hurried note from George saying he had arrived, and all was well.

Cara, impatient and on edge, became restless. She was anxious about what life at court would be like after Anne's death, but she would rather be there, than sit waiting at Willow Manor. At least that way, she would be with George, and they could face it together. Cara yearned for their simple life to return. She awoke one day with a premonition that those peaceful days were over.

The Twin Flame mission was back on in full force, and she must step up to the challenge. Gradually, she was becoming used to being at Willow Manor again, but sometimes it was odd, as though one day she had stumbled in off the street and assumed someone else's life. She missed her own.

Finally, two months later, the letter she was waiting for, arrived.

My dearest darling Cara,

I can't tell you how lost I am without you. The days are long and dull without your laughter and smiling face ever at my side. It's strange to be back at court, but the king is in high spirits like the old days and is happy to have my company. He asks that I bid you join me in the next week, so you may serve our new queen. She wants you as one of her ladies-in-waiting. Fear not. I think you will have a pleasant time of it. Come as soon as you are able, my darling. Give my love and blessings to Thomas and May, and pray tell my parents that I am well and hope to return home for a visit shortly.

Your loving and devoted husband,
George.

Cara immediately went to look for Edward, whom she found in the schoolroom, sorting through papers.

'Edward, I'm afraid I must once again leave the children

in your capable hands. I've received word from Lord Cavendish that it's time for me to join him at court.'

'My dear Lady Cara, you may trust them with me, as you know. I will guard them with my life.'

'I am certain of it, thank you, Edward. It's an enormous burden off my mind that you are here, and we can count on you to keep things in order.'

'Does his lordship mention anything about court?'

'Not much. He says the king is in high spirits, nothing more. I've only had the occasional letter since he left, which isn't like him at all, so the king must be keeping him engaged. I do hope we'll lead a quiet life at Hampton Court and George won't be called away. That's probably too much to hope for, but it will be wonderful to be reunited with him, even if it must be at court.'

'And how are present-day Cara and George?' said Edward, lowering his voice, and glancing over to check the children were out of earshot.

Thomas and May were immersed in playing a board game on the far said of the room, overlooking the garden.

'Since I was whisked back here unexpectedly, I've no memory of travelling to the future, so you likely know more than I.'

'No, unfortunately not. Last time I remember seeing you together was at your wedding.'

They talked nostalgically about their present-day lives, and then Cara said, 'I will leave for the palace tomorrow. I must break the news to the children without delay.'

Cara left for London the following morning, just as first light painted the dull grey sky with broad golden swirls. The roads were wet after days of rainfall and blustery winds, but Hancock, their steward, assured her they were fit for purpose and conditions were no worse than expected for that time of year. Cara wrapped herself up in multiple layers; she felt the cold bitterly after months in their cosy cottage and still hadn't adjusted to the biting cold of Tudor England.

She bid the children and Edward farewell during a hasty breakfast and convinced them to remain inside in the morning chill. Cara couldn't bear to see their distraught little faces as she rode away. It would be a long and exhausting journey, but she was mentally prepared. Hancock would accompany her all the way as it was dangerous for a woman to travel such a distance alone. He was an accomplished rider, and it wasn't long before their horses settled into a steady rhythm.

Her mood had lightened considerably. She felt a delicious stirring of anticipation at the promise of being reunited with George, and even court seemed suddenly inviting. There would be plenty to keep her busy, and the queen would need her support.

Cara consoled herself she would have her dear friend, Margaret for company because George had mentioned in one of his letters that she hadn't been banished and had remained at court following Queen Anne's execution.

Cara consciously committed to do her best to put her mistrust of the king aside, or it would only lead to trouble, which she was determined to avoid this time. It wasn't Queen Jane's fault she had been ordered to marry a tyrant. Cara instinctively knew what the role required, and she would rise to the situation and fulfil her royal duty once again.

Hampton Court Palace, London, One week later - Tudorville

Cara moved back into the familiar Clock Court apartment with George, and despite the harrowing memories of their arrests, she soon felt at home.

One morning, she extracted a dusty volume of a collection of poems from the shelf and passed a quiet half an hour thumbing through the pages. She heard the maids enter the apartment and decided she would finish the poem she was reading and make her way over to the queen's rooms, so they could get on with their chores undisturbed.

Their high-pitched chattering floated into the room and interrupted her concentration.

'I pity her poor ladyship, what with Lord Cavendish besotted with that woman. The word was he and Lady Cara are a love-match, but they seem no more special than any other wedded couple.'

'Men are all the same. The minute your back is turned, they take their pleasure where they may get it.'

The volume of their conversation dropped, and the words muted, and Cara struggled to hear what they said. Her heart thumped and raced; the noise pounded in her ears as though she were drowning. She couldn't catch her breath and she gasped for air.

What woman?

She shoved the book back onto the shelf, her hand shaking as she tried to tune back into the steady stream of mutterings. She made out the occasional word, but by now they had moved on to other intrigues, and she had no wish to alert them to her presence. That would be too humiliating, so she slipped silently out of the bedchamber and went in search of George.

Her mind swirled with unanswered questions. Could what they said be true? She found it hard to believe, but several months had passed until her arrival at Hampton Court. He had been here without her, so anything was possible. He had mentioned little about what had been going on. But still, theirs wasn't one of those ordinary marriages where people cheated, was it? A heavy cloud of gloom enveloped her, and the old violent feelings of jealousy rose up and threatened to strangle her.

She would have it out with him as soon as she could. Cara had no interest in seeking second-hand gossip; she would ask George directly. It was only fair not to assume the worst and to give him a chance to defend himself against the allegation.

Cara's heart raced increasingly faster as she considered the possibilities; she hadn't been this distraught since the painful days when they fell in love in present-day York.

Is it happening again?

She had learned much from the devastating previous chain of events and attempted to consciously rein herself in. She knew she was now in danger of jumping to conclusions and acting on them in anger. But holding back was easier said than done. She desperately reminded herself that things are not always as they seem.

'Have you seen Lord Cavendish this morning?' she asked one of the footmen.

'Yes, my lady. He left on horseback with His Majesty, a short while ago. You just missed them.'

Damn it.

'Did his lordship give any indication of when he means to return?'

'No, none that I know of, my lady.'

Cara's mood plummeted further at the thought of waiting around all day with this dreadful vision lodged in her mind, and the shooting pain threatened to eviscerate her insides. She could barely breathe. The build-up of unanswered questions and fears would be intolerable. No: she would have to seek answers elsewhere, after all. Perhaps she could clear up the misunderstanding, and there would be a simple explanation and no need to trouble George with the servants' tittle-tattle.

Cara entered Queen Jane's apartments and made her way over to the cushioned window seat and sat down next to her companion, Margaret.

After re-joining London court life, she had thought that nothing much had changed in the months they had been absent. Poor Queen Anne had met a tragic end and was instantly replaced by the sweet, innocent new queen, who some implied, the king found to be more amenable to his demands. Even a few of George's old circle of courtiers had trickled back into the fold; although many had lost their heads in the court reshuffle. The king had some fresh faces around him, but the game appeared to be much the same.

Stay always in the king's favour and try not to put your life in jeopardy. Keep the queen sweet, but not too sweet if you are a gentleman, as that would inevitably result in a fresh set of dangers; the king had a jealous nature. Maintaining royal favour was a thin and spiky line to tread, which required the courtiers to live by their quick wits at all times.

'Good day, my dear Margaret. Are you well? How was the queen this morning?' Cara made light conversation and hoped Margaret wouldn't spot the wild panic in her eyes.

'I can't tell you how good it is to have you back with us. Your smiling face is always a pleasure to behold. The new queen is easy to attend—I don't mind the dawn duties. I prayed with Queen Jane, and Her Grace appeared in good cheer.'

Cara forced herself to continue with the polite exchange,

and they talked quietly about how bad-tempered Queen Anne had been in the mornings. They whispered her name—only the old circle dared speak of her at all, for fear of angering the king.

'I sense you are a little downhearted today—you are not your usual joyful self. Is all well with you?' asked her friend, examining Cara's face.

'You are astute as always, Margaret. May I ask something of you in confidence, and trust you won't pass my words onto another soul?'

'But of course. We have always been here for one another, have we not? You may be assured that your secret will not pass these lips,' she said, gesturing that her lips were sealed.

Cara squeezed Margaret's hand and took a deep breath before speaking. Her heart started pounding again, so great was the dreaded anticipation of the answer she might receive. 'Please tell me truthfully, have you heard a rumour about George taking a mistress?'

Cara felt Margaret tighten her grip on her hand. She glimpsed a flash of pity in her friend's sapphire eyes.

Oh, God. It is true.

'I wondered whether you had heard the rumours. I'm sorry, my dear. I won't lie to you. I heard George took a woman called Marianne as a mistress not long after his arrival at court.'

Cara swallowed the hard lump in her throat before her voice emerged as a faint croak. 'Are you certain?'

'Um... About as certain as I may be. I am acquainted with Marianne's sister, and she told me it was so, but I also heard it from other sources which I deem trustworthy.'

Cara was freezing, and she began to tremble.

Margaret drew her friend into her arms, patting her back as though she were a small child. Cara tried to stave off the tears.

'There, there, this too shall pass. George adores you—you know that—everyone knows that. There is many an envious girl who's tried to hold his attention before, and he's only ever had time for you.'

Cara's tears spilt onto her cheeks and she fought to regain her composure. It wouldn't do to fall apart in the queen's rooms.

'If that's true, what could have changed? We were only apart for a few months, which has happened many times before,' she said, hurriedly wiping her eyes with the silk handkerchief Margaret pressed into her cold hand.

'The king now spends his days with George, like in their younger years. And the king's current mistress is a close friend of Marianne's. My guess would be George went along with it to keep in with the king. I'm sure it means nothing.'

Rage consumed Cara as she battled to contain her emotions in the face of such treachery. 'Please excuse me. If the queen asks for me, pray say that I am unwell, and I have retired to my rooms.'

'Of course. Have a rest, my dear. I'm certain you'll recover your spirits soon. All the noblemen at court have a mistress. It means nothing about your marriage.'

Margaret clutched at platitudes in her attempt to restore Cara's peace of mind, and she already regretted being the one to confirm her friend's suspicions. Hampton Court had been awash with rumours for months. The courtiers and the servants took great pleasure in witnessing someone else's misfortune. Margaret had hoped it would blow over without Cara being any the wiser, but she had to tell her the truth when asked.

Pain had quickly turned to anger. Cara was furious. How could George do such a thing? *Her* George, and after all they had been through!

They had always talked as if they would never behave like

other couples. Did he not love her in Tudorville as he used to?

Cara felt the icy cold vortex creep over her skin; she attempted to smile at Margaret, who she believed was a trustworthy friend, trying to do the right thing. Cara vowed to confront George as soon as he returned, no matter the hour. The devious, cheating, double-dealing... But then she was gone.

CHAPTER 3

Rose Cottage, York - Present day

Cara opened her eyes and squinted in the bright early morning sunlight seeping through the cracks in the white blinds. She pulled herself up and saw George was already awake, propped up against the pillows, reading.

'Morning. Sleep well, darling?' he said.

'Morning. Um...no, not really. I don't feel like I slept at all. The strangest things happened.'

George detected the seriousness of her tone, laid his book face down on the duvet, and turned to give her his full attention.

'Like what? You haven't been having those vivid dreams again?'

'Well, if I didn't know better, I'd say yes, that must be it. But no, George, it's started again. I actually time travelled back to Tudorville; I'm certain of it. I met you and the children. And Edward. But then we were back at court. God, it was weird. I had to act as though none of this present-day stuff is happening.'

'What? Oh no, don't tell me I didn't remember.'

'Nada. Absolutely nothing.'

'Did you test me with the Cornelius code?'

'Yep.'

'And?'

'Nothing. It was quite funny, really. You couldn't understand why I would ask about our dog when you'd just received a letter from the king.'

'King Henry?'

'Yes. He's married to Jane Seymour now.'

'What year is it then?'

'It's still 1536, would you believe?' said Cara.

George shifted in bed and pulled himself further up; his book forgotten. 'So, that means time isn't equal in the timelines. A year has passed here but not there. It's extraordinary... Did you figure out what month it is?' he asked.

'Yes, it's October. And I was upset, but I can't remember why.' She shook her head as if it were full of cobwebs. 'Oh, lord. It's coming back to me now. I was angry with you.'

George blinked. 'Angry with me? Whatever for? I'm a lovely chap and I'm always in your good books in Tudorville. It was only here we used to argue like bloody idiots.'

'You won't believe what you did.'

'Go on.' George cleared his throat.

Cara's frown deepened, and she stared at him as the memories whirled into her mind.

'I will say in advance that it's wholly unfair to hold me accountable for anything whatsoever because I know nothing of my doings back then. I'm a model husband now;

let's not forget that important fact,' he added, seeking to charm her out of her miserable black cloud.

Cara smiled, but the sadness reflected in her grey eyes. George always made her feel better, no matter how dire the situation.

'You have only gone and taken a bloody mistress.'

George shook his head. 'No. You must be mistaken. I wouldn't do that.'

'No. I'm not mistaken. I only wish I were. I overheard the servants talking when they came to clean our apartments at Hampton Court. It was awful.'

'Oh, so it must be true, then... You know better than to believe court gossip.' He removed his glasses and closed his eyes, pinching the top of his nose as if he had a raging headache.

The charged silence reverberated between them.

Cara said nothing as she watched him fight to contain his frustration.

Finally, he looked up and their eyes locked. 'You're jumping to conclusions based on a dream.' He sighed heavily. 'I've so enjoyed this peaceful interlude without these ridiculous arguments cropping up. Last year was like living in a Shakespeare play, all misunderstandings and hearsay, over nothing.'

'How can you say it's nothing? You have taken a mistress! Goodness knows how many noblemen she's entertained before you. It's vile to even think of it.'

'Then don't,' he said, his tone sharp and his expression stern. He picked up his book. 'I do hope when you calm down, you'll see how ridiculous this is.'

Cara shook her head and her voice was high pitched. 'I can't believe it. When I think of those lonely months I was languishing at Willow Manor waiting for word to join you; worrying about you, missing you, and all the while you were shagging some hot court-babe and sending the occasional note to keep me sweet.'

George let out a low laugh.

'Impressed with yourself, are you?' Cara snapped.

'No, I'm stunned that you are angry at me for something I apparently did five hundred years ago, something that might even be, well, just a dream. Something that probably isn't true. I've heard it all now.'

'Damn right, I'm angry. It makes me doubt everything we share. How could you do it?'

'And in this dream, did you check there's any truth in these accusations before you built your case for the Crown Court? I mean, do you have any proof, or is it just servant girl gossip with which you're condemning me, I mean *him*?'

'Well, I went to the queen's rooms, and Margaret confirmed it without any hesitation, and she was embarrassed to tell me, poor woman. She said she had hoped it would blow over without me finding out, but she couldn't keep it from me once I asked. Margaret did her best to defend you, saying you love me, and it means nothing.'

'Smart woman. I'm certain it means nothing—that is, if it even happened, which I seriously doubt,' he said.

'Well, that's easy for you to say...off with your fancy woman and keeping the no-good king sweet as he cheats on his new wife. His mistress is this Marianne's friend, which is how you came to hook up with her, by all accounts.'

'I'm speechless.'

'Me too. It's ruined everything. I had such beautiful memories of our relationship there.'

Cara's distraught face was too much for him to bear. He sighed and then reached for her hand. 'Try not to be so dramatic. Can we agree not to jump to conclusions, please? We have to remember we were different people in a different age. If we hold each other accountable for every mistake we made in Tudorville, we're going to make life unbearable.'

'I hope I never return to Tudorville. I'm scared to travel back, and have it confirmed that our love was all a lie. I thought we were the perfect couple.'

'We were—I mean—we are the perfect couple. It would take more than a hot floozy to come between us.'

Cara jumped out of bed and stared at him, her almond-shaped grey eyes blazing. She turned away abruptly and slipped her arms into her silk robe and tied the ribbons, so it concealed her nightdress.

'Where are you off to now?'

'I'm going to take a shower and try to make some sense of this. I feel horrible.'

'Okay. Although, please remember, this is most unfair. We went to bed, and all was fine, and I wake up to this madness, even though I've done nothing wrong and am exactly the same man.'

'I'm sorry. I know it's crazy, but you with another woman is too much for me to bear.'

George shook his head again. It was probably only a dream, but if it were true, what the heck was he supposed to do about George being a bit of a player in Tudorville? He sipped his coffee and resumed reading, but he had trouble focusing on the words.

Hampton Court Palace, London, 1536 - Tudorville

Cara nestled under a blanket in her favourite chair in their bedchamber. She was reeling with shock and struggled to warm up, no matter how closely she huddled to the orange glow of the fire. She couldn't get her head around George having a mistress. As the hours ticked by, her anger smouldered to new and dangerous levels. She wished he would come home before she exploded. There was still no sign of him, and she imagined he was with the gorgeous Marianne.

She wished she could have stayed with George in their cottage in York, even though they were both upset. He wasn't the George who had physically made love to another woman. Now she would have to deal with the consequences of her discovery, and she was exhausted with the flitting back and forth. This is how it had been when she first time travelled—she never knew when she would be swept between timelines. It was incredibly disorientating, and she knew she must resign herself to being at the whim of the vortex.

She couldn't even look up Marianne online. On this fateful day at Hampton Court Palace in 1536, all she had to go on were a few sentences of gossip, and a sad, yet believable confirmation from a friend.

What the hell was he thinking?

Unable to concentrate on reading, she eventually nodded off and awoke with a thudding heart to the sound of the opening door. The dying fire sparks spluttered and popped from the depths of the embers, and her anger rekindled at the sight of George.

'You waited up for me. How lovely.' His face lit up and he crossed the room swiftly to her side and knelt down to kiss her.

Cara turned her face away and his kiss missed its destination.

'Whatever's the matter, my love?'

'Where have you been, my lord?'

George's happy, open expression clouded over. He hated being questioned, especially when she used that tone. It closed him down and provoked him.

'Why do you speak to me so?'

'That's a good question. I speak to you so because I'm wondering whether your day was spent in Marianne's arms. Did you have a gratifying time in her warm bed? I'm surprised you have returned home at all.'

'What the devil are you talking about, woman?' George looked genuinely puzzled. I've spent a long, exhausting day meeting with various ill-tempered parties, in an effort to find a way to quell the ongoing uprising. I accompanied the king at his request because trouble stirs again in the north and he wished to take advice.'

'And what of your mistress, Marianne? Was she unavailable today?'

'I don't know what's got into you. I'm weary, and now I'm angry, so I'm going to rid myself of these cold, wet garments, and trust that your pleasant nature will be restored by the morning.'

George stalked from the room as Cara choked, and began to sob and gasp. The tears flooded her eyes and slid down her cold cheeks. She suspected by the violent way he had responded that there was truth in her allegation, and he merely sought to buy time to come up with a plausible excuse. She had never confronted him in that accusatory manner in Tudorville; there had never been any need. His evasive tone was reminiscent of the present-day George, when they used to argue about their impossible situation.

The agony ripped through her chest and permeated her being. Her emotions were raw, and the trauma of the past hurt still lingered in her soul and resurfaced to haunt her whenever she relived that heart shattering period.

They had been Twin Flames destined to reunite, and as such, there were constant challenges designed for their souls to fully realise their potential. She had allowed herself to believe they had completed that painful cycle and had reached the state of union.

When the timeline reset, they had been free to be together. It was a glorious time, but now it was over. And their Tudorville marriage which had seemed blessed from the start; one of divine love, was now being tested.

How could he betray her when she was waiting at Willow Manor?

Visions of the recent lonely months at their York home, worrying and waiting for news of him, filled her mind.

Cara dragged herself out of the chair and curled up on the four-poster bed. She pulled the sheet over her head and continued to sob quietly. Her intuition told her there was more to this than she knew, but why would he not explain?

She had learned from past experiences that things were rarely as they seemed, but God how it hurt. The thought of him with another woman, after all they had been through, sliced into her soul and the pain was visceral. As she drifted off into a numb sleep, she felt the freezing icy chill of the vortex envelop her. And she was gone. Again.

George stripped off his dirty, wet clothing in the other room, sipped a cup of small ale, and folded his weary body into a chair. He would leave Cara to simmer down. No good would come of him entering their bedchamber now, no matter how much he longed to lie down next to her and enjoy the solace of her company.

He was shocked, and his resentment smouldered at the thought of how she had verbally attacked him and unleashed her wrath. He'd never seen her in such a violent rage. It was no good. He was too upset to join her, so he sat alone, nursing his warm ale for hours as the still night merged with the wispy dawn air.

He couldn't bear hurting her, and yet he had been tempted by the beautiful Marianne when he was lonely.

What a fool he'd been to think she wouldn't hear the inevitable gossip in this venom-filled palace.

He finally drifted off to sleep in the early hours, gloomy and wretched, and desperately wondering if the new day would offer a solution to make things right with his beloved wife.

CHAPTER 4

York - Present day

Cara didn't know what to make of it. How she wished she hadn't been drawn back to Tudorville. If only she hadn't overheard that awful conversation, she'd still be in sweet oblivion, and her heart wouldn't have split open like a gaping wound.

Her memory was updating fast with the frequent to-ing and fro-ing between timelines, but she didn't know what she didn't know.

Cara sighed and sat on the edge of the bed for a few minutes, feeling defeated and wondering what to do next. Resolved, she stood and stepped into a pair of fitted, soft blue jeans and pulled her favourite grey roll-neck over her head. A quick look in the mirror; satisfied, she headed downstairs to find George brewing more coffee.

'How was your shower?'

'Good, thanks.' Cara looked at him and bit her lip. But it

was no good she couldn't restrain herself. 'How could you do it?'

'Do what?' he asked.

'Don't play dumb. You know exactly what I mean.' Her eyes were misty, but she stayed strong.

'I don't know what you're talking about.' George's defensive tone reappeared. 'Cara, you can't hold me responsible for what Tudorville George did. He is—was—a man of his time.'

'So you say, but I don't get it. I can't believe you—he—whoever…had the audacity to take a mistress when I was pining at Willow Manor. It just doesn't seem like something he would do.'

George busied himself pouring the coffee and slid a cup along the kitchen counter towards her.

Cara continued, 'Perhaps heartbreak triggers my time travel and that's why I moved in and out of the timelines so much last year.'

She could sense George's irritation rising. They would need to deal with this unpleasant situation. It wouldn't disappear on its own if he had indeed betrayed her, no matter how many hundreds of years ago.

'I don't know what to say. You're going to have to talk to him. First of all, I can't remember what went on, so there's no point asking me. You know I have only brief memories of Tudorville, and as for this latest event, how on earth can I answer your questions when I wasn't even there?' George sat down at the kitchen table and began skimming *the York Press* as he sipped his coffee.

'And that's all you have to say?' said Cara.

He raised his eyes from the newspaper. 'Yes. Unless I somehow remember, I can't possibly say anything of any significance, other than I'm sorry George took a mistress. I really am. But it's not my fault he's a bloody fool, is it? You'd think he'd know Special Agent Cara would find out, but perhaps he doesn't see it as a problem in Tudorville.'

'Not a problem!' Cara spluttered. 'I'll show him a problem,' she said and then turned and fled from the room.

She shook with emotion. She didn't want to get back into this crazy life where they argued all the time. They had been having a wonderful time with no outside interference and now it was all ruined.

Why is this nightmare happening again?

The following morning after a restless night, Cara wandered through the rain-soaked cobbled streets of York's city centre. Relentless rain drummed onto the small umbrella which protected her from being drenched. She was pleased she'd worn her boots and was able to walk fast. Cara arrived outside the door of Sylvia's office and rang the bell. She peered up at the grey sky from beneath the edge of the dripping umbrella. It was a miserable afternoon and reflected her mood perfectly.

The door buzzed and clicked to unlock. Cara took a deep breath, pushed it open and stepped into the cool interior, carefully closing the umbrella, and setting it down in the cloakroom. She took a seat in the small empty waiting room and picked up a magazine to distract herself. It was impossible to concentrate, and she tapped her hand restlessly on her thigh, hoping she wouldn't need to wait long.

'Hello. It's lovely to see you.' Sylvia poked her smiling face around the door, into the hallway and she ushered Cara into her room.

They embraced and then sat down either side of the table where Cara first learned how Tarot card readings could help her to make the right decisions. It was Sylvia who had conveyed an important message from the Angel Gabriel to warn her that all was not as it seemed.

Sylvia disappeared for a few minutes, and Cara's eyes

wandered around the room, taking in the mystical looking prints on the walls.

'You sounded upset on the phone. Are you okay?' said Sylvia as she placed a steaming cup of herbal tea on a coaster in front of Cara.

'Aw, thanks.' She clutched the cup with her damp, cold hands, paused and then said, 'I've been travelling to Tudorville again. The other day I found myself back at Willow Manor. To cut a long story short, George was summoned to serve the king. I stayed with the children for a few months, and then Queen Jane summoned me to court.'

'Oh, I remember reading about her. Doesn't she bear the king's only legitimate son? Hold on: divorced, beheaded, died, divorced, beheaded, survived,' she said, counting on her fingers.

'Yes, she's number three. I'd better look up when she dies, but hopefully I won't be around to see it. It was awful being there.'

Sylvia raised an eyebrow.

'Knowing she's going to die soon is hard enough to take. But the worst part is, I had lovely memories of our marriage in Tudorville, but now it's all shot to bits,' continued Cara.

'How come?' Sylvia's gold-flecked, green cat-like eyes widened. 'You said it was your dream scenario to witness history in the making.'

'He's taken a mistress!' Cara blurted out.

'The king?'

'No, George. My Twin Flame, my supposed faithful husband and love of my life, is cavorting with an infamous Tudor beauty.'

'Oh, now I see why you're upset,' Sylvia half-smiled. 'Mind you, it could be worse. You know he adores you. He's a product of his time, that's all. It's no excuse, but still...'

'Oh, please don't *you* start with that *product of his time* nonsense. That's what he said.' Cara rolled her eyes.

'I'm sorry. What can I do?' Sylvia said, reaching across the table and patting Cara's hand.

Cara welled up at the kindness in Sylvia's voice. She shook her head and then sipped her tea. 'I hoped you might look into the cards to guide me in the right direction. I feel lost, as though he's betrayed me.'

'But Cara, it's not now. It's not here...' said Sylvia.

'Yes, and logically, I understand that. But my heart doesn't. My trust in him is ebbing away and all the old painful feelings have flooded back. I'm afraid to time travel again, and I'd be so grateful if you could help me to stop.'

'My dear, you know that's not within my capability. Your future and past are unfolding for a reason. You and George are multi-generational Twin Flames, so it's complex. You have multiple past lives to resolve.'

'I hoped the past was over, and we could continue to live a quiet life. It was so lovely. Would you please look into the cards for me and tell me what you see for us?'

'Yes, let's have a look at what message they hold for you.'

Sylvia shuffled her Tarot and Angel Oracle card decks and within minutes she began to sway from side to side, to her inner rhythm.

'Tell me when to stop,' she said. Cara was used to Sylvia's card trance and was soothed by the sight of her as she watched her reveal the cards and flip them over one-by-one.

'Let's start with the wild card that jumped out. It's a Five of Wands, which indicates a total breakdown of communication. Some kind of conflict is brewing, and I see George at the centre.'

'Oh no,' said Cara.

'He seems to be locked into conflict on several fronts. He will have to face an old enemy.' Sylvia pointed to the Tower card next, which Cara recognised as another conflict card. 'The Tower forewarns of destruction and chaos which in Tudorville terms must be some type of war.'

Cara shuddered. 'I feel woefully ill-equipped for another confrontation,' she said. 'Last time, I didn't know what we were up against, and that was bad enough. Now I know exactly how terrifying it is in Tudorville, and it makes it a hundred times worse.'

Sylvia had fallen into a deep trance, and didn't hear Cara's words, but continued, 'Old ego has resurfaced. As you feared, your Twin Flame mission is not complete. There are many things you must still resolve before you're at peace together. You are in the ascension phase, but karma is rising up and must be repaired.'

Cara's heart thudded, and her mind raced. Why did they have to keep being swept back into this drama? She longed for their ordinary life when the main focus of their day was what they would eat for dinner. She had never envied ordinary couples, more.

Sylvia's eyes flickered open after revealing a few more cards. Cara knew from experience that there was no point trying to get her to continue. When it was over, it was over.

'That's it. Was it of any use?' Sylvia often couldn't recall her words after she emerged from the reading.

'What did you see, Sylvia?'

'I saw fire and great conflict; men at arms, some kind of violent battle, and George in the thick of it. I would advise you to take things slowly until we know more about the significance of this vision. One thing is for certain—there's an uprising. An uprising of old pain and wounds, both in the emotional realm and in real-life events.'

'I don't feel ready to face another dangerous conflict,' Cara rested her head in her hands.

Sylvia touched Cara's arm. 'Know that you are always

equipped to deal with whatever is on the cards for you. It is out of your hands, and all you can do is follow your inner nudges.'

Cara raised her head and stared at Sylvia, wishing she had seen something more hopeful for her in the cards.

'This is the stirring up of old pain between you and George in Tudorville. But it will all be resolved. Don't forget the True Love card also showed itself; you must be true to your Twin Flame destiny.' Sylvia tapped the colourful True Love card with her glossy red nails.

They chatted for a few more minutes and Cara finished her tea and left. It was good to confide in Sylvia, but she was even more uptight than when she'd arrived. If it was calming solace she was seeking, that hadn't been on the cards for her today.

Whirring thoughts jostled for her attention as she weaved slowly through the damp York streets, mindlessly stepping around sparkling puddles on her way back to the car.

Hampton Court Palace, London, 1536 - Tudorville

Cara stirred in the early morning chill and opened her eyes. She saw the sumptuous curtains of the four-poster bed and the Tudor beams above her head, and realised she was back in their palace apartment.

She was zig-zagging between the two timelines at a frantic pace and had a flash of a memory of her meeting with Sylvia. She recalled something about George being at the centre of a violent uprising.

'George? George?' she called. No response. She wandered into the other room to find his clothes from the previous night strewn across the furniture, but no sign of him.

Where had he gone? She must warn him.

Several minutes later, the door opened, and he entered. 'Good day, my love. And how are you on this fine, chilly morning?'

Never angry for long, he had the same sunny temperament as he did in the present-day.

Cara crossed the room and threw her arms around his neck and he held her tight. 'Thank goodness you're all right. I had the most awful dream you were in the middle of an uprising.'

'Hush,' he said. 'Everything's fine. I'm here.'

And then the other chaotic memories cascaded into her consciousness. Cara looked into his dark eyes and said. 'Is it true about Marianne?'

George released her abruptly, his open expression becoming instantly guarded. 'Must we do this again, now?' he said.

'Yes,' she replied. 'Your response indicates it's true. Or will you tell me otherwise?' Cara held his stare, unblinking. As forbidding as he made it to challenge him, she would not back down.

He turned away.

Her heart raced, and she felt sick.

George had taken a mistress.

During the weeks that followed, George was frequently away with the king, and he and Cara didn't share more than a few snatched moments. He would appear at odd hours of the day and night, only to rush off again shortly after. The tension at the palace was palpable.

'What's going on in Lincolnshire?' Cara asked him one day when they had a moment alone. There had been excited talk at court of an uprising against the new Church of England. People were enraged over the Dissolution of the Lesser Monasteries, and the king's popularity had not been restored to the level of the Katherine of Aragon years, as he had hoped. Queen Anne Boleyn was never a sweetheart of the masses, but that didn't mean the people didn't object to their queen being executed on what many believed to be trumped-up charges.

'It looks as though the Lincolnshire Uprising, by the grace of God is nearing its end. I fear, however, that the danger isn't over because there is still much unrest in the north. Just because it's been quelled, doesn't mean the cause has been relinquished.'

It had been some years since Cara had studied the specifics of the Tudor rebellions. She recalled there would be several uprisings around this time, but the exact order of events eluded her. The words 'Pilgrimage of Grace' floated in and out of her mind, and she knew it would occur soon.

'Please be careful, George. If there is any way for you to extract yourself from growing ever closer to the king in the role of special advisor in this matter, then please take it. These are dangerous times. The people have just cause to rebel; they are angry at Cromwell's policies. The less we are embroiled in it, the better.'

'Lower your voice, my love. We cannot afford to be overheard exchanging such views.' George ran his fingers through his hair.

Cara moved closer and whispered, 'Must you be so involved?'

George looked at her in surprise. 'Do you imagine I have any say in how I spend my days when I serve the king? Do you think the king asks me whether I'd like to take part? My goodness, I'd much rather be here with you, or at home with the family at Willow Manor. Don't you know that by now?'

Cara held his gaze and said, 'I don't know what to think—since I found out about your mistress.'

'For the love of God, woman. There is no mistress.'

George took a deep breath. He suspected he might be away for some time, and he didn't want them to part on bitter terms; things were tense enough between them already.

'I can't talk about this now. There's too much going on. The king has asked me to travel to York on his behalf to negotiate with a friend of mine who it appears is the nominated leader of another uprising they're calling the Pilgrimage of Grace.'

'Must you go personally? Can't one of the other lords attend to it on your behalf?' Cara hung her head as her emotions bubbled and threatened to overwhelm her.

'You know the king doesn't readily admit the northern lords into his inner circle. He knows Robert Aske and I are childhood friends and hopes that our alliance will allow me to influence him to bid the rebels stand down. And besides, my sympathies lie with Robert; I would like to help resolve matters peacefully.'

'I don't think you grasp how truly dangerous the situation is.'

George raised her hand to his lips and kissed her fingers and then the palm of her hand. 'York is our city. If there is some way I may restore harmony, I must surely do it. You know that my love.'

'But must you play the hero?' she said, desperate to get through to him.

George sighed. 'I'm not playing anything. And certainly not the hero. I only want to help Robert escape the noose, you know he's a dear friend, and I fear for his life if he insists on continuing with this madness. Although, honestly, I don't have any choice.'

'You'll be the most heroic man in the graveyard if you're not careful,' said Cara, her eyes shining.

'Come now, my darling. Let us please not part with such

thorny sentiments. I promise I will take care and be with you again soon. I'll be on the king's business, and as such, I will have the protection of the Royal Army. We'll be on the right side of things this time—it won't be anything like the last debacle.'

There was no point fighting against his iron will. His mind was made up. Cara tilted her head upwards, and he kissed her and encircled her in his arms. She had no desire to upset him, only to warn him. She turned to gaze out of the window at the bustling courtyard below, considering whether she should reveal the future, so he might grasp the magnitude of the situation.

'Please fear not but wait for me in the safety of the palace, passing pleasant days in the queen's rooms. That is how I will imagine you, and the vision of your loveliness will sustain me through the hard days ahead. I will get word to you as soon as I possibly can, my love.' George kissed Cara again and then dashed out of the door to consult with the king and Cromwell before leaving for York. There was no time for her to say any more.

She sat down heavily, feeling bereft. Stranded once again, the long, dull days stretched before her like an ominous stormy skyline with no end in sight. She longed to be back in present-day York, curled up on the sofa with George.

She must find a way to stop the time travel or she would go mad. Every day, Cara prayed that quantum physics professor, Eddie, would figure it out. Only then would they finally be free to lead a normal life.

CHAPTER 5

Rose Cottage, York, Three days later - Present day

After dinner, Cara curled up with George on the sofa in front of the roaring fire. Her wish had been granted, and she was grateful to be back at the cottage. For the first time in what seemed like ages, she was at ease. She'd been furious at George about his Tudorville affair and found it hard to let it go, but she had decided to push it from her thoughts and to enjoy the day.

After all, she reasoned; he wasn't to blame for what he had done five hundred years ago.

Was he?

George tapped buttons and switched channels until he found something that caught his eye. It was a holiday programme about Spain. 'Look darling, it's Seville, isn't it stunning? Oh, I do miss it. Don't you?'

'It is stunning, but I don't remember much of our time

there beyond our first night together. And I don't remember Victoriana at all.'

'I have wonderful memories of Seville,' George continued, swept away by his thoughts, not listening to her.

Cara stiffened. All of her insecurities about his former life raced to the surface.

'Well, at least you remember it,' she said. 'All kinds of trouble's brewing in 1536, and I'm powerless to stop you dashing off to confront the rebels, and you have no understanding of the real dangers. I wish you'd remember what you're doing in Tudorville, instead of reminiscing about your old life in Seville.'

'That's unfair,' he said, his voice dangerously tight and controlled.

'Why? You seemed really rather proud of yourself the other day when I told you about your mistress, as if it's some kind of joke. Is that fair?'

'I'm not at all proud of myself. I curse the damn day I met the woman, whoever she is, and if you're kicking Tudorville George's head in like this, I'm certain he does too. He told you many times you're the only woman he's ever loved. What more do you want? As for me, I don't remember her. Can't you just accept it was a mistake—that is, if it's even true? People make mistakes, you know. We're not all saints like you.'

'I never claimed to be a saint but at least I'm faithful to you. Just because you don't remember, doesn't give you a get out of jail free card to do anything you fancy. Shall I take a lover and we'll see how you like it?'

George's complexion turned ashen. 'Really? You would punish me for a past I don't recollect?'

'No, not now, not here,' Cara instantly regretted her bitter words when she saw the pain etched on his face, but she was on a roll and feeling insecure. 'I mean, I will take a lover in the past. Just like you did. And you...I mean he, didn't tell me anything at all. He didn't tell me I'm the only woman he's ever loved; at least not since I found out about this mistress business. He refuses to talk about it and is always away with the king. Even five hundred years apart, you're remarkably alike.'

George turned the television off and stood up, smoothing imaginary fluff from his black trousers.

'You're being totally unreasonable. I had a life with you in Seville, too, you know. Am I also forbidden to talk about that because you don't remember it?'

She stared at him. His words stung.

'I can't talk to you when you're like this—I'm going for a walk. We both need to cool down,' he said.

'Good idea,' she said, and then burst into tears when she heard the front door close with a snap. Now she had ruined their lovely evening.

It was unfair to take Tudorville George's actions out on him, but she hadn't been able to talk it through with her sixteenth-century husband. She was like a stick of dynamite about to blow. Her discovery had reignited the agonising emotions she had suppressed following the months of trauma before George's former present-day life had disappeared with the timeline reset. Hearing him mourn for that lost life, so closely on the heels of the Marianne revelation, had pushed her over the edge and she was spinning.

The Great North Road, York, 1536 - Tudorville

George and Swifty arrived at the outskirts of York after a long, wet, and tiring journey on horseback up the Great North Road.

George pulled the reins to slow down his horse and beckoned to Swifty to stop. 'Let's find lodgings rather than stay at Willow Manor. My parents will only worry. God willing, we'll find them safe, and none the wiser when all this is over.'

'Aye, my lord,' said Swifty, who had become George's indispensable right hand ever since he had helped Cara and George escape from Newgate Prison. Swifty was no longer a grubby street urchin, but a proud member of the Cavendish household, and true to Cara's promise he had a home at Willow Manor with his brother, Bertie, a stable boy. George had taken him along to court, and Swifty lived up to his name; both in speed and wily wits.

'Where do you plan to meet with Master Aske, my lord?'

'The king thought it would be better to retain an element of surprise, but I sent word to him, so we may meet ahead of the formal negotiations.'

Swifty nodded and rode next to George on horseback as they wound along the muddy track on their way into York. George wasn't one for pomp and ceremony and preferred Swifty to ride at his side rather than bring up the rear in deference to his station.

Later that day, George met unofficially with his old friend, Robert Aske, and they settled down at a quiet corner table in a tavern on the outskirts of York. Some of Robert's men waited nearby for orders.

'George, we have thousand of pilgrims, and thousands more on the way, ready to fight for the cause,' said Aske, one eye blazing, the other blind and vacant.

'I see your passion, and truly, Robert, I sympathise, I do. But in turn, I beg you to consider the folly of leading these insurgents—I don't wish to see you hang for it.'

'Then what do you suggest? The king in his palace in

London is far removed from the suffering the people endure in the north, as you well know. Not only are they taxed beyond reason; the holy relics they treasure are stolen every day. To see the monks and nuns ripped brutally from their homes, and the Church's valuable possessions given to the Crown is to provoke a civil war. How the king imagines he will get away with the plundering and lack of respect of the old traditions and God's servants, I fail to understand.'

George surveyed the other tavern patrons and considered how he might influence Robert. His friend spoke the truth and he didn't know how to convince him to withdraw his support. He gestured to the tavern wench; a busty, vivacious brunette who was busy dispensing drinks, and signalled for another round.

'I don't agree with what's being done to the monasteries any more than you; I wish they would leave them in peace. But you know how wilful the king is, Robert, and with Cromwell at his side, sanctioning and scheming to cater to his every whim, there is little chance of the king reneging on his intentions to demolish the old religion and all that symbolises the old ways,' said George.

Robert took a hearty draft of his ale and drained his glass as he studied George's face. 'I confess I didn't foresee this Pilgrimage of Grace, but it's a natural progression after the failure of the Lincolnshire Uprising. Only a few weeks since, I was a resident at the Inns of Court, but I found myself unable to ignore the cries for help from Darcy and Constable.'

'But why must it be you who leads them? You are a man of law, not a soldier.'

The wench arrived with a flurry, served their drinks, and winked at George, before turning to leave.

'I see you haven't lost your touch with the fairer sex,' said Robert, smirking.

'You risk all you have worked so hard for, not to mention your family's reputation,' continued George, undeterred when they were alone again. 'Could you not advise them rather than lead?'

'I only agreed to step in to lead them because I have the other leaders' word that this is not a rebellion against the king himself, but a protest against Cromwell's heretic policies. It's a call for papist services to be restored, and Mary Tudor to be recognised as the rightful heir. She's the king's daughter, for heaven's sake. His own flesh and blood, and but for his personal ambitions with the Boleyn woman, there would be no new religion. We wish only to restore fairness to our glorious land, or the people will judge us, and it will end in disaster. Mark my words.'

'I understand, and I will see what I can do in presenting your plea. I will get word to the king and await his instruction, although I can't answer for the Duke of Norfolk who has his own way of dealing with matters.'

Robert looked nervous at the mention of the duke.

'I hope that in light of the support you have garnered, and your loyalty to the Crown, the king will consider restoring some of the monasteries and practices the people feel so strongly about. I can't promise anything except that I will do my best for you, Robert. And for York.

'If only they were all like you at court, George, we'd be in a much better position, and it would be a better England. You're a good man.'

George looked at his friend. 'These ongoing uprisings will harm us all. How will the people prosper if this state of affairs continues? I beg you, let us agree to resolve the differences, amicably. In the meantime, do I have your word you won't lead the men to march south, my friend? That would be an all-out declaration of war and the king will see to it that heads roll. It will be a bloodbath if they march on London.'

Aske bowed his head and rested his fingers on his forehead, as if meditating. They sipped their ale in silence for a few minutes, and George leaned his aching back against the hard chair, enjoying the brief respite.

'Cromwell rewrites every law he disagrees with and makes up new ones as he goes along. He pleases no one but himself and has little regard for the greater good of the people. And him a common lad from Putney, with no claim to noble birth, risen so high he no longer glimpses his toes. He should be ashamed, and if we prevail, he is in for a rude fall.'

'That may well be, but I would wager Cromwell is at the Tower making ready for war as we speak. I heard he was lining up the king's armaments and melting plate into coin. And he will not take kindly to you enforcing oaths without the king's blessing.'

George saw Aske was growing more agitated and decided he had made as much progress as he could for one meeting. After exchanging some pleasantries, he stood and reached across the table to shake Robert's hand. 'I appreciate your meeting with me at short notice and for your candour. Stay safe, my old friend, and remember what I said. Please don't let the men do anything hasty. I am optimistic we may resolve this without blood on our hands. I will be in touch.'

Rose Cottage, York - Present day

Cara hung her jacket up in the entrance hall, placed her car keys into the empty fruit bowl on the oak console table, and poked her head around the kitchen door, in search of George. 'I'm home.'

'I'm through here,' he replied.

Cara followed the rich, melodic timbre of his alluring voice through to the back of the cottage and found him sitting on the sofa in the study, glasses on, hardback book in hands. She kissed him and said, 'You look studious. What are you reading?'

He held up the front cover of a large hardback book.

'How did you know?' she asked.

'How did I know what?' he said.

'How on earth did you know that's what's happening in Tudorville?'

'Oh, I see... I didn't know. I don't know. Hang on—what don't I know? I've been reading up on 1536 and I found this book about the Pilgrimage of Grace. You were so upset the other day, I thought I would see if I could help.'

'Oh damn,' said Cara.

'What?'

'For a minute, I thought your memory had updated. I do wish it would all come back to you. But thank you—I appreciate you're trying to help.' She bowed her head. 'I'm sorry I was so bad tempered—it was unfair.'

He smiled. 'It's hard. I found it incredibly strange when I started time travelling and I couldn't talk to you about it. Thank goodness for Eddie, or we may never have understood what was going on.'

'Dear Eddie; that reminds me to call him and see how he's doing, beavering away at the university. I keep hoping he's getting closer to discovering a way for us to control our time travel. I really miss our quiet life.'

George patted the seat for Cara to join him and draped his arm round her shoulders. He pulled her closer, and then kissed her nose, before releasing her.

She nearly slipped off the sofa. 'Easy tiger,' she protested.

'Fancy a cup of tea and a slice of madeira cake?' he asked.

'Oh yum. What a question! I do...you know I do, but sadly I'll have to say no to the cake. I've put on quite a bit of weight; I really must stop eating so much. I don't know where you put it all.'

'Nonsense, you're skinny and gorgeous as ever. But, we'll skip the cake and I'll just make us a pot of tea.'

'You always say the right thing, but my jeans tell a different story.'

Cara kissed him before he ambled off into the kitchen to put the kettle on. What a blessing it was that they had such a wonderful time together doing the most ordinary things. She was even more grateful for the simple pleasures now she was time travelling again and never knew when she would be snatched away and plunged into the inevitable drama of Tudorville.

Cara picked up the book George had been reading, borrowed his reading glasses and leafed through the pages.

He sensed what she needed, even when he didn't know why; it was extraordinary. Cara had intended to look up the Pilgrimage of Grace and memorise the dates, but forgot about this book from her studies. Funnily enough, she'd purchased it in the same bookshop where she met George.

Cara turned the pages and read: "Robert Aske, leader of the most famous Tudor Uprising: The Pilgrimage of Grace, was executed for treason by order of King Henry VIII on 12 July 1537."

'Oh shit!' she said, as George entered the study holding the tea tray.

'What's the matter?'

'Well, you; I mean, Tudorville George has a dear friend called Robert Aske. He's told me about him many times and they are fond of each other. Robert had his back as a young boy and he's never forgotten.'

'Aw, well that sounds all very lovely.'

'Not really...'

'What? How bad can it be? It all happened five hundred years ago, anyway. We can't change it now, so there's not much point getting upset...'

'Um—pretty bad, I'm afraid. Let's just say I don't want to be the one to break the news to you, back then.'

'Oh, no. What happened?'

'Robert was executed for treason in 1537 with the other papist rebels.'

'That is pretty bad. Well, what can we do?'

'That's just it. That's why this is so frustrating. I can't even discuss it with you in Tudorville and so I'm going to have to sit back and watch you jump through hoops trying to save your friend, knowing all along he will die. It's heart-breaking.'

'Can't we save him somehow?'

'You know we can't risk meddling with the timelines, again. You only escaped execution last time because the king had second thoughts. We were close to having our heads dipped in cumin and set on spikes.'

'You do love to paint a gruesome picture,' he said.

'The entire future of Christendom and the Crown could be at stake if we make a wrong move and reset the timeline.'

'Yes, you're right.'

'I mustn't meddle with anything, but how do I know what I would have done if I didn't know the future?' Cara sipped her tea and continued to flick through the book. 'Listen to this: "The Pilgrimage of Grace was a huge rebellion against the policies of Thomas Cromwell and the Crown." It says that the Duke of Norfolk promised a pardon to Robert Aske when he saw that as many as forty thousand men gathered, and the uprising had a chance of being a great success, but then when the rebels, or pilgrims as they called themselves, dispersed, the king changed his mind, or had never intended to keep his word.'

'What a double-dealing scoundrel the king was,' said George. 'Poor Robert. I wish we could do something meaningful to help.'

'You know the rules. If we change anything, there is a real possibility the rebels could succeed to overthrow the Crown, and the country would have reverted to the old religion which would have triggered all-out civil war.'

'Well I don't want that on my conscience,' said George.

'Nor me. We can't risk taking any chances or the past as we know it would be completely rewritten.'

They spent the rest of the day pottering about the cottage and then took a leisurely late-afternoon stroll by the river until the calm blue sky filled with angry dark clouds, and Cara hugged her light cardigan around her as the northern winds whipped into a frenzy. The rain lashed down in heavy stair-rods and George reached for her hand as they raced for home.

In bed that night, Cara shoved lingering thoughts of George's Tudorville mistress to one side and made passionate love to him.

'Wow, what was that?' said George, when they were curled up in each other's arms. 'I saw stars. Did I mention how hot you are?'

'Perhaps once or twice. Seriously, though, we must not take each other for granted. It's easy to grow complacent and forget what we went through to be together. Let's not become one of those dreary couples who only make love on their anniversary, and barely exchange a word,' she said.

'That won't happen,' he said.

'How can you be so sure?'

'Because we're Twin Flames, remember? We've been together for five hundred years. If we're not fed up of each other by now, we're never going to be,' he replied.

'Sometimes I forget.'

He kissed her forehead and pulled the covers over them and they snuggled deeper into the mattress. They drifted off into a blissful sleep, their warm feet touching.

At three in the morning, when all was silent in the winding, narrow lanes around the cottage, George shot up in bed, and shouted, 'We must save Robert!'

CHAPTER 6

Hampton Court Palace, London, 1536 - Tudorville

A footman passed a note to Cara when she was on her way to the queen's rooms. She spotted George's handwriting, and hurriedly broke the seal and unfolded the paper, her hands shaking. She'd barely slept the previous night, worrying about what was going on in the north. Images of George, and his friend, Robert, flitted around her mind and she couldn't settle.

She had a sixth sense where George was concerned, and it didn't help that he'd been gone days and she'd not had any news; she feared she was becoming paranoid. Once the golden boy in the king's eyes, Cara would never have doubted his safety, but she had lost faith in the king and fervently wished George was far removed from the latest political machinations.

George was tender hearted and would not ignore an opportunity to help his friend. Not that he had much choice as he had pointed out: when the king requested he take a trip, he didn't dare make excuses or hesitate. His life depended on it.

Cara, my dearest darling, love,

Fret not. I am well, and it will please you to know that Swifty is at my side, making sure I am well taken care of. I have had a fruitful meeting with my friend, Robert, and am submitting his plea to the king, with the same messenger who delivers this note to you.

God willing, the Uprising will be resolved peacefully. Please pray the king will find it in his noble heart to meet the demands of the rebels, and this will all be over in the coming days. I will return to you as soon as I am able. Take care and know that you are always in my thoughts and forever in my heart.

Your devoted husband,
George.

Cara remembered the details she had researched about the Pilgrimage of Grace, and she knew it would all be coming to a head soon. She also knew that George would not wish to alarm her, and for that reason he would relay only positive news. She was relieved to hear from him but apprehensive about what he was holding back to protect her.

If only Edward were here, they could talk through the potential scenarios, and see whether they might in some way influence those involved in this precarious situation. Alone, she was confused and unsure what to do for the best. Was there anything she could or should do to help, or would she simply risk making things worse?

The weight of history unfolding before her eyes weighed heavily upon her conscience, and she felt woefully inadequate.

'There you are, Lady Cara, I am in need of your calming presence,' said Queen Jane.

Cara smiled and bowed her head. 'Your Grace, how may I be of service?'

The queen linked her arm through Cara's and said, 'Let us take a turn around the gardens while the sun shines brightly this fine and crisp morning.'

'Certainly, Your Majesty,' said Cara, inclining her head. Their long, heavy skirts trailed behind them as they swept across the gleaming palace floor, like giant swans' feathers shimmering on a shining lake.

The queen had recently declared that she enjoyed Cara and Margaret's company most of all, and they had risen effortlessly to the position of her favourite ladies-in-waiting. They were in an enviable spot; all the lords wished their wives, daughters, and nieces to be instrumental in the queen's rooms and sought to influence the king and queen through their kinswomen.

'Tell me, Lady Cara, have you had any word from your husband? I understand he is in York on behalf of the king.'

'Yes, Your Majesty, I received a note; albeit a rushed one, only this morning. I was beginning to fear for his wellbeing as I had heard nothing from him for some days.'

'That is good news indeed. I am pleased your mind is at rest, and he is presumably in good health?'

'He writes that he is well, thank you, Your Majesty.'

'May I enquire if he had anything to say about the new uprising in York? I am most concerned about the situation and wish to speak to the king to intercede for these poor people who have had their rights stripped asunder.'

'That is exceedingly kind, Your Grace; I agree, it is difficult not to be sympathetic to their cause.'

'The king is dreadfully short-tempered if I dare to get involved in his business without understanding the details. What may you tell me of what is happening up there?'

Cara was torn; she learned little from George's note, but she knew too much from her research five hundred years into the future. Here was her chance to assist the queen to bend the king to her will, but what if they succeeded to change the course of history? Would Robert be spared the noose? And if so, what repercussions would she set in motion if she unwittingly rewrote the timeline in her amateur efforts?

Cara turned to look at the queen as they strolled along the path towards the gardens.

'All I know, Your Majesty, is that there is a large group of men; as many as forty thousand, gathered in protest against the revoking of the rights to practise the old religion, the dismantling of the lesser monasteries, and the threat of higher taxes. Oh, and they also demand that the king recognise Princess Mary as his heir. The rebels claim they have been dealt an unfair hand, and many sympathise with their grievance even if they have no loyalty to the Pope. My understanding is that the uprising is not against the king, but rather against Cromwell's policies.'

'I see,' said the queen. A few strands of fair hair escaped from the confines of her gable headdress and shone in the sun. 'I will speak to the king, indeed.'

Cara longed to say, *Yes, plead with him not to break his promise, or the rebels will be executed.* Instead, she guarded her tongue. It wouldn't do to lead the queen into dangerous waters, but she couldn't resist saying, 'The leader of the Pilgrimage of Grace is a dear friend of my husband's and vouches that their intentions are honest, and they are true to the king. I would be grateful if you might beg leniency for Robert Aske, Your Majesty.'

'Thank you, Lady Cara. I do appreciate your candour; you have the advantage of much experience at court, as well as out in the world, so I don't take your advice lightly. It's refreshing not to be treated as though I'm made of glass and may shatter at any moment if I hear one ill word.'

Cara smiled at the queen with genuine fondness, and they continued their turn around the gardens, arm in arm, enjoying the crisp October air, softened by the gentle rays of sunshine.

Cara sighed with relief. Her appointment as lady-in-waiting had worked out better than she had expected, and Queen Jane who had a sweet nature, was far easier to please than Queen Anne who had been volatile and at the mercy of sudden tempers and low spirits. Not that Cara blamed Anne; she'd witnessed what she had been up against with so many people scheming for her downfall.

Rose Cottage, York - Present day

Cara fumbled through the fog of a sweet, deep sleep to switch on the bedside lamp. She looked across at George and saw his t-shirt was drenched in sweat.

'Hush, darling. Wake up. It's only a dream.'

'Where am I? What's going on?' he said.

'It's okay. You must have been dreaming of Tudorville.'

George looked at her and after a few seconds, said, 'I think I remember what's been happening.'

'You were shouting about Robert,' said Cara. 'Tell me what you saw while it's fresh in your mind.'

'It's difficult to know what was real and what was the stuff I've been reading, but it felt like I was there.'

'It can be that way, I get vivid dreams. Eddie's the same. I don't think you've had dreams like that about Tudorville before, have you?'

'No, not vivid like that, as though I was actually there.'

Cara handed George a glass of water from her bedside table and he gulped it down.

'I wonder if you'll remember our life here next time I go back. I've longed for you to remember, but now I'm not so sure it would be a good thing, given the situation with your friend, Robert. I'm trying not to do anything that Tudorville Cara wouldn't do. I mustn't attempt to steer you on a different course. It's just too dangerous,' said Cara.

'I was sitting at a table with Robert in a tavern, discussing the Pilgrimage of Grace. Did you tell me about that?'

'No, not as far as I recall. George didn't give me details of where they met. When I'm back there again, I'll ask you about Cornelius and if you remember, you won't look at me as if I've lost my senses!'

'I saw Robert being executed. That's why I was calling out in my dream.'

Cara stroked George's forehead and kissed his cheek. 'You'd better change out of that damp t-shirt.' She passed him a fresh one from a newly laundered pile on the nearby chest, and then nipped down to put the kettle on. They sipped their hot tea in bed, but couldn't settle down to sleep again, so they chatted until the early hours about the possibility of saving Robert from his inevitable premature death. Whichever way they looked at it, they couldn't see a way to change his fate without jeopardising the fate of the Crown.

'Perhaps Eddie will have a suggestion about what we can do,' said Cara, yawning.

'Did you speak to him since he called the other week?'

'No, it's been quite a while. I've been so busy whizzing back and forth, it's no wonder I lose track of time. I don't remember him calling.'

'What? We were sitting in the kitchen. It was that evening with the out-of-the-blue torrential rain and I was making spaghetti.'

'Ah...that explains it. I think it was the moment I first travelled to Tudorville after so long. Now I think of it, I wondered if the call triggered the vortex. What did Eddie say?'

'Funnily enough, he said he'd been having vivid dreams and it was usually a sign he would travel again. You spoke to him.'

'It's a blur.'

'I didn't know you'd gone at that second,' said George, shifting back down into the bed, and covering them both with the duvet.

'Let's call Eddie tomorrow. I can't speak to him in Tudorville because he's with the children. I can't say a word to anyone; not even my friend Margaret, obviously. She'd think I was crazy,' said Cara.

As the sun rose and the birds tweeted jubilantly in the trees, proclaiming the arrival of a bright new day, Cara and George drifted off to sleep in the comfort of one another's arms.

Grosvenor Square, London, 1848 - Victoriana

When George realised he had been transported back to Victoriana, only a year had passed in present-day time, but eight years had gone by since his previous visit.

Cara had aged slightly but was as stunning as ever. George turned to kiss her goodbye, and she wrapped her arms around his neck, positioning her body against his as they stood in the charming, sunny vestibule of the large elegant townhouse.

'Don't forget we have a dinner engagement tonight with Edward and Carlos,' she said.

'How could I forget those two, my love? I'm looking forward to seeing them. I'll be home in a few hours and we can while away the afternoon together. As long as the queen doesn't have other ideas, that is.'

'That sounds wonderful. I have my own ideas about what we can get up to this afternoon, so please do your best not to be detained.'

George walked at a brisk pace along Park Lane on his way to Buckingham Palace. He had a ten o'clock audience with Queen Victoria. He wondered whether Albert would be there too; the prince had been absent of late, absorbed in his many projects.

When the queen first summoned George, he was surprised to see the royal couple didn't present the same close-knit unit as when they were newly-weds in 1840. The prince and the queen had been besotted with one another back then but seemed to have grown apart.

George had been relieved to witness that he and Cara were as much in love as ever, and their marriage was a tremendous success. All seemed much as he had left it, other than they were now back in London after their sojourn in Seville.

He'd been coming and going between present day and Victoriana for a while now. One day he'd woken up and he was here. George still didn't understand how time travel worked, but he understood enough to know there was no point fighting it because he would lose. If the vortex called, you had no choice but to enter.

He and Cara had dared hope that this part of their life was over, but now he was experiencing the same frustrations as Cara when she travelled between the present-day and Tudorville.

He'd used the Cornelius code, and Cara had no idea what he was talking about. George sighed. It would be so much easier if both of them were conscious of all the timelines all the time. Or would it? Perhaps it was this way for a reason.

George had a philosophical approach to life and liked to believe that everything-happened-for-a-reason, but he struggled to understand the reason for their multiple timeline travel.

Cara's friend, Sylvia said they were time travelling again for their Twin Flame mission, and their souls were being called to evolve in a spiritual sense, and their lack of memory in the timelines signified they weren't fully awakened yet. He thought some of what Sylvia said was a load of romantic poppycock, but he couldn't argue with the reality of time travel.

Sometimes he wished they could live an ordinary life again like their recent happy year in present-day York, but on days such as this he was thrilled with the joy of being alive in 1848. What could be more exciting than serving Queen Victoria in her prime? By some strange twist of fate, he was blessed, and today he felt it.

The footman ushered him into the grand drawing room where the queen liked to receive her callers.

'Good morning, Lord Cavendish,' Queen Victoria greeted him with a warm smile. 'It's good to have you back in London. It seems the past years you've spent most of your time between Seville and York, and while you've been of great service as my spy at a distance, it's far more convenient, and entertaining, may I add, to have you nearby as my confidant.'

She smiled and gestured for him to take a seat on the dark red velvet chair opposite her.

'I'm always honoured to be of service, Your Majesty. It appears we have more than enough troubles in our own backyard to keep us occupied.'

'Do you refer to the Chartists' latest exploits?'

'I do, Your Grace. The uprising could grow more dangerous if we're not careful.'

'Uprising...do you really believe it could grow to be as serious as that? Albert has similar concerns.'

'I do, ma'am, the people want their rights and seem intent on having them, one way or another. This People's Charter has been active and bubbling beneath the surface for years, and as you are aware with the arrival of King Philippe of France; revolution is sweeping through Europe.'

Queen Victoria touched the beads on her necklace and appeared to contemplate George's words.

'And what do you think of these so-called rights, Lord Cavendish? Do you have sympathy for the Chartist cause?'

'I do have sympathy and understanding for them, ma'am. The working-class men have been overlooked in terms of gaining the vote, and I think it will do us no harm whatsoever to extend that right to them. It will strengthen us as a nation and give national pride to the masses.'

'I'm inclined to agree, although I would like to understand exactly what is at stake, and what the far-reaching implications of meeting their demands, might be. I'm not one for giving in to demands without good reason, as you know.'

'Unrest in the city is growing, and I feel it would be wise to be proactive rather than wait until the situation spirals out of control.'

The queen clasped her hands together. 'They attacked Buckingham Palace when you were away, you know. It was terrifying—we thought we may have to flee.'

'Yes, I am aware. The cooking pot simmers; it is my opinion we must do all we can to prevent it from reaching boiling point. That's when the real trouble will commence, and things could turn ugly.'

'You speak wise words, Lord Cavendish, and I am grateful for your counsel. Albert is so preoccupied with his own endeavours these days, it's hard to get a word out of him.'

'There is talk of the Chartists demonstrating again before they present their petition at the Houses of Parliament. We don't want a revolution on our hands which is a real possibility if they feel we aren't taking them seriously.'

'My goodness, you're scaring me rather. Pray tell how we may convey this is not the case. I do not wish my people to think I don't take their concerns seriously.'

'I understand, ma'am, and I did not wish to alarm you. Shall I make enquiries? I fear we are both in our ivory towers as it were, and there is a lot of which we are not aware.'

'What do you suggest?'

'I may pay a visit to where the Chartists are known to congregate and see what I can learn.'

'Do take care; the prime minister warns me some of them are violent.'

George bowed his head. 'Fear not, ma'am. I shall report to you as soon as I have news.'

'Very well. Please make it your priority because I have no

intention of running away to the Isle-of-Wight permanently, as Albert would have us do.'

The queen excused George, and he stood outside the door while he considered the best way forward. A few moments later, he headed towards the rear of the palace and took the stairs, two at a time, down to the lower-floor.

An idea had occurred to him about how to find out what was going on in the heart of the Chartist camp without going far at all. All going to plan, he would be back with Cara by lunchtime, and nothing pleased him more.

CHAPTER 7

Hampton Court Palace, London, 1536 - Tudorville

Cara awoke to the unmistakable sound of thundering hooves in the courtyard beneath her window. She leapt out of bed hoping to see George. She spotted Swifty and sent up a quick prayer that George was with him; she couldn't be certain, but she thought she'd heard more than one beat of hooves.

As she peered through the window trying to make out what was going on, she glimpsed the back of George's head, and as if by magic he looked up and saw her watching him. Their eyes locked and even from that distance a familiar jolt reverberated through her entire being. She waved and signalled that she would be down, before scrambling for her gown and pulling it hurriedly over her linen smock. Cara wasn't at all presentable by strict court standards, but it was still early, and she couldn't wait to slip out to greet George.

All that mattered was that he was home; she longed to feel his arms around her again. She splashed cold water on her face from a bowl on her nightstand, patted her skin dry and smoothed down her wild bed-hair. She saw her anticipation reflected in the mirror. Her grey eyes shone, and a small red patch marked each cheekbone and gave her a flushed, feverish look.

Cara was still amazed by the effect George's presence had on her. She loved who she was when they were together—no matter what the century—their sense of connection was just as strong. Never had she seen so clearly that time was an illusion of the mind.

She rushed out of the bedchamber door, into the dimly lit hallway, and then darted down the backstairs so she could reach the spot where she'd seen George.

Swifty was stroking his horse. He raised his head and his eyes shone as he saw Cara walking towards them. 'Good morning, my lady.'

'Good morning, Swifty, good to see you back. I missed seeing your smiling face around here.'

She was rewarded with his mischievous grin. It was a good day that had brought Swifty into their lives, and she would never forget how he had helped them escape Newgate Prison, and had proved such a support for them in the Tower of London.

'I heard you thundering in; you're quite the experienced rider these days. Where is your master? I saw him through the window, but he seems to have vanished.'

And then a pair of powerful arms encircled her from behind, and George spun her around to face him.

'I was beginning to wonder whether you were a figment of my imagination, so have I longed to see you. I seem to be forever awaiting your return,' she said.

'I know, my love. And I'm sorry for that. I have missed you terribly. What a lovely surprise to see your face in the window at this early hour.'

'I confess I had a sense you were on your way. I couldn't settle last night, and dreams roused me. What a relief to see you here this morning.'

George passed his horse's reins to one of the stable lads and they walked through the courtyard and up the backstairs into their apartment. He captured her hand, and she knew immediately that all was right between them again.

'It's still early; let's steal a few precious hours alone before I must seek out the king and make my report. He will be keen to hear the latest news when he awakes.'

Cara had questions for George, but she could see he was weary and eager to be out of his grubby clothes after the long journey on horseback, so she steered him towards the bed, unbuttoned his shirt and tenderly slid the sleeves off his wide shoulders and down his chiselled arms. She couldn't resist smoothing her hands over his chest, and he raised his head and sought out her mouth with his lips. The kiss was soft at first, but became urgent, and he wound his hands through her long chestnut hair as if to claim her.

'You must be exhausted, my lord, so I thought to help you into bed.'

'That sounds like a perfect idea,' he said, pulling her down onto his lap.

Cara could feel him pressing against her. A thrill spiralled through her body and shook her. They'd not had the opportunity to be together during the past weeks. She had yearned for their physical union, and in his absence, fantasised about him touching her like this. His raw masculine scent inflamed her further.

'It's wonderful to be back in your arms,' she said, then scattered featherlight kisses across his chest and neck, until he shivered with desire.

'Are you cold, my lord?'

'On the contrary, I'm hot—extremely hot, you temptress.'

Cara laughed, and her love for her husband overcame the recent jealousy and insecurity that had clouded her thoughts and hijacked her peace of mind.

Tudorville-Cara's consciousness blended with modern Cara's, and she knew the truth: theirs was true love, and whatever challenges presented themselves, and no matter what either of them did, they would always love each other. Their love was eternal and unconditional, and now she felt it more strongly than ever.

They would be living their lives five-hundred-years into the future, even at this very moment.

Cara was ever wary of the dangers of ruining their hard-won perfect future. They'd been through so much to be together; she couldn't bear it if they lost each other again.

Her heart was aglow with love for him.

George helped Cara out of her gown, tugged her smock over her head and ran his hands slowly over her skin.

Cara groaned. 'You tease me so, I can barely wait for you to take me. It's been too long.'

He reached out to tilt her face toward his and searched her eyes.

'It has been far too long. You were angry with me when I left, and it's stayed with me all the time I was away. I hate to disappoint you, it hurts me as much as it hurts you.'

Sorrow was etched into her features.

'Whenever we are at odds, I feel it so deeply.'

She pulled away from him slightly and studied his face. 'I adore you no matter what you have done, or who you have been with, but at some point, we will need to discuss it, or how will we ever put it behind us?'

George pulled her against him and crushed her lips, and she hungrily returned his kiss. Reality and conscious thought slipped away from them both as the fire that raged between their bodies consumed them.

'Let's focus on this,' he said.

Cara ran her hands through his thick wavy hair, which was smudged with steely grey and gave him an even more dashing appearance than in the present day. His hair was the quickest way to remind herself she was in Tudorville.

She pleasured him in the way she knew drove him wild, and her own excitement built until neither of them could wait. George moved closer to the edge of the bed and their red-hot passionate desire reached fever pitch. George cried out, and they exploded in a pure pool of soul-sex ecstasy.

They lay naked and entwined in each other's arms, satiated and joyful.

'Well, that was worth waiting for,' he said.

He breathed her in and touched her hair which cascaded over her shoulders like an unruly wave. 'Cara, I love you. There has only ever been you since the second we met. And there will only ever be you. That much I promise you. I have no desire to be with other women. Goodness knows, if I did, there are enough of them ready and willing wherever I go with the king. Do you not understand yet that I want only you?'

Cara was silent as she tried to contain her jumbled emotions. His words served as a soothing balm to her hurt, frightened soul. When he was away she had thought she had lost him and been mistaken about the depth of their love. But no; he was saying the tender, reassuring words she'd longed to hear. She knew he spoke the truth and her pain dissipated as quickly as it had arisen to grasp and throttle her spirit.

Her eyes filled with tears. 'That's beautiful. I needed to hear that. Why didn't you tell me that when I was so upset before you left?'

'I was furious when you interrogated and accused me like that. You never behaved in such a way before, and you didn't give me a chance to tell you whether it was true; you simply decided I was guilty. You were the judge and jury.'

Cara saw the flash of pain in his eyes. She bowed her head, and the tears slid down her face. 'I'm sorry,' she said, and meant it. 'Are you saying you didn't go with Marianne, after all?'

'That's exactly what I'm saying. I met her when I was with the king, but we didn't consummate the relationship. Her sister is the king's mistress—the gossips got that bit right, but nothing more. I admit I was tempted for a moment when I was drunk in my cups, but I quickly came to my senses.'

Relief flooded through Cara, and she took his hand and said, 'I shouldn't have believed what I heard so readily. I should have asked you first, and I apologise for thinking the worst. Can you forgive me?'

'Of course, I forgive you. But please don't do it again. If you're upset about something, ask me about it first before condemning me.'

Cara raised his hand to her lips and kissed it. 'You have my word,' she said. 'I seem to have to keep learning the same lesson.' She sighed. Fortunately, they'd not been through relationship turmoil in Tudorville before this misunderstanding, and she was grateful harmony was restored. They rested quietly in each other's arms, dozing to the sounds of the chaotic chorus of chirping birds as the sun rose in the sky, proclaiming a new October day in the year, 1536.

Rose Cottage, York - Present day

The line crackled in Cara's ear; she could hear Eddie speaking but couldn't make out what he was saying. 'Eddie? Can you hear me?'

'Cara...Cara? Can you hear me now?'

'Ah, yes. That's better.'

'I'm on the train so the connection's dipping in and out. How are you?'

'I'm well. Any chance of you coming to stay for a few days?' She raised her voice, so he could hear her over the rumble and screech of the train in the background.

'Not at the moment, I'm afraid. There's too much going on at work.'

'George told me we're having dinner together later in Victoriana; you, George, Carlos and me,' she said.

'How wonderful. Does George remember what's going on in Tudorville too?' asked Eddie.

'No, and it's annoying as hell. He told me you called the other week, but I have no recollection of it. That's when I went back to Tudorville for the first time in ages, so I'm wondering if your call triggered the vortex, somehow.'

Cara pressed her phone tightly against her ear.

'I doubt it,' said Eddie.

'Have you made any progress in your quantum time travel research?'

'I'd love to say yes, but I'm not much further along. The only thing which seems true but is as yet unproven is that when we travel, something big is usually going down in the timelines. It's as though our consciousness wakes us up and we automatically gravitate to where the high drama is in a past life.'

'Like when Anne Boleyn was about to be beheaded, you mean?'

'Yep.'

'I miss our quiet life without all of this intrigue.'

'It must be difficult for you both. How is George coping?' asked Eddie.

'He woke up in the middle of the night shouting about saving his friend in Tudorville, poor thing.'

'That's curious—it sounds as though his consciousness is communicating to him in his sleep. I wouldn't be surprised if he remembers more soon.'

'The thing is, Eddie, I told him what happens, and he wants to save his friend, Robert Aske, who by some fateful throw of the dice is the leader of the Tudor uprising, the Pilgrimage of Grace. The year after it ends, his friend will be executed for treason.'

'What does George suggest?'

'He doesn't know, but he seems determined to intervene. He asked me to help him, and I would like to, but I worry about the repercussions.'

'The chance of his friend's death probably won't affect your future.'

'How do you know?'

Eddie said, 'Um...I don't for certain. There are no guarantees, but unless he's closely entwined with George's future, then it's unlikely there'd be any impact. Unless...'

The train screeched through a tunnel and the connection dropped.

'Unless?' Cara prompted him when he called back a few minutes later.

'Well, if George were to be accused of sympathising with the rebels, that may prove fatal.'

'Yes, that's what scares me. I can warn him again in Tudorville, but the most I can get away with without revealing I'm a time traveller, is to hint at a seer's gift. He doesn't take me all that seriously when I mention my special powers. It's not unusual for women in Tudor times to be seen as having supernatural gifts, but it can be deadly if someone accuses you of witchcraft. I must be cautious, or I'll land us back in the Tower. I'm counting on you figuring this out, Professor, so we're not doomed to the whims of the vortex forever,' she said before they ended the call.

She was only half-joking and didn't know how long she could hold it all together.

Cara and George sat drinking a glass of wine; rays of sunshine warming their faces through the closed bi-fold doors.

'That call sounded completely bonkers. Just as well no one else was listening in. What did Eddie say?' asked George.

'He has an unproven theory that we time travel when something important happens.'

'What, so that we may fix it?'

Cara shook her head. 'You know the rules. Although Eddie only seemed concerned if you directly intervened to help Robert, and the king were to accuse you of backing the rebels.'

George perked up. 'That sounds promising. I don't like to think I'm witness to a gross injustice and can't attempt to help a friend.'

'It does seem like a dreadful waste when we're catapulted back to critical points in history but can't tilt the odds in another direction,' said Cara.

'You said we're together in Tudorville now, right?'

'Yes, you've returned to Hampton Court, but I think you will go back to York soon. According to our research, the Duke of Norfolk delivered the offer from the king, but then double-crossed them as soon as the rebels had their army stand down.'

'Norfolk is Thomas Howard, and a shrewd operator. I know we mustn't try to change history, but I want to help Robert if I can,' said George, gazing at Cara over the rim of his wine glass.

Cara watched his animated face and hand gestures as he made his case for rescuing his friend from the hangman. She was already resigned to helping him; she knew him too well to think he would let it go simply because it was inconvenient.

George said, 'You're going to have to tell me to warn Robert.'

'How do you suggest I do that without revealing I come from the future?'

'How about you say you had a premonition that the king is going to double cross the men, and you think it would be wise to warn Robert?'

'You do know you risk being accused of treason for merely alluding to such a thing? What if Robert mentions it to someone and word gets out that the king's trusted emissary doesn't trust his word?'

'You're right. Hopefully, I won't put my foot in it. We'll have to come up with something more cunning.'

They sat quietly, and he considered his options. He turned to her after a while and said, 'You can tell me I must get him to disassociate himself from the Pilgrimage.'

'You do realise this is you we're talking about, right?'

'What do you mean?'

'Just because I tell you what to do, it's absolutely no guarantee you'll do it. You're just as stubborn in Tudorville, as you are here.'

George looked into her eyes and smiled. 'Ah, right. Well, we'll just have to hope I can see the sense in your suggestion. Try not to be too bossy and I'll be more likely to follow your advice.'

'Bossy, me? I think you mean persuasive.'

George laughed, and Cara snuggled into his arms, grateful they were safely at home together.

CHAPTER 8

Hampton Court Palace, London, 1536 - Tudorville

Cara reluctantly released George from her embrace as he unfurled his long limbs and stood up slowly.

'I must report to the king; he'll have heard of my return and no doubt awaits the latest news of the uprising.'

'All right,' she said, her mood plummeting, despite her efforts to be stoic.

George tilted her chin upwards and looked into her eyes. 'I won't be away long today, and we will dine in the great hall together later. Even if I leave again soon, it won't be today as the king will want us to determine strategy with Cromwell and Norfolk.'

'I don't think it's going to end well for Robert if he persists in leading the Pilgrimage,' she said.

George studied Cara's face as he rubbed his thumb across her cheek and then leaned down to kiss the top of her head.

'What is this, my love? Have you divined some strange power to see into the future while I've been away?'

'Something like that... I ask you to trust that I have a strong sense of trouble for your friend.'

'It's true, you're rarely off base with those senses of yours although what more I can do for him, I don't know. Robert is up to his neck in it. I probably couldn't tear him away if I tried; he's deeply passionate about the cause.'

Cara beckoned him closer and lowered her voice. 'The queen told me the king has no intention of granting their demands. She relayed to me how she beseeched him to restore some of the papist customs.'

George dressed hurriedly in clean breeches, white shirt, and a finely embroidered doublet, always preferring to dress himself unlike the other nobles. 'I don't as yet know the details of what the king intends to propose,' he said. George was secretly worried about the king's intentions but hadn't wished to alarm Cara.

'Henry was immoveable on the matter and rebuked the queen for attempting to intervene in affairs of state,' Cara whispered.

'I have high hopes that what the queen told you will not come to pass. I am most optimistic of a peaceful agreement, and the king granting at least some of their demands. If he double crosses the rebels, I can't see them backing down without bloodshed...in which case you could be right about poor dear Robert.'

George finished dressing, kissed Cara one last time, and said, 'Thanks for warning me, my darling. When I return, we must think of a way to divert him; perhaps we may save him from such an untimely end.'

Cara wrapped her arms round his neck and returned his kiss. 'Hold on, what? You know about Robert Aske being executed?' she said.

George looked at Cara; his confusion reflected in his brown eyes. 'Why, of course I do. We talked of it at the cottage in York. Have you forgotten?' he whispered in response.

'How wonderful you remember, at last. It was so difficult trying to figure this out on my own. We'll talk more upon your return. Do please take care not to let anything about the future slip out by mistake.'

'Don't fret; I'm clear on my role here.'

'I love you,' said Cara.

George turned to face her from the doorway, 'I love you,' he said, and blew her a kiss as he departed.

Cara lay in bed for a while musing over how incredible it was that he was aware of their time travel. The fear she had carried with her, like a hard lump in her chest, dissipated and she jumped out of the four-poster bed with renewed optimism.

Later that day, Margaret turned to clasp Cara's hands when she entered the queen's apartments and sat next to her. 'Are you quite well, my dear? I've been worried about you.'

Cara smiled, and replied, 'All is resolved. George has returned, and we have spoken about the matter. I am reassured that it wasn't what we thought. I was a fool to believe it when I know his heart is true.'

'That's wonderful news. I am happy to hear that the most well-suited couple at court, are reunited. If I spoke false, I am sorry indeed. Please forgive me.'

Cara squeezed her friend's hands in return.

'I know you only said what you'd heard in good faith. Gossip spreads like wildfire—it's difficult to quell the flames once they gather momentum.'

'May I help in any way, my dear Cara?'

'Perhaps you would be so kind as to let it be known that the rumour was false, and Marianne is not George's mistress, as her sister would have the court believe.'

Margaret and Cara passed several uneventful but contented hours sewing in the queen's rooms. Cara's heart was light, and she was at peace for the first time during her recent visits to Tudorville. Adept with a needle, she still had no memory of where or when she had learned to sew other than a few bundled attempts at school in present-day York. She was once again grateful and not a little in awe that she was somehow naturally accomplished in the ways of Tudor aristocracy.

Later that afternoon she entered her rooms and was pleasantly surprised to find George already there. She was excited to find out more about what he remembered of their other lives.

'I didn't expect to see you at this hour. How did it go with the king?'

'Come sit and let's enjoy the time together before I must leave tomorrow,' he said.

'Oh no...must you really leave so soon?'

'I'm afraid so. We are to offer terms to appease the rebels. The king; well, in truth, Cromwell, bade us to leave at first light as he is eager to crush the rebellion.'

Cara poured them both a glass of wine and they settled down next to the glowing fire.

'And did you think of a way to divert Robert from playing such a prominent role?'

George looked at her curiously. 'Why would I endeavour to divert him? It'll all be over when we deliver the king's offer, and God willing the rebels will lay down their arms and call off the Pilgrimage.'

'Oh lord, you've forgotten,' said Cara.

'Forgotten what, my love?'

'Never mind. I don't suppose you've seen Cornelius?' she said, staring into George's confused eyes, already knowing his answer.

'Cornelius? But he's at Willow Manor. Isn't he?'

Buckingham Palace, London, 1848 - Victoriana

George stepped onto the lower floor which was the engine room of Buckingham Palace. Without the servants following the carefully planned operations and procedures from below stairs, nothing would move in the old building.

'May I help you, Sir?' A figure who for a fleeting moment reminded George of Carson from the popular TV show, Downton Abbey, loomed before him.

'Ah, yes, sorry to appear unannounced like this but I'm on a rather urgent errand on behalf of the queen.'

'Lord Cavendish, how may I be of assistance?'

Nothing escaped Smithson, the long-serving butler, and he knew who George was with no introduction. He had admitted him into the queen's presence many times over the years.

'I wonder if we may have a brief word, in private.'

'Yes, of course, my lord, come into my office; it's just over the other side of the parlour. May I call for some tea, perhaps?'

'No, no, thank you—there's no need for any fuss.'

Smithson invited George to take a seat, while he remained standing.

'Please be seated, Smithson.' George pointed to the chair and the butler perched on the arm.

Smithson looked at George expectantly.

'Don't worry; I shan't detain you long,' said George,

detecting the butler's unease at being called away from his duties. George lowered his voice and continued, 'It's rather a delicate matter, regarding the queen. I'm concerned for her safety and I'm trying to get a sense of what's happening on the streets, and I thought, what better place to seek answers than here, below stairs.'

Smithson's bushy eyebrows twitched slightly, but his face remained devoid of emotion which was the result of twenty years in service with the royal family. If he was disturbed, no one was going to guess it from his carefully guarded features. 'I'm certain no one here has anything but love and respect for the queen, my lord.'

'Yes, of course. Forgive me, I didn't mean to imply anyone would wish her harm within these walls—I expressed myself clumsily. I'm keen to know what your opinion is of the Chartists and your understanding of their intentions.'

A fleeting sign of curiosity crossed Smithson's face, but his expression was instantly restored to that of a blank canvas, and then he said, 'I spend so much of my time within the palace I'm not the best person to ask. And as far as the servants go, I expect them to guard their loose tongues, so I fear we will be of little use to you in this regard.'

'I quite understand, Smithson. Is there someone who may be more in touch with what's happening beyond the palace? I wouldn't impose on you if it weren't an urgent matter concerning the queen's security and that of the country.'

Smithson pondered for a few seconds, rotating his thumb back and forth across his lips. 'I'll call one of the junior footmen; if anyone knows what's happening on the streets of London, it'll be him. Please bear with me, my lord. I think he may be above stairs this morning.'

George watched a sluggish five minutes tick by on the mahogany grandfather clock and hoped that Smithson would soon return with his street-wise apprentice. He was anxious to accomplish his mission and to embark on his leisurely afternoon with Cara; but this was important business. He hoped he would leave significantly more enlightened than he had arrived.

A familiar-looking boy hovered in the doorway, and Smithson gave him a gentle push in the small of his back to propel him into the office. 'Go in lad. This is Lord Cavendish, and he has a few questions for you about the Chartists. You're not in any trouble; just tell him what you know.' Smithson discreetly left the room and closed the door.

George saw the young footman didn't recognise him, or if he did, he was a terrific actor. 'Good afternoon. Thank you for agreeing to help me with my enquiries. I'm sorry to have dragged you away from your duties.'

The boy looked startled and stood to attention before George, cutting a fine upright figure in his royal uniform.

'What's your name, boy?'

'They call me Swifty.'

George nodded, doing his best to conceal his delight at unexpectedly meeting his faithful servant from Tudorville.

'What do you know of the Chartists?' George asked.

'The People's Charter—the Suffrage Movement?'

'Yes. I hear more unrest is brewing. I want to know if you have heard the Chartists talk about the queen and the royal family.'

'I know little, my lord. I think most wish only to present their petition to Parliament and are hoping a bill will pass to give working class men the vote.'

George was impressed by Swifty's eloquence and demeanour. He was older here in Victoriana than in Tudorville, and by what he'd seen so far, he was a real credit to the royal household.

Present-day Cara would be thrilled when he told her he'd

met Swifty in the service of Queen Victoria. She had a soft spot for the boy; they both loved him dearly.

'Do you by any chance know where the Chartists gather for their meetings?'

Swifty paused for a second and was thoughtful. 'I do, my lord. I know one of the leader's sons who is active with the Chartists.'

'Swifty, I can't say why exactly, but I feel a certain affinity with you; as though I may count on you. Would you be willing to undertake a secret assignment for me? We would have the blessing of the queen.'

Swifty's eyes widened. 'I am always ready to serve Her Majesty and I am at your service, my lord.'

'I am extremely grateful for your willingness. Come closer; one can't be too careful when discussing such delicate matters.' George leaned towards Swifty and whispered into his ear.

Swifty's face was solemn as he listened. 'Yes, my lord. I believe it is in my power to carry out such an assignment. I have Sunday afternoon off and could go then.'

'Splendid.' George dipped into his pocket and withdraw some coins and pressed them into Swifty's palm. He whispered instructions and Swifty nodded.

'Can you write?' asked George.

'Yes, my lord,' he said, the pride evident in his musical voice.

'Good. Send me a note as soon as you return. Don't write your findings but let me know whether you have learned anything significant.'

George scribbled his address onto a palace notepad and handed the paper to Swifty. 'Here, keep it safe. Be cautious, lad, the Chartists will not take kindly to you poking about in their secret business, but the queen's safety may depend on what you discover.'

CHAPTER 9

Rose Cottage, York - Present day

Cara and George sipped tea and basked in the gentle warmth of the conservatory which overlooked the garden.

Cara cast her eyes over the vibrant flowerbeds, bursting with crimson, red and yellow roses. 'The garden needs some attention. I'd better get out there later if the weather stays dry.'

'I'll help. I could do with the exercise—I can't keep sitting around like this.' He studied the rows of colourful flowers waving and swaying in the soft late summer breeze. 'How are things in Tudorville?'

Cara peered at him over the rim of her china tea cup. 'It's like being with some poor dear old soul suffering from Alzheimer's,' she said, rolling her eyes. 'One minute you knew about Robert Aske's execution, and the next you'd forgotten and were excited about the king's false promises.'

'I remembered for a moment? Well, that's encouraging,'

said George. 'I know how infuriating it is; you're the same in Victoriana. There was that moment last year when you recognised Eddie, but other than that, nothing, so don't be too hard on poor old Tudorville George. Victoriana Cara remembers nothing about our parallel timelines, but she is so lovely, I can't be frustrated for long.'

Living multiple lives was taking its toll on the newly married couple. All they had to go on were their catch-up discussions in the present day.

'I sometimes lose the plot and forget what we agreed to do. And I think you are here with me, when you're not really,' she said.

'Well, short of checking every two minutes, how are we to know? We can't keep asking about Cornelius. We'll drive each other mad,' said George.

'On the bright side, if we don't notice any difference, I suppose we must be much the same,' said Cara.

'Talking of Cornelius how is the beautiful, sweet boy?'

'He was as darling as ever last time I saw him at Willow Manor,' said Cara. 'He took to accompanying me and the children on our daily rides. He missed you terribly when you left for London. Then he sat by your chair every day, looking mournful.'

'Wasn't it wonderful when he appeared at Willow Manor when we stayed at the hotel?' said George.

'Yes, I love it there.'

'Perhaps we could do that again. I had a dream the other night that we lived at Willow Manor and it was ours again,' said George.

'How lovely. Do you know what happened—I mean why it's no longer in the family?'

'I wondered about that, but never really got around to looking into it,' said George. 'Kate might know. She's up on the family history. I'll ask her next time we talk.'

'It would be fabulous if we could get it back again.'

'Funnily enough I've been thinking about it ever since I had that strange dream. It must be incredibly expensive to run, which might be why the family let it go. I don't think we could raise the funds for such an extravagant purchase, without bankrupting ourselves.'

'My father might be interested in investing in it. I could ask him, although I know absolutely nothing about hotels other than how to stay in them,' said Cara.

'Me too. Still, I may look into it and see if it's possible to raise the funds somehow—that's if it ever comes back on the market.'

'Are you getting bored not working?' she asked.

'I'm starting to feel rudderless without a career. I miss the smell of musty old manuscripts.'

'So, being Queen Victoria's spy and King Henry VIII's envoy in two historic uprisings, isn't enough to keep you entertained?'

George smiled ruefully. 'Well, when you put it like that. Although, I still feel like I need something purposeful to do here.'

'Fair enough, whatever you want to do, you know you have my support. It would be fabulous to own Willow Manor, and even to live in it if we could swing it, somehow.'

'You know what—I'll give Kate a call now and see what she knows. Probably best to check, before doing anything drastic,' said George.

'Great idea. I'll be in the study writing for an hour.'

'Perfect. Meet me in the kitchen at noon. Fancy scrambled eggs on toast?'

Cara leaned in to kiss George. 'My stomach's already growling at the thought. Give my love to Kate. I hope she's enjoying some time out of her hectic schedule at Casa Cavendish and making the most of the Spanish sunshine.'

. . .

Cara entered the kitchen and saw George putting the last touches to brunch. She laid the table, and they sat down to eat.

'This is delicious,' said Cara, as she chewed slowly and savoured the scrambled eggs while George wolfed his down as though he hadn't eaten for days.

'I love cooking for you,' he said.

They laughed and chatted in between mouthfuls.

'Did you speak to Kate?'

'Yes—we had a lovely catch up.'

'How's she doing? Did she know anything about what happened to Willow Manor back in the day?'

'She's doing well, and as we suspected, she knew rather a lot. It turns out that one of our ancestors was a bit of a black sheep, and unfortunately he's another one whose name I bear.'

'I knew there had to be a bad egg in the George Cavendish bloodline. You must have made a wrong move somewhere through the centuries.'

'Is almost being executed by order of King Henry VIII, not enough for you, you blood thirsty wench?'

'That was gorgeous,' Cara said, finishing her last piece of buttered wholemeal toast. 'Oh yes, well there is that. But come on, don't keep me in suspense, what on earth did the scoundrel, George, get up to?'

'Well by the sounds of it, he really was a bit of a cad, but I'll fill you in on him later. We've got something far more important to do.'

'Oh—and what might that be?' Cara wiped her hands on a napkin and pushed her plate to one side.

'We're going to reacquire Willow Manor,' said George,

spreading a thick layer of strawberry jam onto another piece of toast.

'Goodness, you move fast. How the heck are we going to do that?'

'I've got an idea; rather an ingenious one, even if I do say so myself. Come on, finish your coffee; we're going on a reconnaissance mission. There's something I want to show you.'

Cara looked at George. 'Oh-oh...you're deadly serious, aren't you?'

'Willow Manor is coming back into the Cavendish family if we can pull this off.'

Cara loved adventures with George, and even more so when they were in the right place in the right timeline.'

She swigged the last of her coffee, grabbed her jacket from the hook in the hallway and they headed out the door.

'Yours or mine?' he said.

'Yours, it's a Porsche day, and anyway you know I love it when you chauffeur me about.'

'That's the trouble with marrying a rich girl,' he said.

'More like Cinderella.'

Cara hadn't forgotten her humble beginnings; her father was one of the wealthiest businessmen in York, but before he visited the children's home and changed her life by adopting her, she had been a nervous, lonely little girl. She was forever grateful and tried never to take her immense good fortune for granted. Occasionally, even all these years later, she dreamt she was alone in her single bed in the dormitory, and awoke in the night, heart racing, feeling scared and unsafe.

'Where are we off to?' she asked.

'Patience is a virtue, my darling. It's a surprise; you'll see soon enough.'

'Perhaps I should have driven, after all,' she said, teasing, as she settled into the soft leather seat of George's classic sports car, and they zoomed off down the narrow lane. She gazed at his profile, and a surge of love consumed her. 'I love you, I'm so glad we've got over our disagreement,' she said.

'Me too. What happened with Tudorville George?'

'What happens in Tudorville, stays in Tudorville,' she said, winking.

'I knew it. Next time you have to trust me.'

'That's more or less what he said.'

'Classy guy, I like Tudorville George.'

A fierce burst of warm wind whipped through the open window and blew Cara's hair across her face. It was one of those perfect moments when she was grateful to be alive, and the future lay before them like the promise of a rosy summer's dawn.

George handled the car with ease and she gazed at the beautiful lush scenery as they darted down the country road. 'We're going to Willow Manor,' she said after a few minutes.

'Spot on.'

'Is the surprise that you booked us into the hotel for the night?'

'No, much better than that. Just wait a bit and all will be revealed.'

She never tired of admiring his beautiful hands, and she did so now as they rested on the steering wheel and manoeuvred through the gear changes.

They swung through Willow Manor's gated entrance which was open, and then George brought the car to a smooth stop on the other side.

'Why are we stopping here?'

'Look out of your window,' he said.

'Oh my God.' Cara looked over at him, her eyes glittering.

'I wanted us to see it for ourselves. It's a sign, all right,' said George, reaching for her hand.

Hampton Court Palace, London, 1536 - Tudorville

George and Cara dined in the great hall that evening, just as George had predicted. It was impossible not to notice the charged atmosphere. The king was ill-tempered and drank even more than usual, and the queen did her best to pacify him with her sweet smiles and alluring manner.

Cromwell beckoned to George and the Duke of Norfolk, to follow him and leave the hall. A while later, when George returned, he whispered to Cara, 'Let us retire, my love, unless you wish to stay longer? I leave tomorrow at first light.'

'You know there's nowhere I'd rather be than alone with you. I've passed many a dreary evening when you were away; and there will no doubt be more ahead.'

The courtiers were determined to show they were having a good time and there was much forced merriment. Cara had already endured quite enough and wished for nothing more than to be with George in their apartment. Who knew when they would be together again, and a ripple of fear shot through her as she thought about how dangerous it was for George to be brokering the Pilgrimage of Grace negotiations between the rebels and the poisonous Duke of Norfolk. The duke had sold out his flesh and blood; his niece Anne Boleyn, and it was obvious he cared only for his own reputation. She shivered at the memory of his betrayal.

When they were alone in their bedchamber, Cara said, 'George, please be vigilant. Norfolk is desperate to get back into the king's good graces and will stop at nothing.'

'You're right. I know him of old and fear I'm being used as a pawn to trick the rebels.'

'It's unfolding just as history reported,' said Cara, the anguish ringing in her voice.

'What do you mean—as history reported?' asked George.

Cara swallowed. 'Do you remember when I asked you to trust me about knowing certain things about the future? I can't explain exactly how I know, only that I do. Norfolk will double-cross the rebels, and they will be executed, next year —1537.'

'But the king has promised he will meet at least some of their terms. Why would he renege on his word in such a fashion?'

George rubbed his temple and sank heavily onto the bed, and then reached down towards his feet. Cara knelt to help him remove his heavy boots.

'I don't know, other than he can't stand anyone getting the better of him. Cromwell is pulling the strings behind the scenes. The people blame him for the Dissolution of the Monasteries and call him a heretic, but lord knows, the king must have personal demons enough. Let's not forget he recently killed a wife and took a new one inside a month. It's a wonder he's able to run the country at all.' Cara spoke in hushed tones. Even alone in their apartments they couldn't be too cautious.

George pulled Cara towards him and whispered in her ear. "This is treason, my love. And those looking to incriminate you would say you seeing the future is pure witchcraft. I know you have visions, but we must be careful. No one other than me must hear you speak so. Promise me...'

Cara looked at George and saw the concern etched on his face and reflected in his kind dark eyes. She nodded.

George sighed and his body visibly relaxed. 'I'm pleased to have your word, or I would be frantic with worry when I'm away. But how is it you see the future so? It's quite incredible.'

She stroked his hair and kissed him. 'It's safer for you if you don't know. One day I promise I'll tell you everything.'

'If what you say proves true, the Pilgrimage of Grace will

end in bloodshed and I am locked into a doomed, unholy mission, engineered by Cromwell, the king and Norfolk. How am I to keep my integrity without endangering us all and seeing Robert in an early grave?'

George had many questions, and Cara unfortunately couldn't give him the answers he sought. She wasn't about to trouble him with tales of karmic Twin Flames and five hundred years of time travel, on the eve of his potentially life-threatening mission to negotiate with the rebels.

She said, 'You know I have had the seer's gift since I was a child—I don't speak of it for the very reasons you state. There's no need to concern yourself—I will be cautious.'

They discussed how George might save Lord Darcy, who was also destined for the gallows.

'I fear whatever you do would only endanger you and risk the king branding you a traitor. Please, my darling, don't be a hero and do anything foolhardy.' Cara was pale and clutched his hand as they talked through what might happen when he reached Pontefract Castle.

It was after midnight, and Cara lay in bed listening to the soothing rhythm of George's breathing. He was exhausted and fell into a deep sleep moments after his head hit the pillow. Cara's mind spun out a thought a second, and she couldn't find solace in the same deep slumber her husband enjoyed. She envied his ability to sleep on demand.

Before George drifted off, he cuddled into her and reached for her hand. In moments like this it was obvious they were bound to each other through the centuries with a fierce love; they were the perfect match. She'd experienced nothing like the depth of this connection in her previous relationships, and here in Tudorville, George was the only man she'd ever loved. They were destined to be together, and in the dark, still hours of that fateful night before he left to confront the rebels, sleep eluded her. Her mind took flight and the thought occurred to her that they may also have been in love in yet another lifetime. Was George the reincarnation of his ancestor, the black sheep in the Cavendish bloodline?

An instant and overwhelming sense of loss ripped through her and engulfed her being; it gripped her entire body like a physical pain, and her heart throbbed and shook. She moved her head as if to free herself of the painful thoughts and feelings, but they lingered.

Cara knew instinctively there must be more to George's ancestor's story, and the intense feeling she'd just experienced made her think she had been involved with him then too.

She made a mental note to find out more from Kate, and to do some research into the mysterious black sheep, once she returned to the future.

Cara drifted off to sleep and dreamed of a different George. She was in a world where something wasn't right between them; he had abandoned her, and she saw herself weeping alone in a beautiful drawing room. Cara awoke and her heart beat so fast, she was breathless. The terror was tangible, and she reached for George to check he was present, and it was only a dream.

But was it?

She tossed and turned, deep into the night, unable to get the strange images out of her mind, until finally she was transported into a blissful, dreamless slumber, her hand entwined in George's.

As the first rays of the new day seeped through the windowpane, George stirred and pressed his warm body against hers. His hands caressed her skin and the thrill of his touch turned her on instantly, and her sleepiness dissolved. She reached beneath the sheets and heard his sharp intake of breath and leaned across to kiss him tenderly on the mouth as he pulled her tighter against him.

'This is Morning Glory at its finest,' she said, and she continued to touch him and saw the dramatic effect that her hands evoked, as the ecstasy danced across the features she so adored.

'You do come out with the strangest sayings, but I won't deny that waking up to this is glorious indeed. Now, come here,' he said, his deep voice husky.

A while later, Cara pushed herself up in bed, covering her chest with the sheet to keep out the dawn chill as George washed and dressed in the pale morning light.

'Please take care, my love,' she said, trying not to show how anxious she was. When he was ready to leave, he sat on the bed and gathered her into his arms. They held each other for a long time; they were as one—no words were necessary.

Cara watched from the window and he looked up to wave and blow her a kiss before he cantered out the courtyard with Swifty at his side, and she was alone again.

CHAPTER 10

York - Present day

Cara stared at the newly pitched red and white *For Sale* sign emerging from a disturbed patch of grass at the entrance to Willow Manor.

'How did you find out it's for sale?' said Cara turning to George, her glossy lips curved in a captivating smile.

'I spotted an article in the paper. If we don't take immediate action, we'll miss our opportunity. Stately homes don't appear on the market very often. I want Willow Manor back in our family, and this is our chance.'

'How exciting...but there's the small matter of funding. On reflection, I don't fancy asking my dad to invest—he's been trying to reduce his commitments since he retired.'

'You don't have to. We'll figure out a way to do it ourselves,' said George.

Cara asked, 'How much do we need?'

'Twenty million to buy it, but that's without any renovations and running costs.'

Cara's eyes widened.

'I thought about going back in time to buy shares,' he said.

'I love that idea.'

'Me too,' he said, raising an eyebrow. 'But then I realised it's impossible.'

'Damn it. How come?' she asked.

'How would we orchestrate the timing when we can't travel on demand?' said George.

Cara sighed and rolled her eyes. 'I forgot about that. What a shame—it would be so amazing to invest in the stock market knowing we couldn't lose.'

'I know, but I came up with something else.'

She looked at him expectantly, as she wrapped a tendril of hair around her finger. 'Go on.'

'I think I can pull it off. The artist, Turner, was alive in London in 1848. I read up on him and he was a bit of an eccentric recluse at that time; he died in 1851, and in his final years, everything went to shit, but he'd already painted his famous works. He was well known, but his gallery had fallen into disrepair and he was living in poverty.'

'How terribly sad,' she said.

'Yes, it is, which is what prompted my idea. This could be a win-win for us all: an opportunity to raise money so we can buy Willow Manor, outright, and at the same time Mr Turner's final years will be more comfortable.'

She nodded. 'Sounds good.'

'I will make a generous offer for a painting we know will fetch a high price from the right private buyer—his paintings are worth a fortune these days.'

'How will you know which one to buy? I'm not up on his work other than knowing he was famous for landscapes,' she said.

'I think our best bet is for me to visit him. It would be amazing to meet him, and that way I could find out which paintings he is still in possession of in 1848.'

'I like it, but what about the obvious dangers of rewriting history?'

'That's why I'm thinking that rather than trying to buy one of the famous paintings which is now likely in the collection at the Tate, I'll see if I can acquire a lesser known one. Maybe we'll get lucky,' said George.

'That is a fantastic plan.'

'I don't know if I'll be able to pull it off, but it's worth a try, don't you think?'

'There's just one small problem.' Cara wrinkled up her nose and her eyes sparkled.

'What can possibly be problematic about locating a dead painter from two centuries ago and then transferring one of his great works of art through time?'

'Let's say you manage to buy a painting. Where will you store it, so we can access it now?' asked Cara.

'Ah, good point. I don't know yet. We're back in London staying in the Grosvenor Square townhouse. Perhaps I can hide it there,' he said.

'If only we'd bought that townhouse; you could store the painting in a cupboard and we could retrieve it immediately. Not that we'd need to; imagine how much that townhouse is worth today. I reckon, we could just sell it and fetch enough to buy Willow Manor.'

'I don't know who owned that house—it may have belonged to the Crown. The palace arranged our accommodation when we stayed in London so there's no easy way to gain access now,' he said.

'I wonder where we lived after that. I have often wondered what happened to us later, but it spooks me a bit,' she said.

'What an awful thought—to know in advance when we're going to die. I hope I die before you.' George looked stricken.

'It's too horrible to think about. I don't want to be stranded in time, hundreds of years ago without you. Maybe timeline amnesia is a blessing, after all.'

George kissed her and said, 'Let's drive to town and grab a coffee and have a think about what I should do in 1848.'

George parked on the outskirts and they weaved hand in hand through the city toward their favourite coffee shop.

There was a free table in the corner and Cara said, 'Sit down and I'll get the coffee.'

As she waited to be served, she stared out of the window into the high street at a row of banks. An armoured security truck rolled up outside and a guard, dressed in black from head-to-toe, jumped out and disappeared into one of the banks. The queue was sluggish as she waited for their coffees to be served. She turned back to look out the window once more and saw the same guard exiting the bank, this time carrying a heavy-looking steel case, which he shoved into the back of the truck and then closed the metal door with a firm click.

'I've got it,' Cara said to George as she arrived at the table holding two steaming cups of coffee.

'A cake, by any chance?'

'No, no cake. Come on, we agreed we're going to lay off the cakes for a while.'

'Spoilsport,' he said.

'I mean, I think I know where we can store the Turner painting, so we can easily access it.'

'Are you going to tell me, or am I to guess?'

'How about you stash the painting in a vault at the Bank of England?' she said.

George paused mid coffee-sip. 'Now that is pure genius. The Bank of England is a dead-cert.'

'I think it could work,' she said.

'There are a few potential niggles,' he replied, after he'd run the idea through his mind for a few minutes.

'Right...'

'Firstly, what the hell will I do with the key, or whatever they give me to access the vault? And secondly, what if I forget what to do with it?'

'Do you think that's likely?' she asked, raising one eyebrow as she sipped her coffee.

'No, I suppose not. Our memories seem pretty reliable when we're the one who travels. It's the one who's already there who isn't aware of what's going on,' he said.

'Yes, I was thinking about that the other day. It appears I haven't yet travelled to Victoriana this time around, or I would remember something. It must be the same for you in Tudorville.'

George nodded and continued. 'I don't know what kind of code or access key they'd have had hundreds of years ago. What if it's not transferable?'

'There's only one way to find out,' she said.

'The internet?'

She shook her head, amused. 'No, I mean we will only know for sure when you try. You're going to have quite the time of it.'

'I hope I can manage it. Not only must I make sure Queen V is safe from the Chartists and I haven't screwed things up somehow with Swifty's intervention, I must also track down Turner and source a painting worth at least twenty million pounds. If we can raise more it would be even better because Willow Manor is sure to be a money pit.' George stared out of the window and thought about what was ahead of him.

'I wish I could come with you,' she said, looking wistful.

'Oh, my darling, I wish you could too.'

'Eddie and I travelled together once when I first met him,

but I'm too scared to try and do it with you, in case it screws things up for us, somehow. Sylvia said we must reach Twin Flame ascension, which is a kind of harmony in every timeline, but based on my recent performance in Tudorville, I don't think we're quite there yet.'

George smiled. 'It's not possible to escape human emotions. If I thought you were with another man, I would go ballistic too.'

Cara loved how he did his best to make her feel better even in the most difficult situations.

'How will I know where to find the amazing Mr Turner?' he said, taking one final slug of coffee, and resting the empty cup back down on the table.

Cara pulled out her phone and tapped Turner's name into the search bar.

'Cheyne Walk,' she said.

'What? An impoverished artist lives in the heart of Chelsea, overlooking the Thames? My—how times have changed.'

'Yep, he lives in Cheyne Walk. I appreciate the internet so much more after being stuck in Tudorville,' she beamed, looking pleased with her instant success.

'I must admit, I rather enjoy the freedom of being off the grid in Victoriana; it's one of its many charms,' said George.

'Perhaps we should consider buying property in Grosvenor Square or Chelsea in Victoriana. We could be multi-millionaires or even billionaires by teatime if you buy the right paintings and houses. Did Chelsea exist in Tudorville?'

'I don't know, but I feel much better about facing the challenges of Victoriana now,' he said.

'The truth is I've been dreading all of this lasting for much longer, but it's good to see what fun we can have when we work together and take advantage of the benefits of our crazy situation,' she said.

'That's a good way of looking at things,' he replied.

'I wonder who I could meet in Tudorville?' she said, an impish smile lighting up her face.

'Let's not forget you were close friends with Anne Boleyn. That's not too shabby as far as famous historical figures go...'

'You're one to talk; best friends with Henry VIII,' she said.

'I don't think I'd class us as best friends just yet, and it is an extremely dangerous friendship. Whomever you decide to seek out in Tudorville when I'm not around to keep an eye on you, please remember one thing.'

'What's that?'

'We agreed we are not to overreach and meddle with history. We must always keep the big picture in mind,' he said.

'Don't worry. I know the rules. It's you who's most in danger of rewriting history. I still don't know whether I succeeded in warning you not to do something drastic to save Robert Aske.'

When they were together, the simplest of things became magical in each other's presence. The future looked exciting again, despite their fears and the unpredictability of the timelines.

'So where do we start?' Cara asked after a few minutes of allowing it all to sink in while a quiet feeling of contentment washed over her. She hadn't felt this at peace in a while. She had almost lost sight of the spiritual principle that everything unfolds just as it should and there was no point railing against life.

'I'll get onto finding Turner just as soon as I'm in Victoriana again. There's not a moment to lose if we're to raise the funds before someone else snaps up Willow Manor.'

'For once, I'm actually excited about you going,' she said.

They rose from their seats in sync, exited the café and passed the bank on their way back to the car.

Grosvenor Square, London, 1848 - Victoriana

Sunday came and went with no word from Buckingham Palace. George was impatient and couldn't sit still. Thoughts of everything he must do whizzed about his mind, tormenting him.

On Monday morning, Cara said, 'You're pacing about like a caged lion. Whatever's the matter?'

'I have heard nothing from Swifty. I sent him on an important assignment and he was supposed to get a note to me yesterday upon his return.'

'Swifty? What a splendid name.'

George stared at Cara, despair reflected in his eyes.

'What?' she asked. 'Why are you looking at me like that? I know that look.'

'I hoped you would remember, that's all.'

Cara hated disappointing George.

'Remember what?'

'Never mind,' he said, shaking his head, trying not to let his mounting irritation show on his face. It wasn't her fault she had no idea what was going on. Victoriana Cara wasn't his quantum time travelling partner. He adored her, but he wished she was conscious of their future life together. He kept a lonely secret and the only person he could confide in was Edward, whom he hoped to see again soon.

There was a loud rap at the front door, and he heard muffled conversation.

The maid tapped on the drawing-room door, and George called for her to enter.

'My lord, a letter has arrived for your urgent attention.'

A small envelope perched on a shiny silver tray which she extended in his direction. George stretched out his hand to retrieve the envelope and then roughly broke the seal as he thanked the girl and nodded for her to withdraw.

'Perhaps this is what you were waiting for,' said Cara.

'Yes, let us hope so as I've become quite anxious about the poor boy.'

George extracted a sheet of notepaper and squinted as he tried to decipher the scrawled handwriting.

Have one thousand pounds ready. If you alert the authorities, we will know, and your boy will die. Meeting point to be confirmed. Come alone.

George slumped against the upholstered back of the chair, the notepaper clutched in his hand as he tried to evaluate the scope of the sudden threat.

'Are you okay, my love? You look like you've seen a ghost. What on earth does the note say?'

'It's a ransom note.'

'Let me see,' she said, extracting the paper from between George's fingers. 'Who is this from? Could it be a joke of some kind?'

'I don't believe so. I think it's a real kidnapping. I shouldn't have sent Swifty on such a dangerous errand. I don't know what I was thinking.'

'Who are these people?' asked Cara.

'You've heard of the Chartists?'

'Yes, of course. Who hasn't? They make such a song and dance; I doubt there's anyone in London who hasn't heard their demands.'

'Well, one of their sinister factions must be holding the palace footman, Swifty. He is a good, loyal boy, I'm certain you would like him. Anyway, they are demanding a ransom of one thousand pounds, or...'

George didn't want to say the ominous words aloud. The thought of Swifty in such peril because of his clumsy request was too much for him to contemplate.

'Are you certain it's for real? Could it not be an idle threat from someone who knows of your connection to the palace and is trying their luck for financial gain?' asked Cara.

George ran his hand through his thick, dark hair, trying to keep a grip on his frustration and not burden his wife.

'They are trying their luck, all right, but I can't take any chances. The Chartists have been pushing their agenda for years and there are signs they're growing tired of being ignored and not achieving their ends. By all accounts, most of them are decent law-abiding citizens who wish only to see the Charter demands granted so that working-class men may vote. But as is the way, there are a few of them...' George's words trailed off as he contemplated the awful reality of what he had got Swifty involved in.

'A few of them...?' prompted Cara.

George shook his head from side to side. 'Well, a few of them will stop at nothing like all zealots pursuing their cause. There have been violent riots, and both the prince and the prime minister are urging the queen to leave immediately for Osborne on the Isle of Wight.'

Cara looked shocked at the prospect of the queen being in such danger she must flee her own palace.

'My understanding is a small extremist group of Chartists has turned to armed uprising and aims to overthrow the monarchy. They were no doubt encouraged by what's been happening in France. The queen welcoming her cousin,

Louise-Philippe to London, has aggravated matters and heightened tensions.'

George had been reading up on the Chartists and knew his Victorian history. Ultimately, if the history books were correct, the queen wasn't in any real danger, but like Cara in Tudorville, he had no way of knowing what part he was destined to play in making sure events unfolded as they originally had. He walked a deadly tightrope where if he took one wrong step, he risked skewing the outcome of preordained events. And conversely, if he didn't take the same action that Victoriana George took the first time around, he could destroy history as they knew it.

Was he putting the royal family in greater jeopardy by interfering? For all George knew, Swifty was only involved because of his bright idea to send him to investigate the Chartists, and now the boy's life was in danger.

George was second-guessing his actions at every turn and panicking that he had already reset the timeline.

'Will there be a revolution in London like in Paris, do you think?' asked Cara. The thought of the poor young boy kidnapped by the Chartist extremists, and George having to rescue him with a ransom made the danger feel suddenly all too real.

'No, I don't think so, but we need to avoid any more riots. The political unrest could spark an all-out uprising if the Chartists' demands are not handled with prudence and sensitivity. Lord Palmerston understands the people, but the prime minister is like a bull in a china shop.'

George rose abruptly. 'Excuse me, my love. I must speak with the queen immediately. Perhaps Prince Albert's hunch is right, and the royal family should leave for the Isle of Wight without delay.'

'Who delivered the note?' asked Cara, looking up at him.

'Now that is a good question. I shall endeavour to find out and then leave for Buckingham Palace forthwith.'

'George...'

'Yes?'

George saw fear reflected in Cara's eyes.

'Take care.' She squeezed his hand in return as he reached for her.

'You too,' he said. 'These are dangerous times, my love. Please don't leave the house unless it is absolutely necessary; in fact, please forgive me for limiting your freedoms, but I beg you not to venture out today. Who knows where these kidnappers may be lurking. Double lock the door after me, and I will return just as soon as permits. Pray tell the servants to be cautious.'

Cara stared after her husband's back as he exited the room and closed the door quietly behind him, her heart fluttering wildly.

She clasped her hands together in prayer and offered a muttered promise that if God would only deliver George home safely, she would stop lamenting her miscarriage, and make the most of their marriage, even if they weren't to be blessed with a child.

Never before had she appreciated how precious their life together was, and she vowed to be grateful for all of their blessings.

Please God, bring him home to me and let the boy be safe too.

CHAPTER 11

Pontefract Castle, Yorkshire, 1536 - Tudorville

George and Swifty arrived in the valley which surrounded the base of Pontefract Castle after an uneventful but gruelling journey and just a few snatched hours of rest along the way. They stopped to catch their breath a while and to drink some ale.

'I can see why the castle has such a fearsome reputation for being impenetrable. It's even more impressive than I'd heard,' said George.

The vast ominous fort loomed before them, topped by majestic towers that gave the illusion that the castle hovered amidst the fluffy clouds high up in the sky. The sandy stone glinted in the pale winter sunlight and the emerald green fields stretched for miles, as far as they could see.

They trudged up the hill and finally arrived at the castle entrance and a pair of patrolling guards came to enquire about their business.

. . .

Lord Darcy, the master of Pontefract Castle waited anxiously for George's arrival and spotted him from the tower window.

'George Cavendish is here, Robert,' he said. 'Let us hurry down to greet him.'

Robert nodded. 'Keep in mind, we are both fond of him and could be overly susceptible to his influence.'

'You make a fair point. George's father has been a dear friend to me over the years, as George has been to you. We mustn't lose sight of the fact we are on opposite sides in this unfortunate situation, even though I have witnessed him to be every bit as trustworthy as his father.'

Robert removed his spectacles and closed the heavy tome of law he had been studying with a loud snap. He stood, stretched his legs, and followed Lord Darcy out of his tower room.

They descended the ancient steep stone staircase; Darcy led the way and continued with his observations. 'That devil, Norfolk would sell his soul for his own ends and if my sources are correct, advances with his army as we speak.'

Lord Darcy gave the guards the nod to raise the portcullis and the iron grid grated against the well-worn grooves, to reveal George and Swifty waiting on the other side, escorted by the guards.

Darcy beckoned them to enter and waved to one of his stable boys to relieve the visitors of their sweaty horses. A weary but enthusiastic George embraced first Darcy and then Robert before his two friends ushered him inside to take refreshment.

Doncaster, Yorkshire, 1536 - Tudorville

The following afternoon, George rode alongside Robert and Lord Darcy on the muddy track, with Swifty following closely behind, as they headed to the arranged spot to meet with the Duke of Norfolk, who had travelled from London with his hastily recruited army.

Swifty took the horses to be watered and the three men waited for the duke in front of the Rose and Crown.

They didn't have much time to pass before the duke and a small band of soldiers turned the corner and rode slowly towards them. The duke dismounted and bade his men to wait for him nearby. Introductions were frosty, and George's diplomatic skills were stretched to the limit. George led the impressive looking bunch into the inn, and they swept passed the dark oak bar and the gleaming panelled walls and moved towards a corner table in the dim interior. A fire blazed and the men removed their cloaks and sank into the leather seats, grateful for the warm respite from the Yorkshire chill-to-the-bone cold.

All eyes were on them. It wasn't every day the Rose and Crown enjoyed the custom of noble high-ranking clientele, obviously on official business. Ears twitched, and the esteemed gentlemen didn't want to risk being overheard in their efforts to reach an agreement to disperse what would go down in history as the most serious uprising of king Henry VIII's reign.

After thirty minutes of quiet discussion, the Duke of Norfolk said, 'So what is it to be?'

'What is what to be?' said Robert, looking vague; he was an experienced lawyer and assumed a poker face as second nature.

'You surely don't expect to continue on with this rebellion, and for the king to look the other way after we've come all this distance to meet with you?' said the duke, in a goading, arrogant tone.

'My understanding was that you have come with a fair offer from the king which I may relay to the forty thousand men-at-arms, ready to march on London to preserve the religious freedoms of this fine country, should our demands not be met. The Pilgrimage, as we have assured the king repeatedly in our communications, is not against the Crown, but nevertheless it is the king alone who has the power to consent to our demands.

The duke took a slug of whisky and pulled a sour face as it burnt his throat. He glowered at Robert as if daring him to continue.

'It is His Majesty who must ultimately temper Cromwell's heretic tendencies and disrespect for the old ways,' Robert paused to draw breath, his face flushed.

The duke rested his glass on the table, took a deep breath and said, 'Robert, you have not misunderstood; we do indeed bring word from the king who is eager to resolve matters and restore peace and harmony to the north.'

Robert appraised the duke and continued. 'Aye, then that is good news. But do you, Your Grace, a known adherent of the Roman Catholic faith not agree with the cause? I imagine that's why the king selected you to negotiate on his behalf.'

The duke made a snorting sound. 'Whether I agree or not, is irrelevant.'

'What does His Majesty offer in lieu of the terrible injustice the people have endured as a result of our houses of worship being attacked and decimated?' asked Robert.

'His Majesty promises that all involved will receive a general pardon should you do the right thing and have your men stand down and drop arms forthwith, with no more threats of marching on London or uprising and insurrection anywhere else for that matter,' replied the duke.

George remained silent, sipping his wine, and watching as the conversation unfolded. He and Darcy exchanged several looks, both hoping the two men would reach an agreement, and the conversation wouldn't turn nasty.

'And if we should agree, what more may I tell them we will receive in return, other than a pardon?' asked Robert.

The door opened to reveal some new customers and a cold draught hissed through the inn, causing the fire to spark, and several of the candles to be extinguished.

'The abbeys will receive a reprieve in the meantime until a parliament is held here, at York, within the year, as you requested. That way we can review matters in line with the law and with a calm head instead of amid rioting and disorder spreading through the country,' said the duke, hunching closer to the fire.

'And what of the princess? Will her rightful recognition as the heir to the thrown be restored?' interceded Lord Darcy, as much to give Robert a break from the harsh discourse, as to learn the answer.

'That, I'm afraid, I cannot say, but the king will consider it in due course. Let's not forget his marriage to the new queen, as he expects to soon be blessed with a son, so Princess Mary's position is somewhat of a moot point,' said the duke turning to Lord Darcy.

'Queen Jane has interceded on the pilgrim's behalf; she is in favour of Princess Mary being restored as heir, and the traditions and respect for the old religion to be renewed,' said George, taking his cue from his friend Darcy.

'We know exactly how much notice His Majesty takes of his wives,' said Robert, his tone bitter.

The duke snapped, 'Don't be a fool, man. The king is

willing to meet you more than halfway. Don't throw it in his face, or you will be sorry for it.'

'Is that a threat? I do hope not. You know as well as I that we have the numbers to overcome your troops here today, should the situation warrant it,' said Robert, squaring his shoulders, and raising his torso in the chair as he stared at the duke with his one bright eye.

George reached out and touched Robert gently on the shoulder. 'Calm down, my friend. It is better all round for us not to allow things to blow out of proportion. Let's not risk more bloodshed because we are stubborn but instead let us come to an agreement where everyone wins.'

'It's a good offer. I advise you to take it. Disperse your marching rebel bands and as soon as we see that the king's request has been honoured, the pardon will be granted so you need not fear reprisals, and we will set events in motion for the parliament to be held within the year in York, as promised,' said the duke, unmoved by Robert's violent reaction.

'And what reassurances do we have that the abbeys, monasteries and convents will cease to be stripped and their inhabitants no longer cast out with nothing to show for their lives of devout service?' asked Robert.

'I give you my word, backed by the king's promise that the Dissolution of the Monasteries will be on hold until matters have been reviewed,' said the duke.

George held his breath.

After several seconds of silent contemplation of the dregs of his warm ale, Robert replied, 'Allow us to consider our position, for a few moments, Your Grace, if you will.'

The duke nodded, and Robert beckoned to Darcy to follow him as he rose and left the table.

George looked at the duke and said under his breath, 'How reliable is this pardon?'

'Don't concern yourself with the details, Cavendish. We must have these men dispersed; they are a danger, and they make the king look foolish. He must offer whatever it takes to make them stand down, or we look weaker than we already do, and it endangers the whole country.'

'But will the leaders be pardoned?' pressed George.

'In truth, I do not know. You know as well as I, it depends on what side of the bed the king gets out as well as on Cromwell's machinations on the day the decision falls. For now, let us move forward on the king's orders.'

There was a tight knot in George's gut as he contemplated the earnest face of his dear friend Robert.

He will hang if what Cara says is true, but is there a way for me to save him without putting us all in danger?

George's head ached, and he was overcome with a sense of powerlessness and despair.

The men returned to the table, and discussions resumed. George avoided looking at Robert, suspecting the offer was merely a ploy to trick him into having the men leave the region and return home until the king could move more troops up north to prevent any future threat of the rebels marching on London.

'Let's take a short break; I am ravenous,' said the duke.

They ordered food and a fresh round of refreshments. As they tore at the bread and hungrily demolished the selection of cold meats laid before them, Robert moved closer to George and spoke quietly in his ear while the duke was preoccupied exchanging loud pleasantries, in between mouthfuls, with the innkeeper who was anxious to make sure his affluent guests were content.

'May I trust his word, my friend? I hope you know I trust you implicitly. Unfortunately, I don't feel the same about the duke, and I am hesitant to put the pilgrims' hopes and dreams in his hands after we have come so far and arrived at this point where we at least have some leverage with the king.'

George considered his response carefully, aware that the future of Christendom and the Crown could depend on his words.

'You must follow your conscience, Robert. I wish I could do more, but I fear I may only tell you what I've heard. In all honesty, I do not know the king's true motives. I do however, beg you to cease this uprising. The king is adamant it will end.'

Dusk drew in, and Robert, Darcy, and George stood and shook hands with the duke. They had reached an impasse—there was no more to be said until Robert laid the king's offer before the rebel-pilgrims.

'We will stay in the vicinity until we hear from you,' said the duke before he bid them farewell.

George nodded and headed back to Pontefract with the others. How he wished he were at Willow Manor with Cara and the children, not brokering a deal for what if her visions proved true, would end in a murderous and bloody rebellion.

Pontefract Castle, Yorkshire, 1536 - Tudorville

That night George slept poorly, despite his comfortable quarters, and rose before dawn to write a note to Cara. He couldn't give much away without endangering her, but he knew she would be waiting to hear he was safe.

My darling, Cara,

We arrived in Yorkshire, and I am invited by Lord Darcy to stay at Pontefract Castle until matters are resolved. The castle is quite as splendid as its legendary reputation.

We have already been in negotiations with the duke. You will no doubt hear that the rebels have captured the castle, but do not fear for me. They are reasonable men, and I am safe, thanks to Darcy's gracious hospitality. Please pray for a peaceful resolution and I will return to you as soon as we have word that the rebels pledge to the duke they will not march on London.

I have not as yet found a way to address our particular dilemma, but I aim to think of something before I leave, or I will find it hard to live with myself. Truly, I know not what to do, and wish you were at my side, for it is always easier to think clearly when we are as one. I long for nothing more than for us to be passing our days at Willow Manor with Cornelius at our heels as we wander around the grounds, with May on her precious Nutmeg, and dear Thomas reciting his poems.

Take care, my beloved. Your loving heart sustains me through these difficult days and long nights.

Your devoted husband,
George.

George signed off with a bold inky flourish and went in search of Swifty to ask him to find an errand boy to dispatch the note to Cara.

Darcy invited George to join him to break their fast in his private rooms in the magnificent King's Tower at the top of the fortress-castle. George looked out of the turret window and let out a low whistle at the sight of the rolling fields surrounding the stone fort. 'It's a remarkable view from up here.'

'Aye, it is. I believe it to be the most awe-inspiring castle in all of England. I am indeed blessed,' replied Darcy.

They grazed on a light meal and Darcy enquired after George's father before they got down to the serious business of the day.

'May we trust these terms from the duke?' asked Darcy.

'It is a difficult situation. I can only say, the king commanded us to end the insurrection and to restore peace.'

'I don't know,' said Darcy. 'My gut is uneasy; something feels off.'

'We find ourselves in a tight spot. This is bigger than both of us. It was out of your hands the second the rebels entered the castle. I fear for your safety should you continue to back them. Is it true you took the Pilgrim's Oath?' George lowered his voice to a whisper.

Darcy stared at George before dropping his eyes and staring at his plate. 'Yes, does the king know of it?'

'He heard you admitted the rebels to the castle of your own free will,' replied George.

Later that morning, Darcy wrote a note to the duke, saying he and Robert would speak to the other leaders and he pledged to recommend they accept the offer of a general pardon.

'Do you think you can influence them? The less you are

seen to back them, the better; for your own, your family's and this magnificent castle's sake,' said George.

'I can't promise,' Darcy said. 'The men are riled up and ready to march—they've been hurtling towards this moment and things have come to a head. And I confess, I have great sympathy for the cause. I'm not at all certain I will be able to divert them from marching, even if I use all of my powers of persuasion. Robert doesn't trust the duke, and he was still for marching last we spoke.'

'I urge you to tread with caution,' said George.

'Yes, but if we submit now, when we are in this powerful position, we stand to lose everything for which we have fought. We will not get another chance to turn the tides in favour of the true religion,' said Lord Darcy.

CHAPTER 12

Rose Cottage, York - Present day

Cara came downstairs in the morning to find George sitting at the kitchen table, reading, as he scrolled on his phone. The rain sluiced against the glass, flooding the window panes. She straightened the blinds and peeked out and noticed the moody sky. 'So much for summer.'

'Um, it's shocking,' said George.

'What are you so engrossed in?'

He looked up. 'I'm reading about the Chartists and trying to understand who the bad guys were.'

'What's happening in Victoriana?'

George laid his phone on the table. 'I'm as uninformed as you on that score. I don't remember a thing since I told you about the riots and we made our plan for me to visit Turner. I'm guessing I haven't been back again yet, but it could be that for some reason my memory hasn't updated. I want to organise the funds for Willow Manor, so I need to see Turner, and I'm also concerned about the queen's safety.'

Cara filled the kettle and switched it on, then turned to him and said, 'I keep thinking what if either of us does something that has an unexpected knock-on-effect for the future, and I come home one day to find you're not here.'

George looked at her over his black-rimmed glasses, which gave him an air of a studious professor. 'Or I come home, and you've vanished. Have you considered that scenario?'

'I know it's just the same for you, but you already disappeared once, and I can't shake the memory. I wake up in the night and it spins around my mind. Besides, you take it all in your stride.'

'Oh darling, I worry too, but I try to shut those thoughts down as soon as they appear. I lost my former life, you know, which was rather an ordeal. I certainly don't want to go through that nightmare again.'

'But, if you hadn't, we wouldn't be together.' Cara busied herself making tea.

'We don't know that; it would have sorted itself out, but let's not get into all that again. It only upsets you.' He gave her a stern look. His reading glasses now rested unevenly on the bridge of his nose and his hair stuck up in an unruly just-out-of-bed fashion.

'Well, I'm sorry, but it's bloody difficult. I thought I had mastered living in the moment, but lately I can barely sleep.'

'I've told you to wake me when you can't sleep,' he said, his voice tender.

'I don't have the heart to disturb you. Your head hits the pillow, and you sleep so soundly; it would be unfair to bother you. Anyway, you're a dreadful fidget when you can't fall sleep, so I just cuddle into you instead.'

George smiled and patted the seat. 'Come and sit down, darling.'

Cara sat down next to him and kissed him on the cheek. 'You really are marvellous, even when you're a tiny bit cross.'

'I've been told that many times.' He pulled a comical face.

'It's just as well, because modesty certainly isn't one of your virtues.'

They laughed and drank their tea.

'Okay, marvellous man, enough of the George fan club, shall we have some toast?'

They sat side by side in the warm kitchen, munching on toast and jam, sipping tea, and listening to the rain strumming on the window.

'Feeling better?' asked George?

'Yes, thank you. I wish we could stay here like this, forever. You always know how to get me out of a funk.' She squeezed his arm and thought how lucky they were to have found each other, no matter how many obstacles they must overcome.

Cara shivered as they completed the newspaper quiz. 'Is it just me or has it suddenly got really chilly in here?'

They looked at each other and both said, 'The vortex.'

'Be careful, darling!' called Cara, her face clouded with apprehension.

'We'll meet back here, soon. I love you,' he said.

I love you too.

But then they were gone; her words were lost in the ethers. George arrived in Victoriana and Cara in Tudorville. To their knowledge this was the first time they had entered the vortex simultaneously. Were they destined to always be separated by centuries?

Anyone entering the kitchen would find them doing the quiz like any ordinary couple passing the time on a rainy summer morning.

Things would stay just as they were in the present day—as long as neither of them made a fatal error in their past.

Buckingham Palace, London, 1848 - Victoriana

George had requested an audience with Queen Victoria, and as he entered the drawing room, he saw Prince Albert was present just like the old days.

'Your Majesty,' George said, bowing to the queen, and then inclining his head towards the prince, 'Your Royal Highness.' They were a dashing pair, and George thought how incredible it was to witness this historic couple in action.

'Lord Cavendish, my wife tells me you have been quietly investigating the Chartists, to gauge the level of danger to our family.'

'Yes, and I'm afraid I have rather unsettling news.'

George felt two sets of eyes bore into him, and he composed himself in an attempt to convey his message in the calmest, most effective way possible.

'In what now seems like a hasty decision, I commissioned one of your footmen to gather whatever information he could about the Chartists. I thought he would blend in with the men on the street much better than I, and it would be the best way to ascertain what they are planning.'

'Why was I not aware of this?' asked Victoria.

'Your butler gave his permission, ma'am, and it didn't seem like something to bother you with.'

'I see,' said Victoria, pursing her lips. 'And, what is the unsettling news?'

George remained standing and moved the brunt of his weight onto his other foot. 'This morning I received a note threatening the boy's life if I don't deliver one thousand pounds.'

'But that's out-and-out kidnapping,' said the prince.

'Yes, I'm afraid it is, and I must ask for your support in rescuing him.'

'What do you mean to do?' asked the queen.

'I am awaiting word from the kidnappers as to where and when I must take the money.'

The queen crossed the room and stared out of the window in silence. Then she turned, and said, 'I must forbid you to risk your life. Let us involve the police and have them deal with it.'

George withdrew the note from his pocket and passed it to the queen, and the prince read it over her shoulder.

The queen sighed and sat down. 'There is never a dull moment. Thank goodness I already gave birth.'

'Indeed, ma'am. And how is the princess, Louise? Lady Cavendish sends her blessings and intends to visit you, soon.'

'The little princess is well, thank you. And how is my dear, Lady Cara? I trust she is restored to good spirits. Please tell her she is welcome to return as soon as she feels well enough. She is missed, and her absence is keenly felt.'

'You are most generous, ma'am. She is considerably better. I shall relay your kind words.'

'May you be blessed with a child soon, my lord.'

George inclined his head.

'And in the meantime, what are we to do about these damned kidnappers?' the prince asked.

'We must involve the police without delay,' said the queen, and the three of them continued their discussion.

Hampton Court Palace, London, 1536 - Tudorville

One thought lingered in Cara's mind as she realised she was back in Tudorville.

Would their past always be their future?

She was tense and tired but knew she must find out what was going on with George. Had the rebels proceeded to march on London, and if so, was he imprisoned at Pontefract Castle or had he been embroiled in the rebellion? She prayed the rebels hadn't turned against him because he was the king's envoy. Cara had no way of knowing whether things were unfolding for George as they did the first time.

Cromwell hurried into the king's privy chamber and bid him good morning before the king proceeded to grill him on the latest news about the Pilgrimage of Grace.

'Your Majesty, Lord Darcy is an old friend of the Cavendish family and George Cavendish and Aske are childhood friends. If I'd realised it when we dispatched him to join Norfolk in negotiations, I would have recommended another take his place. It doesn't bode well when there is a long-standing personal affiliation.'

The king gestured for Cromwell to take a seat.

'I'm not certain I agree with you, Thomas. I'm inclined to think Cavendish's influence could go a long way with Darcy and Aske and remind them of their loyalty to their king. I had thought that was precisely why we sent him, and you know I would trust him with my life, despite your doubts,' said the king running his hand through his fading red hair.

Cromwell shuffled his papers and addressed the king, his eyes solemn. 'Perhaps ordinarily that would have been the case, but I regret to inform Your Majesty, I have confirmed that Darcy is for the rebels and has presumed to take their treasonous oath. I did not wish to share such sorry news without confirming it first. No doubt, Darcy thinks we won't learn of his two-faced ruse, and he can play both sides as it suits him.'

The king rose and limped across the room to stare out of the window. He eased himself down onto a seat next to the window, causing the upholstery to sag under the heavy weight of his girth. He sighed and said, 'I am tired, Thomas. I am tired of the constant infighting and uprisings. By Christ's bones, is a king never to enjoy a quiet moment in his kingdom even when he is newly wed to a sweet bride chosen and blessed by God himself?'

Cromwell composed his features into a suitably sympathetic expression. 'I am sorry for your discomfort, Sire, and wish to resolve these unpleasant matters. Do not worry yourself any further; I will handle these so-called *pilgrims* and show them who is in charge.' He spat the word out as though it would infect his mouth. 'Now I urge you to rest, Your Majesty.'

'Lady Cara, I beg you to accompany me on a turn around the gardens. Forgive me, but you and Lord Cavendish are the Earl and Countess of Gloucester, are you not? I confess I am not yet familiar with all the grand titles of my ladies.'

'It is of no consequence, Your Majesty. Cara will suffice if it pleases you. I confess, I am not as impressed by my title as others.'

'And that's why I am so fond of you, dear Cara. You're not like the others,' she confided in a low voice as they walked down the large wooden staircase on their way out to the gardens. 'You have a certain wisdom beyond your years, which I find extremely reassuring as I tread this fresh path.'

'Thank you, Your Grace. I sometimes feel as though I have lived for hundreds of years.'

You have no idea.

'The sun shines today, and that is, I hope, a good omen,' said Cara.

'Do you have a need of good omens, my dear? I have heard the situation up north has only been aggravated by Norfolk's attempt to negotiate with the offer of a pardon from the king.'

'Then you are much better informed than I, Your Grace. The last I heard was that my husband has arrived and is being accommodated at Pontefract Castle, by Lord Darcy. I fear he may be caught up in this dreadful uprising and may even have been taken hostage by the rebels at the castle.'

'This is why I wished to speak with you alone,' whispered the queen.

Cara's eyes studied the queen's sweet face. Her heart began to thud. She knew this must be serious for the queen to say such a thing.

'What is it, ma'am? Pray tell me what you have heard, or my heart shall beat itself out of my chest.'

'Let's move deeper into the gardens and walk by the river,' she said, looking back up at the windows. A curtain twitched —someone always had their eye on the queen, and she was quickly becoming accustomed to it.

Cara threaded her arm through Queen Jane's, and they walked in silence for a few minutes, admiring the shrubbery and the bright flowering borders of the meticulously tended lawns. The River Thames sparkled before them in the sunshine.

'What troubles you, Your Grace?'

'This is for your ears only, Cara, and I risk telling you only because I hold you and your husband in such high esteem. I remember what befell your family when we were both ladies-in-waiting, and I know the king regretted his hasty decision. He is too easily led,' she whispered, and patted Cara's hand, her eyes full of fear.

'You can trust me, Your Grace. I understand the magnitude of your words and will do everything within my power to protect you.'

'I do trust you, Cara. I believe Secretary Cromwell and his minions engineered your past troubles; the king loves you both dearly and at the time I found it odd for him to turn on you as viciously as he did.'

'I am most grateful and humbled by your kindness. Pray continue, Your Grace.' said Cara.

'I overheard a conversation between the king and Cromwell, and I believe your husband is in danger of falling foul of another of Cromwell's ingenious plots to undermine the king's most trusted confidants...'

Cara tried to steady her racing thoughts and control the rising panic threatening to engulf her. She walked along the river bank in a daze and her five-hundred-year future flashed before her as a wedge of snow-white swans glided through the blue sky and landed smoothly on the surface of the water. It should have been a perfect day.

What the hell am I going to do now?

CHAPTER 13

Rose Cottage, York - Present day

Cara swung into the yard and the wheels sliced through the dusty gravel as the car came to an abrupt halt. The orange sun hovered low in the pink sky, just visible over the thatched roof, the sun beams dancing on the ivy leaves nestling in the crevices of the decorative half-timbered Tudor-style cottage.

George grabbed Eddie's holdall from the back seat and they jumped out of the car and piled in through the heavy wooden door.

'Oh, it's nice to be back,' said Eddie as they wandered into the cosy kitchen.

'It seems ages,' said Cara.

'It does—I've been dying to see you both.'

Cara made coffee and they sat around chatting about nothing in particular, enjoying being reunited in the way old friends do.

'I hear you've been hard at it in your lab in London. How's it all going?' asked George, a while later.

'Pretty good, although I still haven't made any headway with the TTS. It was such a mess last time, I don't know what to do next.'

'TTS?' said George.

'Time Travel System,' replied Cara. 'Remember, it's what we were testing when I disrupted the Tudorville timeline and we had our little stay in the Tower of London.'

'Oh yes, when you were trying to catapult Cara into the future to save the world?'

'Sounds a bit hubristic when you put it like that, but yes; that is pretty much what we were up to,' said Eddie with a wry smile which lit up the craggy lines of his face.

'I was supposed to travel to 2100 to report back on the state of the planet, so Eddie could study the data and we could avoid a future catastrophe.'

'What happened to not meddling with the future?' said George.

'Ah well, it seemed like extenuating circumstances. I'm afraid if we don't course correct and make the right decisions for the planet now, we may not have a future,' said Eddie.

'On a personal note, I'm hoping you'll figure out how we can control if and when we time travel,' said Cara.

'That would be a lucky break. All this coming and going is tough—which reminds me—I wanted to bring you both up to speed on Victoriana,' said George.

They sat around the kitchen table, a warm glow of camaraderie in the air, another round of steaming coffee cups in hands, while George told them what had been going on with the Chartists in 1848.

'There's been a kidnapping.'

'What?' said Cara and Eddie, simultaneously.

'You won't like it, which is why I didn't mention it sooner. Didn't want to upset you.'

'What's going on?' said Cara, looking worried.

'It's Swifty; he's a footman at Buckingham Palace. When I asked who could go on a scouting mission for me, the butler produced Swifty. I was gob smacked, and now I'm kicking myself for involving him because he's been kidnapped. If I hadn't recognised him, he wouldn't be in danger now.'

'Poor Swifty,' said Cara.

'It's extraordinary,' said Eddie.

'What is?' asked George.

'Swifty is also in Victoriana.'

'I hadn't fully appreciated it, with the shock of hearing about him being kidnapped,' said Cara, nodding.

'I had the bright idea to deploy him to spy on the Chartists to see how much danger the queen is in, given the recent overthrowing of the monarchy in France and riots in London,' said George.

'How do you know he was kidnapped?' asked Cara.

'I received a ransom note. I told Queen V, but she was adamant the police must handle it. She forbade me to search for him.'

'Thank God. I love Queen Victoria—such a sensible woman,' said Cara, touching his hand.

'I feel terrible though—it's all my fault,' said George.

Eddie stood and paced around the kitchen. 'That's not necessarily true,' he said.

'How so?' asked George, intrigued, his eyes following Eddie as he walked.

'Well, think about it. We have no way of knowing whether you would have done what you did even if you didn't recognise Swifty.'

'I don't follow you,' said Cara.

'Nor me,' said George.

Eddie scratched his head and sat back down. He waved his large hands around as he talked; and looked every bit the archetypal professor. 'The biggest challenge we have when we cross into other timelines is to live; or more accurately, to re-live our lives in the way we would have done the first time. We don't know what we would have done so we can only follow our gut and hope it's the same action we took originally.'

He paused and looked first at Cara and then at George to gauge their reaction.

'The problems start when we learn something about the future that we wouldn't have known before. Then, I believe, we have an immense responsibility to decide whether we will choose a different course to try and change the outcome, or whether we step back and allow the future to unfold without attempting to disrupt it.'

Cara and George both contemplated his words.

'It's a genuine test of following your gut, and it takes nerves of steel,' continued Eddie.

'It makes sense, but I sometimes wonder whether the purpose of us being given these *do-over* opportunities isn't to steer things in an alternative direction?' said Cara.

George looked at her as she spoke, nodding agreement.

'Sylvia says the purpose of Twin Flames is to develop higher consciousness as our souls learn their spiritual lessons, and so wouldn't we naturally take different actions the second time around?' asked Cara.

'I think there's something in that, but there's also the weight we carry as time travellers. There are many questions we must ask ourselves, such as, will we attempt to change the past to create what we see as a better future? Will we do so only for the greater good, or will we also use our gift to change the future for ourselves and for the people we love? And of course, the big one: how do we even decide what is a *better* future?' Eddie paced around again, stopping to draw imitation speech marks in the air with two sets of fingers to stress the point.

'It's a minefield because we don't know the future implications of our actions,' said Cara.

'Yes,' said Eddie, turning his attention to George. What's critical to consider when you think about Swifty, is that if you followed your gut, which you seem to have done, then you did the best you could.'

George raised his head. 'So, you mean if I had decided not to send him—to ignore my gut—even though I recognised him as an ally, that could have messed things up even more?'

'Potentially.'

'Now you sound just like Sylvia, Eddie. Who would think a quantum physics professor and a psychic would give such similar advice?' said Cara.

Eddie grinned at Cara. 'Don't forget it was Sylvia who introduced us in this timeline.'

He addressed George, 'I would wait to see whether the police find Swifty.'

'I was afraid you might say that,' said George. 'Although I wouldn't go against the queen's wishes, so I have little choice. I only hope the police have located the lad or I'll never forgive myself.'

'Swifty is smart; if he's anything like Tudorville Swifty, he's difficult to out-fox. I have a good feeling about it,' said Cara, reaching for George's hand.

She hated seeing him so upset.

'Carlos and I loved our dinner with you two the other night,' said Eddie.

'It was brilliant seeing you both,' said George.

'I have major fear of missing out,' said Cara, rolling her eyes.

'Never fear. If you're meant to remember, you will. It'll all come back. Although, I'm not convinced we're all supposed to be aware of every timeline...I think sometimes we're just sleeper travellers,' said Eddie.

'I was happy to hear you and Carlos are still together. It must be eight years in Victoriana time since we first met in Seville. Looks like there's a happy ending for you, after all, Eddie. You were quite forlorn when we first discussed your love life,' said Cara.

'That devil, Carlos, broke my heart in Tudorville, but ever since you stumbled upon him working at Willow Manor, we've been together here too. I've no idea whether I'll see him again in Tudorville, but two out of three ain't bad,' replied Eddie.

'I bet if you had a reading with Sylvia, she would find that you two are also multi-generational Twin Flames. Perhaps it's your destiny to reunite in all the timelines, too,' said Cara.

Eddie scratched the side of his nose, as he reflected on his complex five-hundred-year love affair with Carlos.

'It's a bit far-fetched, but it could be the case,' he said.

Cara threw back her head and laughed. 'Hold on, is this the guy who is creating a time-travel-on-demand system, saying that being in love with the same soul through multiple generations is far-fetched?'

Eddie raised his hands in mock surrender. 'Nothing is beyond the realms of possibility, given what we've seen. I still think harmony in two out of three timelines is pretty good going, but maybe I'll talk to Sylvia when I get a chance.'

'Talking of which, have you guys made peace in Tudorville, yet? Last I heard, George was a wrong-un, and it had all gone to hell between you.'

'Oh, that's old news, Eddie,' said Cara. 'You advised me to trust him and you were right, as usual.'

'That's fantastic,' said Eddie, beaming at them. 'I can't

stand it when you two are at odds—it makes my life very difficult.'

'I'm afraid, we have much bigger fish to fry in Tudorville, and your life might be about to get more difficult,' said Cara.

Eddie rested his head on his hands on the wooden table and looked at her expectantly.

'George is involved in the most dangerous uprising of the Tudor period,' she said.

Chelsea, London, 1848 - Victoriana

George hurried on foot to Cheyne Walk. He'd exited the carriage as they entered Chelsea and walked the rest of the way to enjoy the breath-taking view of the River Thames. Gentle rays of sun skimmed the water and reflected off the river's surface, bathing the landscape in a comforting golden glow.

What a wonderful photo this would make to show Cara.

As he walked along the river bank, he mused that maybe he should do what Cara suggested, and figure out how to purchase riverfront property. It would be an incredible investment; houses and flats in Chelsea sold for multi-millions of pounds in the present day and were in great demand.

From what he had read briefly on the internet, Turner and his long-time companion and common-law wife, Mrs Sophia Booth, had purchased a little house here so Turner wouldn't have to keep travelling to Margate to visit her, and they could live a life of quiet anonymity. George hadn't been able to glean much more in his brief search as it appeared the master-painter had been a secretive man, led a double life, and there appeared to be many versions of what he did, when he did it, and with whom. George was curious to see what the reality would be like, and excited to meet the renowned painter.

He arrived at 6 Davis's Place hoping to find Mr Turner at home. He need not have feared because the glossy black door stood wide open; perhaps for the couple to enjoy the stunning view of the river that snaked in front of their house.

George was familiar with this area of Chelsea in the present-day where there was now an embankment. In the future, the Davis's Place address would become part of the prestigious Cheyne Walk.

George rapped on the door and waited. He heard muffled voices and a minute later, a stout, jolly looking woman appeared in the doorway. 'May I help you, Sir?'

'Good day, you may indeed.'

'I am looking for Mr William Turner. Is he at home by any chance?'

Mrs Booth looked surprised, and then said, 'I'm not sure if he's available. Who may I say is calling?'

'My name is Cavendish, Lord George Cavendish, and I'm an ardent admirer of Mr Turner's work, and am keen to increase my art collection.'

'Right, I see. You'd better come in.' She took his hat and coat and ushered him through a small vestibule and into a pleasant, bright front parlour with windows overlooking the Thames. There were flowers in a jug which gave the room a cheery feel. 'Please bear with me a moment, Lord Cavendish, while I see if Mr Turner is amenable to a visit. He's not in the best of health, you see.'

'Oh, I am sorry to hear that. Please assure him I mean to only keep him for a short while, and I will not waste his time as I am a serious art collector.'

Mrs Booth disappeared for several minutes, and George waited and looked around the room. Contrary to what he had read, Turner lived in extremely comfortable conditions, and there was nothing remotely squalid about this house, if this room was any indication.

George's eyes were immediately drawn to a painting of what looked like a view of the river from the front window. The master painter had depicted the glorious glowing light which George had admired on his way over. Perhaps his wish for a picture to show Cara would be granted, after all.

A while later, Mrs Booth entered the room with a rattling tray, weighed down by a silver teapot, and three fine china cups. She set her load down on the table carefully, wiped her hands on her apron, and then turned to him and held out her hand which he shook warmly.

'I'm Mrs Booth, Sophia; it's a pleasure to make your acquaintance. Please excuse the delay, Lord Cavendish; may I offer you some tea while you wait for Mr Turner to join us?'

'That's very kind, ma'am; most kind. I'll take a cup; without milk, please.'

She straightened her frilly bonnet, poured the tea, and presented him with a cup and saucer in her outstretched hand.

'Mr Turner is most intrigued as to how you knew to locate him at this residence, when his official address and gallery is in Marylebone.'

'I do hope I'm not intruding, ma'am, as that was not my intention. I made discreet enquiries and was told that the gallery in Marylebone is closed. A gentleman whose name escapes me, was kind enough to give me your address. You may rest assured I will not pass on your whereabouts to anyone, as I quite understand the desire to enjoy a little privacy, being so well known.'

Mrs Booth nodded and sipped her tea. 'I'm sure he will appreciate your interest; he should be down shortly. He doesn't move too quickly these days, now he's getting on, poor Mr Turner, although he is no less gifted with his pictures. Look what he painted the other day, with only his limited paint and brush selection on hand...he grows ever more talented by the year.'

She pointed towards the painting that George had admired.

'If I'm not mistaken, this glorious work of art depicts the fine view from this very window, is it so, Mrs Booth?'

'Indeed, it is, Lord Cavendish; he doesn't work as much now, but he has produced a few fine paintings in the neighbourhood, of late, when he's been feeling invigorated. There's another similar one you might like in the other room. Perhaps he would be willing to part with one of those —he doesn't have much to show here, with most of his work already exhibited in the galleries or adorning the walls of clients.'

George heard the creak of the stairs and the slow shuffle of approaching feet. The door squeaked open to reveal Mr William Turner.

George was excited and rose quickly to offer his hand to Turner but tried to appear nonchalant, as if meeting one of the most famous and celebrated dead painters from two hundred years earlier, was the most natural of events.

'How do you do, Sir? Thank you for taking my unannounced visit,' George said. 'I am grateful and most keen to see your latest work, if you would do me the honour of allowing me to view it.'

'It's good to meet you Lord Cavendish, although I'm afraid I have little to show you of my work at this address.'

Mr Turner shuffled towards a chair and sat down with a heavy sigh, as if he might never get up again. 'What type of painting are you looking for, Lord Cavendish?'

Mrs Booth poured Turner a cup of tea and placed it on the table in front of him.

'The beauty of this fine painting on the wall, struck me. Is that for sale, by any chance? If so, I would love to buy it.'

Turner took a slurp of his tea and grunted. 'You have a good eye, my lord. That has not yet been seen by a soul outside these walls. I pass the time painting purely for pleasure these days. It is the view from this window, and I named it, *Chelsea at Dawn*.'

'It is beautiful and depicts the scene so wonderfully. On my walk over here, I wished for a way to capture the beauty of the morning light on the river and you have done it effortlessly, Sir.'

Turner slurped his tea and replaced a rattling saucer on the table. He raised his head to look directly into George's eyes. 'Effortless,' he barked. 'Oh, it is never effortless, my lord, but I confess to being rather pleased with my efforts on this occasion.'

'I am in no desperate need to sell my work these days and am blessed to be in the fortunate position of being able to work only when the muse takes me.'

'My wife would adore this painting, if you would consider parting with it. I am happy for you to name your price. She has had a sorry time of it lately, and I would love to cheer her by bringing home such a gift.'

'A good husband, you are, Lord Cavendish, and a fortunate wife she is. Go on, Mr Turner, let the man surprise his lovely wife.'

Mr Turner smiled at his lady love, and said, 'The painting isn't registered in my collection at the gallery. I grow increasingly weary of making the trip into town. Mrs Booth is right; you're obviously a good sort and may buy whatever you wish from the small display here at the house. I can tell you are a man of fine taste and my work will be appreciated by you and hopefully by Lady Cavendish in her time of distress.'

They chatted a while longer and arranged the purchase before George bid them farewell.

How George would have loved to have told the painter that in the twenty-first century, not only would the huge art collection he so generously bequeathed to the British nation be on show at the Tate, but one of his paintings owned by a private collector would be auctioned at Sotheby's and fetch an astonishing forty-seven and a half million dollars.

George whistled as he sauntered back along the river bank, one priceless watercolour in one hand, and the second under his other arm. He had discovered something far better than a photo to bring the light back into Cara's eyes.

CHAPTER 14

Pontefract Castle, Yorkshire, 1536 - Tudorville

The mood had grown uglier since George's arrival at the castle; rebels piled into the courtyard, and the army's growing numbers were apparent. George hoped the duke wasn't planning to visit the castle, for he feared he would not enjoy a pleasant reception.

'I beg you to reconsider your affiliation with the rebels and to withdraw and distance yourself,' said George.

Lord Darcy reached out and patted George's arm. 'It's too late for that, George, although I appreciate you trying to help. I'm afraid I'm too far in to extract myself now.'

'I must warn you; it's my belief this will not end well for the rebels and all who support them. If they march on London, it will be out of my hands and I won't be able to save you. I hate to see you mixed up in this folly. I know your heart is in the right place, but I fear the king won't see it that way if you cross him in such a public manner.'

George was weary, but his tone was urgent and compelling. Cara's warning words reverberated through his mind. The clock was ticking and soon it would be too late to save his old friends from certain death.

'My disagreement isn't with the king, but I believe it's the right thing for the northern lords to make a stand and back the pilgrims against Cromwell's regime. We have an army gathered which is as great as forty thousand strong. I wouldn't have believed we could raise such a number if I hadn't seen it with my own eyes. The pilgrims are ready to march south and show the king they are resolute, and it would be a tragedy to waste this opportunity.'

'Surely you do not plan to march with them? You realise it would be a declaration of war on your part?' said George.

Lord Darcy sighed. 'I haven't decided. My health isn't what it was; my spirit is willing, but my body may not be up to the journey.'

'I am sorry I cannot dissuade you from the cause,' said George.

'I am most grateful to you for your concern. Please give my best to your father when you see him.'

They shook hands and George left the room and headed out to the courtyard. Groups of men clustered in and around the castle, awaiting instructions.

A man shouted, 'We will march under the banner of the five wounds of Christ,' and the men cheered and waved their makeshift flags.

George spotted Robert Aske and weaved his way over to him.

'Good day, George. How are you fairing?' he greeted him with a smile.

'Good day to you, Robert. Not as well as I would like. It seems we may be past the point of negotiation if this manic crowd is anything to go by.'

'I warned you we have large numbers ready for action,' said Robert.

'But what about the king's offer? Are you to insult him and risk all-out war in the name of the pope?' George directed his considerable persuasive powers at his old friend. He'd failed to influence Lord Darcy, but there was still a chance to change Robert's mind.

'We are not fighting for the pope, George. We're fighting to regain the beating heart of our country. We wish to worship with the time-honoured customs of old. What's happening to the monasteries is an absolute disgrace and the people won't stand for it,' said Robert, equally impassioned.

'But the king has pledged to meet your demands. Will you not urge the men to give his offer a chance in the name of peace?'

Robert sighed. 'I do not know that I have the power to urge them to back down at this point. Resentment has been bubbling for so long, the lid is about to blow, and the men demand action.'

'Robert, I know you are a man of peace; a barrister, not a warmonger. May I at least have your word that you will endeavour to dissuade them from marching immediately against the king? I strongly advise against moving forward in haste. You have large numbers but when you reach London, you will be up against the full might of the king's men.'

Robert pushed his hand through his messy hair, and his one eye assessed George.

'Right, you are, my lord. You do not desist easily; I'll give you that. I will call a meeting and talk to the other leaders once more, to see whether they will reconsider. I don't disagree with your assessment of the situation. It may very well end in a bloodbath.'

George raised his head, looked upwards towards the sombre grey sky, and inhaled the fresh Yorkshire air. Such was his angst he had forgotten to breathe. Relief flooded through him. 'Thank you. The Duke of Norfolk awaits your official response to the king's offer, so I will advise him of your position. If you do not accept, I know not what his next move will be. I am not privy to the plans in the event of what they will interpret as a declaration of war.'

'As you wish, my lord. You have my word I will do all I can.' Robert thanked George and turned to leave.

'The hour grows late. How long will you need?' asked George, catching him before he moved away.

'I don't know. I'll come and find you when we're agreed whether to accept the offer.'

'The duke will demand a deadline; let's say I'll come and find you at dusk when the first candles are lit, if I haven't received word from you before then.'

Robert nodded and hurried off, and George stared at his back until he lost sight of him. He prayed Robert would push them to accept the king's offer, or all hell would break loose. The duke wasn't a man who took failure with grace. He was set on restoring the high favour he'd enjoyed with the king before his niece, Anne Boleyn, fell from power. He had sat on the council that had sealed her sorry fate, but still his fortunes had declined by association. He would not accept defeat without a fight.

George walked into the castle through one of the back entrances after taking a walk to try and clear his head. He would go to his room and have a quick nap. Whatever the outcome with the rebels, he would need all of his wits about him.

He sank down on to his mattress, exhausted, and soon drifted off, and dreamed of a ragtag army clutching the Five Wounds of Christ banner as they marched on London waving pitchforks and searching for Cromwell, the heretic. They were determined to have their way, or they demanded

Cromwell's blood. George tossed and turned, and next he saw Darcy, his head shrouded in a black hood which could mean only one thing.

He shuddered in his sleep and then opened his eyes. His damp shirt clung to his body, even though the room was winter-cold.

He wished Cara were beside him, so he could protect her. The thought of her stuck in London with the queen filled him with dread. He rose and looked out of the window; a feeling of doom gripped him. The castle was eerily quiet—the courtyard was empty apart from a few guards, and the hordes of rebels were nowhere to be seen.

Were they preparing to disarm and accept the king's offer, or were they readying for war? Was it a good sign, or was it the calm before the battle?

Grosvenor Square, London, 1848 - Victoriana

George held Cara as she wept. Teardrops rolled down her cheeks and splashed on to his shirt. He had returned from Chelsea feeling upbeat. He had checked in with the police and they assured him they had located Swifty and there was a plan to rescue him later that day. He had two stunning Turner works of art in his possession, and he was excited to show them to Cara. He yearned to see her smile like she used to, and he tried to distract her from her melancholic mood at every opportunity. But when he dashed in the door, calling her name, he found her standing by the window in the parlour, her chest heaving and silent tears trickling from her eyes.

'Hush, my love. Let it all out. It'll be all right. These things happen.' He didn't need to ask what was wrong.

'I'm sorry,' she sniffed. 'You've got so much on your mind, what with the missing boy, and the threat to the queen. I thought I was getting over it but worrying about the kidnappers must have brought it all up again.'

He cradled her in his arms and soothed her like a distraught child.

'Shh, my darling...I'm fine as long as you're fine. Everything else is in hand. Don't worry about these other matters.'

George led Cara towards the sofa and they sat down. Her head nestled on his shoulder as his hand continued to pat her hair.

George rang the bell, and when Rose, the maid, entered, he asked for tea.

'Yes, my lord,' she said, bobbing a quick curtsy before rushing back to the kitchen.'

They ran a small, happy household, just him and Cara and a couple of members of staff to serve them and keep the elegant townhouse in order. The house's proximity to Buckingham Palace allowed them to slip back and forth to the palace, without being away from home for days at a time. Cara would resume her duties as lady-in-waiting once she was up to it.

She had been so distraught about her miscarriage that the doctor had given her a draught to calm her, and she'd not been her usual bubbly self for months. George worried and was at a loss for what more to do to restore her spirits.

There was a tap at the door and the maid entered, clutching a tray stacked with a teapot, cups, and an impressive cake.

'Thanks, Rose. I'll pour,' said Cara. 'Are you not visiting your family today?'

'If that's still all right, my lady, I'll be leaving soon.'

'That's perfectly all right. Have fun and please give your mother my warm regards.'

George and Cara kept things as informal with their staff as the etiquette of the era permitted. George loved that about Cara; she knew nothing of their modern life, but she treated the servants respectfully. He occasionally wondered whether her consciousness was more connected to the future than they realised.

When the door closed, Cara handed George a cup of tea and a slice of cake, and said, 'Here, try this. It's Cook's latest creation and is all the rage at the palace, apparently. Imagine having a cake named after you.'

'Victoria sponge, how marvellous. I hadn't realised.'

'Realised what?' said Cara.

George sipped his steaming tea and took a huge bite of cake. A dollop of raspberry jam and cream slid out from between the moist cake layers and plopped onto his trouser leg.

'Hadn't realised how good it would be,' he said, covering his slip-up. 'Damn it, bloody delicious, though. I must say, it's worth the terrible mess I'm making of it.'

His lives blurred, and he found it difficult not to reveal more than he should about the future. He didn't want to arouse Cara's suspicions—things were difficult enough.

'Was your trip to Chelsea a success?' She had composed herself, but her cheeks were still pink and puffy.

'Indeed, it was. I located Turner at the address the fellow at my club gave me, and it was a perfectly lovely visit.'

'I hear he's a strange one,' she said. 'A bit of a recluse.'

'Yes, that may well be...but he paints like an angel. And that reminds me; I have a wonderful surprise for you.'

George slotted his cup back onto the tray, extracted his long legs, which were curled up beside the sofa, and raced out of the room. 'Hang on,' he shouted. 'You're going to love this!'

His joie de vivre was infectious—it was impossible to stay

down for long when he was around. And besides, Cara loved surprise gifts.

I'm the luckiest woman in the world.

Even though she still experienced moments of intense sadness about the loss of their baby, her mood lifted when she was with George, and she believed things would work out as they were supposed to. If they weren't destined to have children, then so be it if that was God's will. She'd rather be childless with him than have a gaggle of children with someone else.

'Close your eyes,' he called out from the hallway.

'Closed,' she shouted.

'No cheating.'

She giggled. 'They are closed tight. Come on! Whatever is it?'

George removed the painting from its covering and lay it down on the table.

'Open your eyes, my darling.'

Cara gasped. 'The colours are breath-taking,' she said.

'I present to you *Chelsea at Dawn*. Like it?'

'Like it? I love it! It's divine. I know little about Turner's paintings,' she said.

'Me too. I noticed it when I was waiting for him and immediately fell in love with this beauty. Fortunately, he was quite happy to part with it. Says his best work is at his London gallery, and this is just the pottering about of an old man in Chelsea.'

'My goodness. Well, if that's the case, we are blessed indeed. Where shall we hang it?'

'First we'll need to organise a frame. How about here, or in our bedchamber?'

'Yes, that's it. Our bedchamber—that way we'll see *Chelsea at Dawn* every morning as we awaken. What a perfect way to start the day.'

She turned to George and kissed him. 'Thank you so much. I adore it. It's the most gorgeous picture I've ever seen.'

'I knew you would love it,' he said. 'I wished I could take a photograph of the river for you when I was on my way over, and then I found this.'

'A photograph. How on earth would you take a photograph? You need all kinds of special equipment for that, don't you? I was reading about it recently.'

'Yes, it's such a shame. In the future, we'll all have camera's in our pockets, but for now we'll enjoy this glorious painting instead.'

'A camera in our pocket? However, do you come up with these strange notions?'

George laughed, and said, 'Never mind about my vivid imagination, let's drink our tea and then go and see about a frame, shall we?'

'That sounds lovely. Is the danger over, then? Is Swifty safe now?' Cara asked.

'I think we are all safe now that the police are onto the gang who kidnapped him. I spoke to the Chief of Police who is an excellent fellow. He said they have a handle on where they're holding him, and that they are petty criminals. He doesn't believe there is any serious danger, and they are going to rescue him later.'

'The poor boy must be terrified,' said Cara.

'I have every faith in his fortitude. The police are hoping he will lead them to the ringleaders who they suspect are planning more serious attacks across the country and against the Crown, so they're monitoring them carefully.'

'You talk as though you know the boy well. I had understood you'd only met him briefly for the first time at the palace, the other day.'

'Let's just say, I get a sense about some people, and I knew immediately we could trust him.' George shrugged.

'Well, I hope he feels the same, after his terrible ordeal, or he may wish never to see you again.'

'Oh, he'll see me again, all right,' said George.

Cara studied her husband's smiling face. Sometimes she was curious about his strange responses—it was as though he knew something she didn't; as if he could see far into the future. She trusted him one hundred per cent, so she shook off her suspicion.

Rose Cottage, York - Present day

Cara and Eddie waited for George to return from taking a phone call in the study, so he could fill them in on more details of his Turner escapade. So far, all they knew was he'd been successful in purchasing a painting.

'George must have inadvertently created a quantum time loop,' said Eddie, rubbing his thumb back and forth across his bottom lip.

'A what? What on earth is that?'

'It's a virtuous circle of time, whereby what originally happened has now been rewritten. George buying a Turner will carve out an alternative history and reset the course of the previous timeline. If my theory is correct, it will now be as if the painting wasn't recorded previously. We have no way of knowing what happened to it in the first round of events or whether it was ever exhibited.'

'Does it matter?' asked Cara, frowning.

'Let's hope not,' he replied.

'Oh no, that sounds dark. Do you think there will be repercussions from such a small tweak of events?'

'As in, aside from you being able to sell an undiscovered Turner work of art for millions of pounds?'

'Um, well, yes...when you put it like that, it doesn't sound like a small tweak,' said Cara.

'To answer your question—honestly—I don't know, but we will see soon enough as things unfold.'

Cara looked at Eddie and considered his prediction of a quantum time loop. 'Why didn't you mention this before?'

'I didn't want to worry you unnecessarily,' he said.

George wandered into the kitchen.

'Tea, darling?' said Cara.

'Yes, please, and what have we to eat? I'm ravenous.'

'Nothing new there, then... By the way, Eddie thinks you may have created a quantum time loop.' Cara scoured the cupboards for a suitable snack.

'Goodness...how did I do that?' asked George, pulling a face.

'If Eddie's hunch is correct, then buying the Turner painting will have rewritten history.'

'Ah yes, about the painting...'

Cara stacked a pile of crackers on a plate and set it down on the table next to a pot of hummus, for the hungry quantum-time-travellers.

'What about it?' she said.

'I actually bought two paintings,' replied George.

Eddie raised one eyebrow mid-cracker.

'How come?' said Cara.

Eddie's expression was puzzled as he heaped hummus onto his cracker.

'That's just it. The Victoriana-you, fell in love with the other one, so we're going to keep it and hang it on the wall of our bedchamber.'

'I don't know whether to be pleased or jealous,' she said.

'Pleased,' he said. 'There's nothing to be jealous about, my darling. You have a far better life than Victoriana-Cara. That's why I wanted her to have the painting.'

Cara looked at George, wondering what he wasn't saying. She knew when he was holding back, but she didn't press. Now wasn't the moment. There would be plenty of time after Eddie went home to find out what else was going on in Victoriana. There was no need to involve Eddie in more of their personal difficulties. He took it hard when they disagreed, and it sounded as though something deeper was going on than merely gift-giving.

'When do you want to collect the painting from the Bank of England?' she asked.

'As soon as I put it there,' he replied, after crunching through a cracker.

'I thought you'd already done it,' said Eddie.

'Nope. Haven't had a chance yet. I was tearing about locating Turner and then talking to the police about Swifty's kidnapping. And to complicate matters further, the military is on standby in London and is armed and ready for Chartist unrest.' He shook his head.

'I wish I could eat like you when I'm worried,' said Cara.

'It's a skill,' he replied. He spread a dollop of hummus onto a cracker and handed it to her, with a smile.

CHAPTER 15

Grosvenor Square, London, 1848 - Victoriana

George and Cara, who had recently retired to their bedchamber, and settled into bed, heard a loud rap from downstairs.

Cara engrossed in a new novel; *Jane Eyre,* raised her eyes. 'Who could that be?'

'I don't know but the servants must have retired by now, so I will go down and see.'

'Be careful,' said Cara.

It was unusual for anyone to knock on their door at this hour.

George layered a silk robe over his long white nightshirt and walked downstairs. As he approached the front door, he called out, 'Who's there?'

'It's Swifty, my lord.'

George opened the door and saw the boy's filthy face and torn clothing.

'What a surprise. I didn't expect to see you here. Come in, come in,' he said, standing aside to usher the boy in.

'You look cold. Are you hungry?'

'Yes, my lord. They didn't give me much to eat.'

'Follow me down to the kitchen and let's see what we can find.'

George boiled water for tea and hurriedly sliced some bread and cheese and put it in front of Swifty. He placed a blanket around his shoulders. 'You look freezing, but you should warm up soon; it's still hot down here from the ovens. Eat a few bites and then tell me how you got here, if you will.'

Swifty devoured the bread and cheese and slurped his tea, barely stopping for air.

'Better?' said George after a few minutes.

'Yes, my lord. Thank you.'

'Now tell me what's going on. I know they kidnapped you, and the police were about to rescue you.'

'The queen is in terrible danger, my lord.'

'How so? And who are these men who were holding you?'

'They're a small extremist group who have broken away from the Chartists and are plotting to take matters into their own hands to overthrow the monarchy.'

'Do you know their plans regarding the queen?'

Cara arrived in the doorway, holding a flickering candle, her long hair plaited, and a robe thrown over her nightgown. 'What's going on?'

'Ah, there you are—just in time to hear the latest. This is Swifty,' replied George. 'He's somehow escaped his kidnappers and has come to warn us about a plot against the monarchy.'

'Hello, Swifty. I've heard a lot about you. You look older than I imagined.'

Swifty looked at her in surprise. 'I think I know you,' he said. 'I feel as though I've met you before—it was the same when I met my lord.' And then his words turned to mumbles, and he bowed his head, embarrassed.

'It's all right, Swifty,' said Cara. 'You look familiar to me, too.'

They both looked at George.

'Perhaps you saw one another at the palace,' he said, not missing a beat. He wasn't going to get into trying to explain how they were fellow time travellers.

'Let's not worry about that now. We must secure the royal family's safety, at once. Pray tell us all that you know, without delay,' said George.

'Yes, my lord. They are angry at the slow progress the Chartists have made with suffrage. They demand more than just equal votes and the six-point Charter. They say they want a new England where every man is equal, and they want rid of the queen and all she stands for.'

'My goodness,' said Cara, sitting down on a kitchen bench. 'Do you know what they plan to do?'

'They have been making a bomb and are going to break into Buckingham Palace and plant it in the queen's rooms to kill her. I heard them plotting.'

'When is this to happen, Swifty?' asked George.

'That's just it. Tonight, I think. I came as soon as I could to warn you. They were distracted, and there was some kind of hold up with the bomb, so I slipped away. I'd been pretending to still be tied up until I saw a chance to break free.'

'Do they know you heard them talking?'

'I can't be sure, but I don't think so.'

'We must warn the palace,' said Cara.

'I'd better get over there immediately. Swifty, we'll go together, and you can tell them all you know. You can fill me in on more of the details, on the way.'

'What if they're at the palace and have already planted the bomb?' asked Cara.

'Good point. I'll see if I can find a bobby on the way and alert the police.'

'I'm coming,' said Cara.

'No, you stay here, it's too dangerous.'

'That's exactly why I must come. Three of us are better than two. You might not find a police officer, never mind proper back up.'

'I can't stop you coming, can I? I know that look in your eyes.' George sighed, and rubbed his tired eyes.

'If I can be of service to the queen and help keep you safe, then my place is at your side. I'm no help waiting here and will just go out of my mind with worry.'

'Very well. I dare say Her Majesty will appreciate your company and is likely to be shaken up when she learns of the plot.'

They hurriedly dressed and five minutes later they exited the house and then ran silently through the dark, sleepy streets, hoping they weren't too late.

'Let's go in the back way,' George whispered as they approached Buckingham Palace, which lay under a dense black sky apart from the bright silver moon twinkling overhead like a piece of crushed satin.

They headed round the back and lined up ready to climb over the wall, panting from the exertion of the long run.

Swifty said, 'Allow me to go first, my lord, and I'll help you down—I'm used to sneaking in this way when I'm late back.'

They heard Swifty's feet touch the ground on the other side, and they paused, listening. Then they heard a growling voice. 'There he is. There's the lad who got away. Stop him! He's going to alert the queen.'

Then came the sound of pounding footsteps, followed by

an eerie silence.

George looked at Cara and pressed his finger to her lips, and they stood unmoving, waiting in the wall's shadow.

Rose Cottage, York - Present day

Cara and George lounged in the garden, drinking tea, and enjoying the last of the warm afternoon rays.

'I have to say, I was surprised when I found Turner. I read that he lived in squalor until his death,' said George.

'I suppose it's a classic case of don't believe everything you read on the internet,' said Cara.

'He wasn't at all desperate for money, and from what I could see he was totally loved-up with a wonderful woman called Sophie Booth, and they seemed like the perfect match.'

'How lovely. Well I'd rather that than the other depressing version of events.'

'Although it makes one wonder how much of what we think is history, is simply a load of mumbo-jumbo,' said George, crossing his legs, and repositioning himself in the sunchair.

'In my official historian's capacity, sadly, I can confirm that a great deal of it is mumbo-jumbo.'

'It's eerie knowing exactly when people are going to die, isn't it? I found it unnerving talking to Turner and knowing when his last day on earth would be.'

'It is strange, but it's great to hear he's making the most of his final years,' said Cara, rubbing suntan lotion onto her face, and passing the bottle to George. 'What's your next move?'

'London is under tight security, with public buildings being guarded from potential Chartist attacks. I tried to get the painting into the Bank of England to store it in a vault, but I was swept away in the rallies on my way over there. The bank is one of the spots where the military is quartered and it's swarming with troops, so I don't know when I'll be allowed in. The city was in chaos.'

'How about asking the queen for help?'

'Now, that's an idea. I hadn't thought of that.'

'It's sort of her bank anyway, isn't it?' Cara tilted her head and smiled at him.

'Yes, I suppose it is. Although, I'll need to handle any questions about the painting. Remember, Turner was already a renowned painter and I've got an as yet unknown painting in my possession.'

'But you purchased it legally?'

'Yes. I gave him more than his asking price, and I did as you suggested and asked for a receipt, and a signed note to state the paintings are his originals.'

'There's our strategy, then. When can you ask the queen for help?'

'I don't know. The last thing I remember, we were tearing over to Buckingham Palace to foil a plot to erase the monarchy by blowing them all up. Hardly the perfect time to be asking for favours.'

Eddie wandered out to the garden. 'Did I hear correctly? You're foiling a plot against the queen?'

'That's right,' said George. 'Well, in the middle of trying to, anyway.'

'Oh dear,' said Eddie, raising his eyes skywards, and shaking his head.

'What?' said Cara and George, both staring at him as he walked across the lawn.

'What's the matter? You're scaring me,' said Cara.

'By the sounds of it, you are creating quantum time loops, right, left, and centre in Victoriana.'

Cara shook her head. 'But wait a minute—someone had to have foiled the plot—there was no mention of an explosion at the palace when I researched it.'

Eddie and George waited for her to continue.

'All hell broke loose following the rejection of the third petition of the Charter by the House of Commons. There were riots throughout the summer and the Chartists tried to organise an armed uprising which became known as the Orange Tree Conspiracy. They met at the now infamous Orange Tree Public House to cook up their plan, but they were arrested in the August of 1848.'

Cara had hit her stride and her face was animated with a historian's zeal.

'Many of them were later deported to Australia for life, which finally disbanded the Chartist movement. Think about it: working-class men only got the vote at the same time as women—shortly after World War I.'

'Yes, we knew all that, didn't we, Eddie?' said George.

Eddie chuckled. 'I don't know how you remember all those details.'

'That's rich coming from a quantum physics professor,' Cara quipped.

'Seriously though, what the hell do you think is going on, Eddie?' asked George. 'Am I creating new problems by being back in Victoriana?'

'I'm not sure, but if you're acting differently than how you would have done the first time around, then anything could happen. There could be an unpredictable outcome, and the more you risk changing things, the greater the chances the timeline will shift.'

'It really is the most infuriating thing. I understand the dangers and implications, but what else can I do?' asked George.

. . .

Windsor Castle, 1536 - Tudorville

My dearest, darling husband,

I miss you so much and you are always in my thoughts. I wish I could be there with you. It's hellish not knowing what is going on and whether you are safe. I pray this letter reaches you and that you will be on your way home to me soon.

The king insisted that the queen and I accompany him by river to Windsor Castle where he says we are safer if the rebels march on London. He says we are preparing for war and my blood runs cold at the thought of you in the midst of it. I pray the pilgrims will see sense and realise they are endangering everyone's life by rebelling against the king. They must accept his offer, or the future will be bleak.

I beg you heed the conversation we had before you left. The rebels must not underestimate Cromwell. The army is on standby and food supplies and war essentials are made ready in haste. The atmosphere is tense, and we are all anxious. I must go now, as the queen has summoned me.

Take care, my love. I await word from you as soon as you are able, and I am desperate to see your face again and be in your loving arms. Above all things, please stay safe and I beg you remember the importance of treading carefully with your friends.

All my love, your wife, Cara.

In the letter, Cara did her best to embed the message about future death sentences she had warned George about before he left, and she hoped he would not do anything foolish.

The lesson of knowing when to do nothing, but to simply surrender to what was destined to happen, had been a difficult one for Cara to grasp. She was a doer and a fighter. And this time around, it seemed George was the one to be tested and he must learn the same karmic lesson. She wondered whether he would resist his natural inclination to be the hero and try to save Robert and Lord Darcy.

Cara feared he would be back in the Tower if he failed to understand the importance of letting go of his attachment to his friends' destiny. Anyone who was seen resisting the king's orders would pay a heavy price during the future culling of the prominent rebels.

Let George not become one of them in his quest to do the right thing.

He had only their brief discussion about her seer's gift to go on—he wasn't aware of their five-hundred-year story. The waiting was excruciating; all Cara could rally herself to do after she dispatched the letter to Pontefract Castle, was stare out of the window at the river. Each endless day dragged by as she prayed to see his beloved figure riding up the hill on horseback.

Cara passed a solemn afternoon in the queen's rooms, seated beside the queen near one of the exquisite oriel windows.

'Lady Cara, have you any news of your husband?'

'I haven't, Your Grace. I don't know whether he's still negotiating at Pontefract Castle. Lord knows where he is; I only hope he doesn't get swept up in the Pilgrimage of Grace if they march.' Cara leaned towards the queen and whispered her reply. You couldn't be too careful, and the situation was precarious with the castle residents on edge waiting to hear whether the rebels would accept the offer.

'There is sympathy for the papist cause; my sources tell me that some of the priests frighten the people with dire predictions of burning in hell if they forsake the pope, their statues, holy days and other customs. I am frightened of the consequences,' the queen whispered back, looking about her. 'I know I can trust you to keep my secret.' The queen's complexion was pale as clotted cream.

'Are you feeling quite well, Your Grace?' asked Cara.

'I confess I have sorry news which I find I cannot bear alone.'

Cara reached for the queen's hand and rested her arm around her slim shoulders. 'You may confide in me, Your Majesty. It's not good to keep it all to yourself.'

'This morning I had some bleeding.' The queen looked at Cara and then lowered her eyes, her pale cheeks now stained with delicate pink dots.

She was but a young, naive women; a virgin before her marriage to the most powerful man in the world. The queen and Cara knew that the marriage's success depended on her bearing a son for the kingdom. That was the king's only request.

'Do you believe you were with child, Your Highness?' Cara whispered in her ear.

'I had thought so, yes. These past weeks it filled me with hope, but then this morning my courses returned.'

Cara held on to the queen's hand. 'I am sorry for your distress. Does the king know?'

'No, I didn't want to tell him until I was certain.'

'That was wise.'

The queen looked at her, tears brimming in her eyes. 'I so wish for a child to take this dreadful pressure away. I can't move without being quizzed about my relations with the king.'

'I can only imagine, Your Grace. But you did the right thing, and this could be a good sign.'

'How so if I cannot sustain a pregnancy?' asked the queen.

'What you describe is extremely common in the early stages. I am confident you will be fruitful and bear the king the male heir he so desires.'

The queen stopped crying and stared at Cara. 'How can you be so sure I'll bear a son? You speak with such certainty.'

Cara had to think quickly. She rebuked herself for letting her prediction slip.

'Let's just say I have a good feeling about it and I'm rarely wrong about these matters.'

'It's true then...'

'What's true, Your Grace?'

'I have long heard that you are special.'

'Special—in what way do they say I'm special?'

'They say you have the sight,' the queen whispered, her voice dropping even lower.

They huddled together, knowing that speaking of such things in a divided land on the brink of religious civil war could mean a death sentence for them both.

When Cara bid the queen farewell that evening and walked back to her lonely Clock Court apartment, Thomas and May dominated her thoughts. How she missed their adorable little faces. After comforting the queen about her dashed pregnancy hopes, her children seemed all the more precious. If it weren't for Tudorville, she wouldn't know what it was to love her children so deeply she would do anything to keep them safe.

Cara fell into a restless sleep. Images of George's face loomed in her mind, and her head throbbed with the tension of incessant worry. After hours of drifting in and out of sleep, she opened her eyes, her heart racing, the taste of terror lingering in her parched throat as she stared up at the intricate carvings on the oak ceiling of the four-poster bed.

George is in danger. I must go and find him.

CHAPTER 16

Buckingham Palace, London, 1848 - Victoriana

Several moments passed as they listened for more movement behind the palace walls. Then George turned to Cara and pulled her into his arms and hugged her before releasing her reluctantly.

'I must go after Swifty,' he whispered.

'Must you?' replied Cara, her heart thumping.

'They might blow up the palace.'

'Yes, and you along with it. Can't we go and seek help, first?' said Cara.

'By the time we get help, it could be too late. We can't risk it. Don't worry. I have the element of surprise on my side because they think Swifty is alone. Go around to the front of the palace and tell the guards what's happening, and that I've gone in after the lad. Ask the guards to come in quietly. Oh, and tell them they have a bomb which they mean to use.'

'Please be careful,' she said.

'I will, but make haste, my love. I'll come and find you as soon as the queen is safe.'

Cara watched George pull himself up onto the wall and slide over the top. She heard a thud as his feet touched the hard ground on the other side. She scooped up the skirts of her gown and raced as fast as she could in her dainty slippers. The frosty night air rushed into her mouth as she ran and made her eyes and throat sting. She arrived at the front of the palace and waved at one of the sleepy guards on night duty, next to the entrance. It took a while for him to spot her, and she waved again impatiently. She didn't risk calling out to him for fear of alerting the intruders that they were about to have company.

The guard approached the gates, and she told him what was going on. Fortunately, he recognised her from her years of service to the queen and let her enter the grounds through a discreet side gate.

'So, you're saying intruders have entered the palace from the back, and as we speak, your husband, Lord Cavendish, is on his way to warn the queen? Is that correct, my lady?'

'Yes, that's about it. Please hurry. Oh, and Swifty; one of your footmen, is also in there. They may have captured him again. I don't know. They have a bomb and mean to blow up the royal family.'

The guard was slow to process her words.

'You know we frequently receive dramatic threats like this, ma'am, especially with the recent riots. It's probably nothing, but I'll call for back up and check it out.'

'Please,' she said. 'Please, the queen and my husband are in there. A bomb could go off at any moment, I tell you. This is an emergency. You must hurry!'

The guard studied her startled eyes and then beckoned her to follow him. Cara entered the palace doors behind him and he alerted his sleepy colleagues. After several minutes, men milled quietly about the grand entrance hall, and weaved in and out of the adjoining ground-floor rooms, searching for the intruders. Cara cast her eyes around, hoping to catch sight of George.

A policeman approached and asked her to repeat what she knew. As she was running through the details, the sound of a gunshot boomed around the hall, and she froze. After a few seconds she turned away from the policeman and began to move in a daze towards where she thought the sound had come from, but he raced after her and held her arm to restrain her.

'You won't be helping anyone by getting yourself killed. Please let us deal with this.'

He guided Cara away from the centre of the room and gestured for her to sit down on an upholstered, wooden-framed chair. 'Please stay there, miss, and as soon as we have news you'll be the first to know.'

Cara sat on the chair, shaking and terrified that George had been on the receiving end of the bullet.

Her lips moved as she prayed, her hands clasped together, and her nails sliced into the tips of her icy fingertips. The only pain that registered was in her heart.

Rose Cottage, York - Present day

Cara buzzed about the kitchen tidying up, and Eddie entered, carrying his bag.

'Must you leave so soon?' said Cara. 'It's been brilliant having you with us.'

'Yes, I'm afraid so. I need to get back to campus, and I pre-booked my return ticket to London.'

Cara nodded.

'What's the latest?' asked Eddie.

Cara wiped her hands on a tea towel and grabbed her car keys and jacket. 'George won't be back for a while, so I'll drop you at the station. We can chat on the way.'

She filled Eddie in on the latest news as they crawled across town in the direction of the train station. The ancient York city walls were an ever-present reminder of Tudorville.

'It's all kicking off, isn't it? Uprisings in two timelines, but so far, from what you've said, nothing major has occurred,' said Eddie.

Cara rolled her eyes. 'Just as well; I don't think I can handle another disaster. We've only just recovered from the last one.'

Cara turned into the busy train station car park and edged the car into a short-stay spot. Eddie jumped out and Cara followed. They hurried toward the platform and saw they wouldn't have long to wait. Five minutes later, the London-bound train hissed to a sharp stop on the tracks, and the wind blew Cara's hair into her face.

Eddie turned to hug her. 'Thanks again for everything. I had the most wonderful time. Take care and come and see me in London when you get the chance.'

'I hope to see you in Tudorville before that,' she said.

He boarded the train and Cara waited for him to be seated.

'Give my love to George,' called Eddie, waving, before tucking his head back into the carriage. He sat by the window and blew her a kiss.

She waved him off as the train grunted slowly along the tracks and slid out of the station. She shivered and clasped her thin jacket around her as the storm clouds, which had hovered in the sky all afternoon, opened abruptly and icy rain lashed down on her head.

She made a run for it back to her car and called George as soon as she was on the road.

'Perfect timing,' said George.

'I just saw Eddie off. I'll miss him.'

'Me too. Mind you, I'll probably see him again soon in Victoriana.' His voice echoed on the car speaker.

'I think I'm still holed up at Windsor Castle, waiting for news of you in Tudorville. I miss having him around, especially with you in danger.'

'When will the rebels surrender? It must be soon,' said George.

Cara paused to think, as she turned the car and joined the busy road. 'As long as nothing's changed because of the quantum time loops, Robert Aske will accept the king's offer towards the end of October and agree not to march on London. You're about to witness a critical turning point in the history of Christendom. The rebels had the numbers if they had marched, and the papists may well have prevailed and had a good chance of succeeding to restore the old customs.'

'I only hope I've not messed things up,' said George.

'If you've messed it up it's my fault. I'm the differentiator in the timeline,' said Cara.

'What do you think will happen to Henry if the rebels succeed to take London in this new order of events?'

'The monarchy could be overthrown, and the Church of England cast aside completely. Princess Mary was the Catholics' choice for the next monarch so perhaps she would have come to the throne earlier and reigned longer. Who knows what today's England would look like?'

George shook his head as he talked to Cara from the kitchen back at the cottage. 'Henry was such a stubborn character, I can't imagine it coming to that. He would not retire with any grace. I feel sure he would fight to the death even if it meant harming his own daughter.'

The rain hammered on the windscreen as Cara drove slowly through the busy streets, and they discussed what was at stake if things went wrong.

'What if something's happened to you at Pontefract Castle? I won't even know until it's too late.'

'I'll be fine. I must be. I'm alive now so it must have worked out.'

'Yes, but the timeline could still reset. What about the quantum time loops? All it takes is for either of us to put one foot wrong and we could lose everything—like last time. If we change the course of history it could eradicate our future,' she said.

George kept her company on the phone until she arrived home and he came out to meet her in the rain. They hugged, and he kissed her freckled nose. 'Don't fret so, my darling. Whatever happens, we'll figure it out. I promise you won't get rid of me that easily.'

Windsor Castle, 1536 - Tudorville

Cara entered the queen's bedchamber, and after several minutes of idle conversation, she said, 'I am sorry to have to ask, Your Majesty, but I must seek your permission for a leave of absence from court.'

The queen looked startled; her breakfast cup froze mid-air before she recovered herself and moved the ale towards her red lips, took a sip and then said, 'But where will you go? Why would you go now? War is likely to break out at any moment.'

'I asked Master Secretary Cromwell, to bring me word as

soon as they received news of George. The king has received a dispatch from the Duke of Norfolk in which he reports he hasn't heard from George since their meeting with the Pilgrimage of Grace leaders. The duke's men were refused entry to Pontefract Castle and he suspects the rebels are holding George prisoner.'

'I am so sorry to hear this news.'

'Thank you, Your Grace.' Cara bowed her head and waited for the queen to speak again. A courtier wasn't permitted to take leave of service without the monarch's blessing. Cara was impatient to be on the road, but she knew she must play by court rules and wait for an audience with the queen, or risk paying a high price upon her return.

'My dear, is it wise for you to leave now? While I understand your concern, I don't see what you will do. Is it not better for you to stay here in the safety of the castle and wait for this madness to pass?'

Cara moved closer to the queen and whispered the highlights of her plan in her ear.

'But it's folly of the highest order! I can't imagine even dreaming of doing such a thing. You're either terribly brave or terribly foolhardy,' she spluttered, her jewelled fingers clutching her cup.

'I can't just wait, Your Grace...sitting here at Windsor, in my fine clothes, while the rebels hold my husband. He may end up dead in a ditch somewhere if I don't get him away from them. Besides, I would surely go out of my mind. I hope you understand.'

The queen nodded. 'Very well. You have my blessing. I confess, I find your courage extraordinary, and I'm proud to count you as one of my ladies.'

Cara thanked the queen, assuring her she would return as soon as she could. 'I've spoken with Lady Margaret who has agreed to take over my duties, so my absence will not unduly inconvenience you, Your Grace.'

'I will pray for you to be reunited with Lord Cavendish and that all will be well. My knees are raw from kneeling on my prie dieu, there is so much to pray for in these dangerous days.'

The queen reached out to clasp Cara's hands, and they stood in sisterly communion for a moment, enveloped in the warmth of their mutual affection and respect.

'Take care, my dear Lady Cara. Know that you will be in my thoughts, and you will be missed by your queen. You have become quite indispensable. Please take anything you need to make your journey comfortable.'

Cara curtsied and edged out of the queen's rooms backwards, before turning and fleeing out the door. She longed to be on her way before anything or anyone else could delay her from carrying out her bold plan.

Cara careered down the corridor, taking the bends in the most unladylike fashion, hoping no one would see her. Back in her rooms, heart beating fast, she rifled through some of George's items, looking for a particular outfit she had brought with her. Even with the Tudor fashion of just-below-the-knee breeches, George's would drape down to her ankles, and his silk shirt wouldn't do; it would drown her slight frame and draw attention to her. But the spare outfit she had saved for Swifty might just meet her requirements.

She dressed in a hurry; the black breeches fitted well, but the ruffle-collared white shirt accentuated her bust and would make her conspicuous. She pulled the shirt off and wrapped a pale silk scarf around her chest to bind her inconvenient breasts, so they wouldn't get in the way. The blue waistcoat fitted sufficiently, and she pinned her shiny chestnut locks up on to her head and then shoved the page's jaunty cap on top.

Fortunately, she had brought her black leather boots from Willow Manor for riding in all weathers. She surveyed herself in the large mirror and concluded she looked the part of a royal page, but she would freeze to death without something warm around her when she was on the road.

Cara grabbed one of George's thick fur-sleeved cloaks, threw it over her shoulders, and tied the silky ribbons neatly at her throat. It smelled of him and for a moment she closed her eyes, weak with longing; but she knew she must rally all of her resolve or she might lose him forever.

The smell of him would comfort her as she made the dangerous journey. Smelling like a man was perfect for her disguise. She grabbed a few items and stuffed them into her saddlebag, including the bread supply she had smuggled from the kitchens. Cara scanned the room one last time to check she had forgotten nothing, and then, heart pounding, she rushed into the hallway, closing the door softly behind her. She didn't want to alert anyone to her sudden departure.

CHAPTER 17

Buckingham Palace, London, 1848 - Victoriana

Cara shivered as she sat waiting on the upholstered chair in the grand entrance to Buckingham Palace—she was petrified and chained to the spot. No one appeared on the wide sweeping staircase since the boom of the gunshot filled her head with terrifying, unwanted images. The policeman who told her to wait had disappeared up the stairs and the entrance was buzzing with palace staff anxiously awaiting news of the queen and the royal family.

There was a loud explosion and Cara screamed. She sprung up off the chair and raced upstairs in search of George—to hell with the consequences. She would rather die trying to save him than sit there being useless.

The upstairs landing was thick with dense black smoke, and she saw pieces of debris strewn across the plush carpets. Her heart pounded as she inched forward, holding her hand over her mouth to stop the foul-smelling, polluted air from rushing into her lungs. She couldn't hear any sound and tentatively pushed open the first door she came upon, hoping she wouldn't be walking right into the hands of the perpetrators. Cara looked around the large deserted sitting room; renaissance paintings by the grand masters jostled for space on the tightly-packed walls. Cara turned around to leave and as she approached the door, there was a crash and she heard loud voices.

'There he is. Grab him. I've got the other one in here,' a gruff voice shouted.

Cara poked her head around the door, and saw two policemen closing in on a small, shifty looking man in a grubby, once white shirt, being held down by Swifty, who was clearly much stronger than he appeared.

'Please, please,' the man cried out. 'It's not my fault. I had to do it, or they said they would kill me.'

'Tell it to the judge,' snapped the policeman as he bent down to relieve Swifty of his prey. 'You're a hero, my boy. You've saved the queen from this villain and his explosives.'

Swifty unfolded his wiry limbs and stood up.

'Where is Lord Cavendish?' said Cara, her words barely audible. There'd been no sign of George since the sound of the gunshot.

Before Swifty could answer, another one of the policemen called to him and said, 'Be a good lad and let the others downstairs know the queen is safe. They can come up now and secure the area and we need to get his lordship to hospital quickly; he's in a bad way.'

'Where is he?' shouted Cara, feeling as if she was drowning.

'Come with me, my lady.' Swifty showed her into a room further down the hallway.

George lay there unmoving; his eyes closed, and the pale carpet soaked by a pool of his blood.

'Oh my God, is he dying?' To her own ears, her words sounded as if they were coming from underwater. She was woozy with exhaustion from the events of the night, but there was no time for weakness. Cara bent down and touched George's wrist, checking for signs of life. She caught a faint pulse, and then he shifted slightly and turned his head, muttering and delirious.

'George, my love, can you hear me? Please say something.'

His eyes flickered open for a second and then rolled back in his head and he slumped into silence before blacking out with the pain.

Swifty ran into the room and knelt down beside them. 'How is he?'

'He's been shot and lost a lot of blood. There's no time to get him to a hospital. Please run downstairs again and ask for the palace doctor. Bid him come immediately before it's too late. And ask the servants to bring up some clean bandages so we can stem the flow of bleeding.'

Cara sat next to George, holding his clammy hand, and feeling helpless. Tears filled her eyes, and she tried to calm herself. They still had so much to do together.

Let him live, let him live...

The mantra ran through her mind like a relentless ticker tape. A few minutes later, she heard a movement on the landing and thought the doctor must have arrived, but to her disappointment it was the policeman again.

'Was that a bomb that went off, earlier?' she asked.

'Yes, my lady. It exploded in the queen's apartments. Thank God she and Prince Albert are safely at Windsor Castle and these rogues didn't get wind of their whereabouts or they might have saved their attack for another day. Her Majesty stayed at Windsor yesterday instead of coming back as originally planned.'

'And the children? Are they all right?'

'Yes, ma'am. They are at Windsor with their governess.'

'Oh, thank goodness. The whole royal line might have been wiped out if these rogues had their way.'

'Yes, and if it weren't for your husband and the lad's heroic actions, the palace; the symbol of the heart of the monarchy would now be burning to the ground.'

A few minutes later, she was relieved to see the familiar face of the palace doctor and he knelt down to examine George.

'He's lucky to be alive,' he said, his expression grave as he peered at Cara through his spectacles. 'The gunshot narrowly missed his heart.'

The Great North Road, 1536 - Tudorville

Cara spurred the black palfrey on as if she were riding to the ends of the world. Rain hammered down on her head and she was grateful for George's heavy cloak and the pageboy cap, or she would already be soaked. The horse, one of Windsor's finest, was saddled and hurriedly readied for her by a stable boy who had developed a crush on her during her recent days when she had been riding with Queen Jane. She told him she had the queen's blessing to take the horse, and he was happy to assist. Cara considered asking the boy to accompany her, but she decided it would be better to press on quietly alone in her disguise as a young page. She didn't want to attract attention.

As she rode, she used the hours to think things through and try to make sense of events, so she could plan how to handle the situation with George and the Pilgrimage of Grace. She hadn't dared mention her concerns to the queen or Cromwell, but she secretly worried that George may have been swayed to the side of the rebels—there were a great many northern leaders involved, of which he was one. He shared a deep lifelong bond with them and naturally had empathy for their grievances; despite his close alliance with the king. Black thoughts ricocheted around her mind, gripping her as she pushed on through the freezing rain.

What if they had somehow forced him to take the Pilgrim's Oath, or even worse, if he had taken it of his own free will?

She shuddered at the memory of George shrouded in the hangman's hood on the brink of execution earlier that year.

She shook her head in an attempt to shake free of the calamitous web of thoughts and to bring herself back to reality.

No: he wouldn't have taken the oath.

Her mind was playing tricks on her again. They were both bound to the Crown and George wouldn't risk their lives in such a cavalier manner. Even so, she was concerned that his lack of communication meant the rebels had taken him hostage.

Surely, they wouldn't dare harm him when he was at Pontefract Castle by invitation of his friend, Lord Darcy, and by order of the king.

Who knew what desperate men might do to procure their means? The very future of England depended on what the rebels did next.

After some time of being caught up in her anxious thoughts, she managed to snap back to the present and noticed the rain had stopped and the day had considerably brightened. Pale rays of sunshine reflected in the muddy puddles as the horse's hooves sped along the track. The hour was still early, and so far, she hadn't seen a soul on the road which was good news. The fewer people she met, the less chance of raising suspicion. Her stomach rumbled, and her throat was parched from the exertion of riding at a breakneck pace, so she reined the palfrey in, slowed to a stop, and fumbled around in her saddlebag until her fingers closed over a portion of hard bread. As she chewed, she resolved to keep riding for as long and as fast as she and the horse could bear, without taking a break. Her plan was to make it to Madame Alicia's tavern on the outskirts of York, where she would rest for the night before continuing on to Willow Manor. Madame Alicia, as she was known, had proven herself a formidable ally in the past, and Cara trusted her with her life even though she knew she would doubtless be for the rebels.

Cara would need her wits about her and all the energy she could muster if she was to find a way to rescue George without endangering both of them by double-crossing the king or provoking the rebels.

Rose Cottage, York - Present day

Cara entered the kitchen, removed her gardening gloves, and washed her hands.

'Good session?' asked George.

'I enjoy it once I get stuck in,' she said. 'It's a bit hot and sticky out there today, though.'

'Yes, it looks like there might a storm on the horizon. By the way, I need to travel to Richmond tomorrow. Would you like to come along? We could stay over for the night and drive back the next day.'

'As in Richmond, London?'

'Yes. I thought it would be nice to have a wander around. Fancy it?'

'Absolutely! It'll be lovely to have a change of scene.'

'Splendid! That's settled then. I'll need a couple of hours

to meet someone—a business associate. You're welcome to join us, or I thought you might want to pop into town.'

'That's okay—it's perfect timing. The National Archives are nearby, in Kew, and I've been toying with the idea of visiting for a while.'

George turned to Cara, eyebrow raised. 'Oh?'

'I have a special pass; I used to go there frequently to do research.'

'Are you looking for anything in particular?'

'I want to see what I can find out about the key players in the Pilgrimage of Grace.'

George frowned. 'I thought we agreed we wouldn't poke about in the past because we don't want to know what happens in the future. It could influence the actions we take, and we risk rewriting the timelines.'

'I know we agreed, but I've been reconsidering. I wouldn't go there without discussing it with you first. But we have a dangerous situation.'

'You mean at Pontefract Castle?' he said.

'Exactly. I'm on my way to York, but what if I'm over-reaching and doing the wrong thing? The queen was shocked by my leaving, so I don't know whether Tudorville Cara would have dared take such bold action.'

George sat down at the kitchen table and listened as Cara explained her thought process.

When she paused, he said, 'So, I take it you mean if you discover in the archives that we will live a long life then we may be best not interfering and just allowing events to unfold?'

'Yes, pretty much. Perhaps I shouldn't try to rescue you after all? I'm on my way to York, and I'm counting on my memory updating or I won't get the archive information in time anyway.'

'I see. Well, breaking me out of Pontefract Castle from

under the noses of the rebels sounds dangerous, so I won't argue against you having second thoughts. You're impossible when you get a crazy idea in your head. I don't imagine I could stop you.'

Cara chuckled. 'I won't be alone. I plan to get Eddie's help,' she said, pulling some cups out of the cupboard and resting them on the counter. 'Tea?'

George nodded. 'What if you discover something terrible at the archives?'

'We'll just have to deal with it and decide what to do from there. I'd rather know what we're up against before we go looking for you.'

'Okay. We'd better move fast. I'll book a room at our favourite hotel on Richmond Hill.'

'Perfect,' said Cara.

'I probably won't find any mention of us—it's all so long ago, but I want to check,' she said, reaching for George's hand.

'I sort of hope you find nothing. I don't want to know when we die. There's such a thing as too much information.'

Their eyes locked as they both contemplated what she would discover.

CHAPTER 18

Windsor Castle, 1848 - Victoriana

The carriage wound through the pretty streets of Windsor, and the sparkling sunlit waters of the River Thames flowed nearby like a constant companion. The imposing castle built by William the Conqueror, towered over the old, majestic river town, visible from almost every angle. The carriage dragged them up the steep hill towards the castle which looked truly magnificent against the backdrop of wispy clouds in the azure blue sky.

'I love Windsor—not only because it's where we first met but also because it always feels so familiar to me. It's almost like I've been here before in another life,' said Cara, wistfully, turning to him. 'Do you know what I mean?'

George studied his wife's glowing face, pondering when or whether he might tell her she had indeed been at Windsor Castle in another lifetime—serving as lady-in-waiting to Jane Seymour.

'Yes, I do,' he said carefully. 'I sometimes experience a similar feeling, especially at the palaces. I suppose it's only natural that their history will rise up to give one a sense of connection to the past.'

Cara squeezed George's arm, her small hand encased in a black velvet glove. They were dressed in their finest clothes in honour of the grand occasion, and Cara bubbled with excitement.

'I love how I can tell you even the strangest things and you never make me feel ridiculous.'

George weighed up the odd predicament he found himself in. He recalled that several years earlier in Seville; she had briefly recognised Eddie from another timeline, but since George had returned to Victoriana, Cara had displayed no awareness of another life. He concluded they must only have access to memories of another timeline when they were the one time travelling. This would explain why he had no awareness in Tudorville apart from the odd sense of deja-vu, much like Cara was experiencing now. George tried to avoid thinking too much about the mechanics of how it all worked because invariably, when he did, he ended up feeling frustrated. George gallantly pressed his lips against Cara's glove and said, 'Ready for an audience with the queen?'

'Yes, I'm ready! I've missed her and I'm curious to know why she summoned us.'

A footman dressed in a smart red tunic sprang into action the moment the carriage came to a halt outside the main entrance of the castle. He opened the door with a flourish for George and Cara to alight.

George winced slightly as his feet hit the hard ground; his left upper arm still bandaged from the bullet wound. He had been warned to take it easy until it healed.

'Dear Lady Cara,' said Queen Victoria, after they were shown into the opulent Crimson Drawing Room where the queen awaited their arrival and they observed the usual formalities. 'It's so good to see you after all this time. You look well.'

'Thank you, Your Majesty. I am feeling much better and was thrilled to receive your invitation and have the chance to see you again. How are the children?'

They exchanged the latest news for a few moments before Queen Victoria invited them to sit. 'You're a wounded hero, Lord Cavendish, and I understand you must rest for a speedy recovery.'

'Not at all, ma'am. They fuss so, but I assure you I am quite well.'

'Let's all sit, nevertheless. It's always a pleasure to see you both, but you must wonder why I expressly invited you to Windsor today, rather than waiting for my return to Buckingham Palace.'

'I confess, it had crossed my mind,' said Cara.

'Well, as you may know, the renegade Chartist faction has been dismantled and they are safely behind bars, thanks to your brave intervention. I can barely believe they wished us dead—the thought of such venom against their sovereign chills my soul. And for that reason, I would like to request that you keep the plot to yourselves. After some reflection, Prince Albert and I came to the sober conclusion that the less our people know of how close those rebel Chartists came to murdering us in our beds, the better,' said the queen, her hands rested neatly on her knees.

'I see the wisdom in your decision, ma'am. My only reservation would be that there were quite a number of police and members of security, not to mention the palace staff who witnessed the attack. Are you convinced we will be able to prevent it from leaking into the public domain?' said George.

'My security and staff are sworn to secrecy, and I trust them implicitly. As for the police; if the truth about how close the intruders came to blowing up the palace and Britain's monarchy along with it, they would be a laughing stock. And I don't need to tell you they wish to avoid that,' replied the queen.

'Good point, ma'am. Well, I hope you know you may trust us to guard the secret with our lives.'

'Indeed, although as you very nearly already paid the price of your life to save me, I do hope that won't be necessary,' said the queen, smiling at them both. 'I was frightfully worried when I heard you had been shot.'

'Thank you, ma'am. You are too kind. I was only doing what any royal servant would do in the circumstances.'

'And you, Cara, I understand you accompanied Lord Cavendish and the footman on their midnight mission and alerted the guards.' She held up one hand as she spoke. 'And before you say it's what any off-duty lady-in-waiting would do, let me assure you I have not found that to be the case. I am forever in your debt and await your return to my side just as soon as you both feel well enough to resume your positions.'

'Thank you, Your Majesty. I am relieved we were able to intervene before anything dreadful happened, or we would never have forgiven ourselves,' said Cara.

'Now we've got all of that out of the way. I would like to formally express my gratitude and that of all of my family, to you both, for your bravery and service to the Crown. And with that in mind, is there something I may arrange for you that would go some way to adequately showing our appreciation?'

'Why thank you, ma'am. It's quite a coincidence that you should ask because there is something that Cara and I spoke of recently that would be of great assistance to us.'

'Go on,' she said, her hands resting neatly on her lap.

'Well, I've been trying to open a vault at the Bank of

England to store a valuable item, a painting to be precise, ma'am.'

'Yes, that's wise considering the current unrest. And how may I assist you?'

'I haven't been able to access the Bank of England because of the military quartered there.'

'Ah, I see. We do have a royal vault and I'm certain we can organise something similar for you. I'll have a word with my man, Cuthbert, and he'll see to it. Reach out to him and he should be able to arrange it. Well, that's simple enough. Is that all?'

'Cara?' said George.

'I was thinking about Swifty, the footman. He was terribly courageous and suffered at the hands of the kidnappers for days.'

'Indeed, and I haven't forgotten him. My head of security made it very clear that without Swifty arriving to warn you, they may have succeeded in blowing up our private apartments. Thinking about how easily they entered the palace, sends shivers down my spine.'

'We are all fortunate to have escaped this incident with our lives,' said Cara.

'Swifty will be promoted to the position of a higher-ranking footman and will accompany us on our next holiday as a special show of gratitude, so he is recognised accordingly for his heroic act. I always like to keep an eye out for those in my service who display that extra-special something.'

'That sounds perfect. He's got an extra-special something all right. Thank you, ma'am. I'm sure he'll be honoured,' said George.

'And talking of the Isle of Wight, I would very much like you two to join us. I feel we all deserve a little holiday after this trying time. May I count on you?'

They accepted her kind offer and then the queen rang the bell for them to be escorted out in time for her to receive her next visitor.

Cara and George held hands as the carriage swept them down Windsor Castle's steep drive and back out onto the pretty cobbled streets of the town.

'We're in high favour,' said Cara.

'We are indeed,' said George, relieved to see Cara relaxed and cheerful.

As they trundled and bounced along in the carriage, he wondered whether he had managed to maintain high favour with Henry VIII. The very fate and future of Christendom had somehow unexpectedly fallen onto his sixteenth-century shoulders, and even worse, he didn't remember a thing about it.

He adored nineteenth-century Cara, but he longed to see his future wife. They had work to do. And besides—he missed the other Cara, terribly. He was torn—it was as though he was in love with two women and destined to always have to live a double life.

Rose Cottage, York - Present day

Cara awoke to the gentle humming sound of the early morning and stretched luxuriously like a lazy cat. She turned to look at her still sleeping husband and wondered how George was getting on in Tudorville, and when the vortex would transport her back to 1536. As much as she loved being with him in the here and now, she was terrified their life would be wiped out with one wrong move in the past.

The last thing she recalled was galloping along the Great North Road towards York to enlist Edward to help her to save George from the rebels.

George stirred and reached for her hand.

'Good morning, darling,' she murmured.

He leaned over to kiss her. 'I couldn't fall asleep last night. I kept thinking about whether my actions in Victoriana caused the plot against the queen. What if it's all my fault? If I hadn't recognised Swifty, he wouldn't have been kidnapped and perhaps they wouldn't have had the idea to blow up Buckingham Palace.'

'It's tough. I'm in a similar spin about Tudorville. On the one hand, I'm worried I haven't done enough to stop you, and on the other, perhaps I've interfered too much. I worry you're determined to stop the rebels from meeting the gallows. If I hadn't told you about the doomed uprising and how the king reneges on his promise, and the rebels meet a bloody end, the odds are you wouldn't even be considering how to divert the course of history. You wouldn't know your friends were in immediate danger, would you? You'd think you're helping them by convincing them to accept the king's offer.' Cara pulled a face as the various scenarios whizzed through her mind.

'Gosh, you poor thing; it sounds like you're having an awful time of it.' George yawned and stretched. 'I have an idea,'

'Go on...I'm out of ideas at the moment. Whichever way I turn, we seem to be up against it,' she said.

'Let's take a break. I'll make us some coffee, and you relax for five minutes. Try and stop churning it over and over, will you, darling? That's what I'm going to do,' said George, climbing out of bed.

'Okay, you're right. Although, you know it's much easier

said than done. When I try and stop thinking about something, it immediately dominates my thoughts.'

'Yes, but if we continue on like this, we're going to go quite mad. The best solutions always come when we least expect them. You know that.'

'True, but lately I've been falling back into my old habit of taking fast action.'

'We're both giving ourselves a hard time and we're not getting very far, so I vote for a more relaxed approach.'

'You sound just like Sylvia, now,' Cara said. 'Which reminds me, I must go and see her. She was incredible last time we were in danger—she channelled a message from the Angel Gabriel, who told me that things were not as they seemed. That's what saved us from a life in exile.'

'Sounds like Angel Gabriel knows his stuff. Perhaps I should seek divine guidance, too,' said George.

'Oh, I think that's a marvellous idea. I'll book us in for a double session—maybe she can even see us this afternoon.'

'Hmm, I was kidding.'

'I know, but it's an excellent idea, nonetheless. We need all the help we can get.'

'Right-ho; but not today.'

'Why not?'

'I knew you'd forgotten.'

'What? What have I forgotten? My head is in 1536.'

'We're going to Richmond this morning, remember?'

'Oh, yes!'

'I'm still nervous about what you're going to uncover in the archives. Are you certain you want to go ahead with it?' he asked.

She nodded. 'Going to see Sylvia after my visit makes more sense. I need her to help me locate you—you've gone missing since your arrival at Pontefract Castle.'

'Okay, are you ready to stop thinking about it for five

minutes, and come down to the kitchen for a coffee and breakfast before we head out?'

'Now that's an invitation I can't refuse.' Cara hopped out of bed and pulled her robe off the hook on the door. She pushed her tanned feet into her slippers before following George down the narrow staircase, her hands resting on his broad shoulders. 'We're staying over in Richmond, right?'

'Yes, it'll be fabulous this time of year.'

'Brilliant. Mind you, it's fabulous any time of year.'

George drove them to Richmond, and Cara leaned against the worn leather seat and relaxed as the radio chit-chat washed over her and the car effortlessly hoovered up the miles. If only the London to York trip was this quick and convenient in Tudorville—two hundred miles was a heck of a long way on horseback, and she would have had to make multiple changes.

When they stopped for a coffee, Cara wondered whether she'd made it to Madame Alicia's yet. Time lost all meaning when she travelled between timelines. She might not become conscious of what was happening in Tudorville for days yet. There was just no way to know what to expect, and because of that she frequently experienced a sense of panic.

Cara rested her hand on George's thigh as he drove. 'Do you sometimes feel like everything is out of control when you're going back and forth to Victoriana?'

He glanced at her and nodded. 'It's one of the most disarming things about it. Terrifying actually, as you never quite know what awaits you on either side.'

'How did we get ourselves into this dreadful mess?' she asked.

'I don't think we got ourselves into it at all. We just found ourselves in it.'

'I've been reading up on Twin Flames again.'

'Oh-oh, and?' George said.

'Mystics say our ancient twin souls made a spiritual contract thousands of years ago to go through multiple lives together in our commitment to reach our most awakened selves.'

'If it wasn't happening to us, I'd say whoever came up with that theory was a bit of a chump.'

'Classic you,' she said.

'Either way, there's no point us getting so worked up over something we have no control over,' he continued.

'Yeah, but when it all gets too much, I can't help thinking about it. If only Eddie would have a breakthrough with the time travel system, we could at least have some say on when we travel. Imagine how much simpler our lives would be if we could choose to leave and return when we want instead of when the vortex decrees?'

'I imagine it would be a double-edged sword. It'll all work itself out, and don't forget, if we can pull it off, we'll soon be able to put in an offer on Willow Manor. I'm excited about that—it will give us something positive to focus on,' he said.

An overwhelming sense of love welled up in Cara's chest as she looked at him. 'You're right, that is so exciting.' She took several deep breaths and resolved to be more philosophical. She had been gripped by intense feelings of doom intermittently since the previous day.

'I considered cancelling my visit to the archives, but I think I should go,' she said.

'You really don't have to, you know,' he said, looking across at her and covering her hand with his.

'I know, but I think I should have a poke around and see what I can find out about our past lives. We've never actually looked at any records at all. Maybe we're missing something critical that will help us.'

'Okay, whatever you think is best,' he said.

Cara always felt safe with George. She relaxed and dozed off to the gentle hum of the engine and dreamed of Tudorville. She saw herself riding hard on the Great North Road; the old Roman road that ran parallel to the one they were driving along now, five centuries into the future.

CHAPTER 19

Richmond, London - Present day

The Porsche pulled into the hotel car park on Richmond Hill, and Cara awoke with a start. 'Goodness, we're here already!'

'Nice snooze?' George asked.

'Lovely. Thanks for driving us.' Cara checked her appearance in the mirror and glanced at the time on the exquisite old clock face set into the sandy coloured brick of the hotel tower.

11:11, of course...we've arrived at the perfect time.

Sylvia had told Cara that Twin Flames typically noticed many signs as their consciousness and intuition heightened. 11:11 was one of the most symbolic.

That afternoon, after they checked into the hotel, Cara was deep in research at The National Archives. She hadn't yet found anything of interest related to the Cavendish name, even though it was a popular old surname. The further back she went, the records were unsurprisingly, either missing or illegible. She was just thinking she was wasting her time when a paper slipped out of a dusty binder, swooped through the air, and landed at her feet. She stooped to pick it up and then looked around—she had a peculiar feeling she wasn't alone, but she couldn't see anyone else in the silent room.

Cavendish, George Oliver, died...

She blinked, disorientated. Cara scanned the paper for the date of George's death, feeling sick, her throat dry and her head bashing. George was right, it would be terrifying to see the reality of his death. But she was certain there had been numbers on the paper before she'd been able to make out the figures—they had disappeared before her eyes.

I shouldn't have come. This was a dreadful mistake.

She concluded she must be imagining things and went to put the document back, but as she clutched the paper, still looking at it, a new set of numbers slowly appeared, one by one, filling the blank space. Cara blinked and shook her head.

What the hell...

A new date formed on the paper. She stared at the shifting form of the digits, transfixed; her heart drumming in her tight chest, unable to catch her breath as the numbers 1 5 3 and then 7 appeared in a faded black ink.

George would die next year in Tudorville.

Cara let out a strangled scream, and the paper slipped from her fingers, fluttered through the air, and landed on the hard floor near where she had retrieved it. She leaned heavily against the wall, shaking, and stayed there for a few minutes.

Cara took a couple of deep breaths and then raised her head. Her eyes locked onto a pair of bright blue ones. A man stared at her from across the cold room. She hadn't heard him enter.

She would leave now—this place was spooky—she should never have come. She shivered, and a feeling of sheer terror spiralled through her body.

Who was he and where had he appeared from?

She longed to flee, but first she must take a photo of the paper. Even now, it seemed far-fetched. She snapped a photo with her phone and shoved the paper back into one of the binders.

Cara picked up her bag, and as she turned she saw the man still watching her every move, making no attempt to hide his surveillance. His blue eyes bore into her soul with a sardonic expression, and she shuddered as an icy chill rippled down her spine. She tried to say something but couldn't form the words.

A woman entered the room, breaking the hypnotic spell as she hovered near the entrance, temporarily obscuring Cara's view of the man. When the woman moved, he was no longer in the room. Cara ran to open the door, poked her head out and looked down the corridor, but there was no sign of him. It was as if he had vanished, and she'd imagined the whole thing.

But there had been something familiar about his eyes. The thoughts flew around her head in a chaotic mess.

Why was the blue-eyed man watching her?

She fled outside the building and then forced herself to calm down and walk slowly, looking around, half-expecting the man to jump out at her. She stopped and fumbled in her handbag to extract her phone and clicked to open the photo library. She gaped at the screen. There was no record of any photo taken that day, no matter how much she scrolled. Cara moved in a daze and slumped on a low wall near the river, waiting for her racing heartbeat to slow as she tried to make sense of what had happened. Her pointy shoes pinched her toes, but she didn't notice.

. . .

Outskirts of York, 1536 - Tudorville

Cara arrived at Madame Alicia's establishment, exhausted after two days of gruelling travel. She had left the black palfrey at the first posting house on the long route. It was impossible to cover two hundred miles with only one horse, so she'd made several stops, but only for short breaks before continuing on with her next steed.

'You must be worn out,' whispered Madame Alicia, not wanting to give Cara's disguise away, when she saw her mud-stained breeches and cloak. 'My goodness, have you come all the way from London alone?'

Cara nodded. 'I am on an urgent mission and could only rest a short while.'

The madam ushered Cara inside, helped her find a spot next to the roaring fire, and promptly brought her some hot stew, bread, and wine.

'Here you are. You look in dire need of warming up through to your bones, so pray eat this while I organise your room for you, my lady.'

Cara was too tired to speak as she slumped into the chair, warmed her freezing hands next to the fire, and then fell ravenously upon the meal. She had depended on receiving just such a warm welcome from Madame Alicia, who had become a good friend to her and George when they escaped from Newgate Prison after being accused of treason and were on the run with a price on their heads and the king's soldiers on their tail. The brothel-tavern was the perfect place to keep a low profile. She would be grateful for a comfortable bed for the night and a chance to rest and think through her options.

Cara finished the simple, wholesome meal and sipped at the wine as she enjoyed a few peaceful moments.

Five centuries into the future, she knew she was in Richmond. Cara saw herself, as if watching a movie, at The National Archives, holding the record which confirmed George's death.

1 5 3 7

That meant her worst fears had been realised and they would kill him along with the rebels during the mass executions.

How could she tell sixteenth-century George they were time travellers and had been soul mates for hundreds of years, in multiple lives? No, there wasn't time to explain. She would have to get through to him without revealing their centuries-old secret. The truth would only confuse and further complicate the situation.

George told her he couldn't bring himself to tell Victoriana Cara about their other lives, and now she empathised all the more. They were back in the catch twenty-two they'd originally found themselves in.

The ability, or the curse of time travel, as Cara sometimes viewed it, had been unlocked on that first fateful meeting in their present-day lives. Those early days had been a magical, yet heart wrenching period. They'd fallen for each other the second they met and then spent months driving each other crazy as they attempted to untangle their complex lives.

'My lady, how was your meal? The colour is restored to your cheeks. You looked deathly pale when you arrived,' said Madame Alicia.

Cara jumped. She'd been miles away. 'Madame Alicia, thank you for your wonderful hospitality. I feel much better, thank you. I was so relieved to find you here as I'd hoped.'

The glamorous madam pulled a chair nearer to Cara and

sat down. 'Pray tell me—why the man's costume? What is this urgent mission, you spoke of?'

Cara moved closer and dropped her voice a notch.

'Last time I heard from Lord Cavendish, he was trying to negotiate an agreement with the rebels on behalf of the king. He was with his friend, Robert Aske, the Pilgrimage of Grace leader, and they were at Pontefract Castle. I think my husband is in danger and I'm on my way to find him.'

'The rebels are strong in number, my lady. I have heard they are ready to march on London and not considering the king's offer.'

Madame Alicia was well-connected to the northern lords, many of whom had been loyal to the House of York, and opposed King Henry VIII's father, Henry Tudor, when he had claimed the throne. The unrest had continued even after the houses had united upon Henry Tudor's marriage to Elizabeth of York.

'I see. That confirms my suspicions,' said Cara.

'May I assist you?'

'I hate to impose on you, but I wonder if I might borrow a horse to take me to Willow Manor? I'll have one of the stable boys return it to you.'

'Of course, my lady, It's no trouble at all. I'll get my man to organise it, ready for you to leave at first light, if you wish?'

'Yes, that's perfect.'

'I heard Lord Darcy had gone over to the side of the pilgrims,' said Madame Alicia in an equally low tone.

'I heard that too, which is what worries me. George's father is good friends with Lord Darcy, but I think the rebels may have overruled him and are holding George prisoner.'

That night Cara fell into an exhausted sleep and felt closer to George than she had since he left on his mission. She dreamt of the last time they slept together in this room—

it was as though his presence watched over her and kept her safe through the still, quiet hours.

After a rushed breakfast, courtesy of Madame Alicia's maid, Cara set out for Willow Manor. A while later she rode up the familiar driveway, hoping for a glimpse of her children. She hadn't sent word that she was on her way and hoped to surprise them. In the back of her mind had been the fearful thought that it was better they didn't expect her, just in case she didn't make it.

At the stables, Swifty's brother, Bertie, greeted her and took the horse's reins, helped her down and then led the mare to water before removing the saddle from her sweaty back.

'Last time I saw Swifty, he was in good health,' said Cara.

'Is he with Lord Cavendish in London, ma'am?'

'No, the last I heard, they were both at Pontefract Castle which is why I have come.'

Bertie paled. 'With the rebels, my lady?' he whispered.

'Yes. Lord Cavendish is under the protection of the king and charged with negotiating terms of a peace agreement. Swifty accompanied him, but don't fret, I will go there shortly and no doubt we'll find all is well.'

'May I be of service and accompany you, my lady?' he asked.

'That's unnecessary, but kind of you to offer. I must talk with Tutor Edward, and then we shall decide what's best. Do you know of his whereabouts?'

'I believe he is in the schoolroom at this hour.' He ducked his head as a sign of respect and then led the weary mare to join the other horses in the nearby field.

Cara skipped up the back-door step and entered the

house via the kitchens, still wearing her page boy's outfit, her cloak over her arm.

'Good morning, Mrs Talbot,' she said.

Cook's mouth flapped open as she turned mid-pummel of the dough on the counter in front of her. 'By God's grace! Lady Cavendish is it really you?' she said.

'I've no time to explain, but I must see Tutor Edward and the children. Are they in the schoolroom?'

'Yes, they are—last I heard of them, they had gone up for their lessons,' she replied with a stunned expression. She'd never seen her mistress, or any woman, dressed like a man. She was used to seeing Cara in fine silks, satins and brocades and the vision of her disguised as a boy knocked her off balance.

Cara fled up the backstairs as quickly as she had erupted into the kitchen and for a moment Cook wondered whether she had imagined the episode. Later that morning, she said to her husband, 'She was like a phantom possessed, I tell you.'

Her husband nodded. 'It'll be something to do with the rebels that brings her home in such a flurry. Mark my words. They're about to march,' he replied as his wife's mouth dropped open for the second time that day.

Grosvenor Square, London, 1848 - Victoriana

George raced upstairs in search of Cara and found her pottering about their bedchamber, still wearing her nightgown.

'There you are. I was wondering whether you would like to accompany me into town,' said George, kissing her.

'Ooh yes, please. What a splendid suggestion,' she said, excited at the prospect of an outing. There was nowhere she'd rather be than mooching about on her handsome husband's arm.

'Perfect. Make haste and dress, my love—I've arranged to meet Cuthbert at the palace and we'll go from there in his carriage.'

Cara raised a dark eyebrow. 'We really are getting the royal treatment.'

'Indeed. Well, it's not every day a crazed assassin tries to take the queen's life, and that of her family, is it? She does like to show her gratitude and given the atmosphere and tight security in the city, I must say I'm pleased to have her support.'

Cara kissed George and then crossed the room towards her wardrobe. The shock of almost losing him had jolted her back to herself and made her realise life was too short for regrets. 'I'll be ready shortly,' she called as she surveyed her gowns and decided what to wear.

George whistled quietly under his breath. Since the palace attack, she had been different.

There was nothing like having everything nearly snatched away to make you appreciate what you have. Whatever the reason for her buoyant mood, he was relieved.

His mind flitted to thoughts of future Cara, and he wondered what she discovered at The National Archives. He was torn between a natural curiosity and the fear of learning their fate.

The Bank of England, London, 1848 - Victoriana

They rode with Cuthbert in one of the royal carriages and alighted at Threadneedle Street in front of the Bank of England.

'I'll accompany you and make sure you are given access; security is even tighter since the recent riots in the city,' said Cuthbert.

The street was just as busy as when George had tried to reach the bank alone and had been pushed aside by crowds and almost lost the precious painting. The military had cordoned off the area near the bank, and Cuthbert showed his identification before they were permitted to enter.

'It's a fine thing you're with us or I see I would have made another wasted trip.'

Cuthbert smiled and nodded his head in assent as he beckoned Cara and George to follow him past the grand pillars and through the entrance hall of the most famous bank in the world.

'Have you ever been here before?' asked Cuthbert, a chatty, pleasant individual.

'I can't say I have. Although I see it's quite as impressive as one might imagine,' replied George.

He paused a moment to soak up the reality of the moment. His eyes moved to Cara as she smoothed the skirt of her fashionable gown, which accentuated her tiny waist, and she straightened her velvet bonnet, before throwing an impish smile in his direction and claiming his arm. As usual, she drew admiring glances everywhere she went: she must know the spell her presence cast, but she also had a beguiling innocence.

Here he was in 1848, entering the Bank of England with Cara on one arm and an undiscovered Turner masterpiece under the other. Living a double life was a tough business, but occasionally he was present enough to acknowledge the greatness of his peculiar situation. And this was one of those moments.

He couldn't wait to tell Cara about this when he returned to present day. But there was one big problem. He couldn't seem to get there. Time here wasn't equal to time in the present-day, and sometimes it seemed like he had only been gone for a minute while months had passed in Victoriana. Lately he hadn't been back at all. And now he was plagued by a dangerous thought that hadn't occurred to him before.

What if I can't ever get back to the future?

CHAPTER 20

Richmond, London - Present day

Cara and George sat at a table on the terrace in front of their hotel, overlooking the vibrant green meadows and verdant woodland which rolled all the way down to the meandering River Thames. The river glinted like a shimmering blue lake in the mild afternoon sunshine.

After a few minutes of admiring the famous view, George exclaimed, 'Did you know this is the only English landscape view to be protected by an Act of Parliament?' He stretched out his arm and swept his palm from left to right, to present the view to Cara.

'I don't know where you come up with your never-ending facts but that is a good one.' She pushed her sunglasses up onto the top of her head and smiled at George.

'Can't beat a good fact.' He took a gulp of cold beer. 'Turner painted it, you know. It's called *The Thames at Richmond*, or something similar.

'And talking of Turner, what's going on with the painting? You haven't mentioned it in a while,' she said.

'Unfortunately, that's true. I didn't want to worry you, but I've come up against a slight problem.'

'What's happening?'

'Well, it's more a case of what's not happening. I can't remember anything about what's going on in Victoriana. I've no idea whether I managed to get the painting into the vault or not. It's as though my connection has been turned off overnight.'

'I shouldn't worry. That happens sometimes. I don't always remember everything—it can take a while for our memories to catch up, or for our software to update, as Eddie calls it,' she replied.

'What if I'm stuck here indefinitely?'

Cara studied the face she loved so well as she processed his words. 'But how can you be? You're aware of what's happened in the past.'

'True, but when we're here we're always aware of the other timelines, but it doesn't mean we have access to knowledge of the latest events.'

Cara's grey eyes probed his as he talked.

'I've got a feeling something's changed, but I don't know what or why. All I know is when I began travelling to Victoriana again, I bounced back and forth frequently, but it's been more than a week since I woke up with anything new in my head.'

She reached out to touch his arm.

'Let's hope I've got it wrong and something comes to me soon, so we can retrieve the painting,' he said, kissing her hand.

She nodded. 'It would be a shame not to be able to get Willow Manor back, but if you have stopped travelling permanently, that would be exactly what we've been hoping for, wouldn't it?'

Wait until you hear about the other problem...

'You're right. I've been so focused on our plan, I forgot that.'

He rubbed his hand across his stubble. 'How was your visit to the archives?'

Cara's heart lurched—she couldn't avoid telling him any longer. He had been at his meeting when she'd returned to the hotel, head spinning, not knowing what to make of the strange experience at the archives. She had taken a nap, followed by a hot shower, and tried to calm down, but she dreaded the impending conversation.

How can I tell him I know the date of his death?

He had exploded into the room in enthusiastic George-style, sharing the latest news from his meeting, and she hadn't wanted to pierce his bubble by telling him what she'd found. She could barely believe what had happened to the paper in front of her eyes, and she regretted her over-zealous probing and wished she hadn't insisted on going.

'Darling, I'm not sure how to tell you this, but I think we have bigger problems than funding the purchase of Willow Manor...'

George's liquid brown eyes moved to meet hers, and intense emotions bubbled in her chest. He still had that effect on her, even though they were together continuously; in one life or another.

This must be what soul mate love is: a never-ending feeling of being in the right place at the right time with the right person.

Cara shook herself out of her daydream.

'I'm almost afraid to ask. What did you find?' he said, pursing his lips.

She took a few calming breaths. She didn't want to alarm him more than necessary.

'You'll probably tell me I went against your advice and shouldn't have gone to the archives,' she said.

George reached out and covered her hand with his.

'No, I won't. What would be the point? As you have often said—sticking our heads in the sand doesn't change reality so it's better we know what we're up against. And if I have gone and changed the future with my impetuous actions, then we must find a way to change history back to what it's supposed to be.'

Cara released her pent-up breath.

George continued to prompt her gently. 'Go on, please tell me, darling. There's nothing we can't handle together.'

'I love you so much. Thank you for being so solid,' she said.

George pulled her against him, his arms holding her cocoon-like. The stress and tension of their recent comings and goings between timelines and trying to figure out what was going on had eroded her resilience. And then the incident in the archive room had pushed her over the edge.

'It will all be okay. I promise. Now please tell me what happened.'

Cara hugged him and then drew back into her chair, and took a sip of her wine, before she began to recount the strange events she'd experienced.

When she paused, George sat quietly for a few minutes as he held her hand and then he said, 'I think this is our cue to pay Sylvia a visit. Let's see what she can tell us about this man and the shifting date.'

Cara nodded. 'Okay. But hang on—I didn't tell you the most disturbing thing about him yet.'

George waited.

'Well, I only saw him for a minute, but he came from the past.'

'What do you mean?'

'He was dressed Tudor-style, with a heavy fur-trimmed cloak draped around his shoulders. It was as though he'd stepped right out of Tudorville.'

George stared at her. 'A fellow Tudor time traveller? But how can that be? When we move through time, we merge with our past selves. Travelling with clothes through time is impossible. Isn't it?'

The man's sinister, piercing blue eyes filled her mind. 'I don't know, but I have a feeling I've met him before.'

The Bank of England, London, 1848 - Victoriana

Cuthbert was true to his word and made an introduction to the bank, which instantly opened both metaphorical and physical doors. It wasn't a simple procedure to acquire a vault at the Bank of England.

'It sounds as though you need a private vault. We'll open one in your name forthwith by invitation of the queen to avoid any delays,' said the clerk, appraising George through his tiny spectacles, which rested precariously on his large, bulbous nose. The dapper, suited clerk then tucked the vault register under his arm and beckoned them to follow as he led the way through a maze of cool corridors. 'Follow me please, Lord and Lady Cavendish.'

George noticed Cara's sparkling eyes and could see she was enjoying the novelty of the occasion. It wasn't every day you got to see behind-the-scenes of an iconic building.

The network of rooms occupied a cavernous space, and they continued walking for several minutes, threading in and out of the shadows and around countless closed doors. Then the clerk came to a halt outside a heavy grey door and fumbled with a big set of keys before turning to them and scanning their faces.

'This is it,' he said. 'Have you your items you want to store in the vault?'

'Yes,' said George, indicating the wrapped painting for the clerk to see. 'It's just this for now.'

'Very good,' he said. 'There are several private vaults in this room. I know exactly which one to allocate to suit your purposes.'

They walked through the narrow door, following him into a small room that was empty apart from a gleaming wooden chair and a small matching table. The walls were lined with silver doors, and drawer handles protruded from them. The clerk leant down to open one of the vault doors and unlocked it with a silver key.

He opened the door and pointed to the vacant storage vault. 'Is this to your liking?'

'Indeed,' George replied. 'This will do splendidly.'

'Very good. I shall step outside and leave you to your business. Take as long as you need, and I'll be waiting to lock up and sign you out.'

Cuthbert followed the clerk out of the vault-room, and George and Cara's eyes met.

'This is terribly clever,' she said.

'Yes, it's very impressive.'

'Is the painting really so valuable to warrant keeping it here?'

'Not yet, but it will be. It's best to keep these types of collector items in a safe place out of the house unless we want them on the walls for pleasure.'

'It's all very top-secret,' she said.

'It'll be useful for us to have a private vault—especially if we travel for an extensive period again and don't want to leave our valuables in someone else's care at home.'

George removed the layers of paper from the Turner masterpiece and rested it against one wall for a final look. He stepped backwards to the other side of the room and reached for Cara's hand. He wanted to view the painting one last time before storing it in the vault. If he'd got this right, he would soon be back to retrieve it in present-day, but if not, it could be the last time he saw it.

'Isn't it glorious?' he said.

'Absolutely breath-taking. I'm so happy we have *Chelsea at Dawn* for us to enjoy on the wall at home.'

'Me too. This one is called *Chelsea at Dusk,*' he said. 'The pair are equally stunning, but I particularly love the optimism of the dawn painting.'

'It was so thoughtful of you to surprise me like that,' she said, turning to kiss him in the privacy of the vault room.

He returned her kiss as he held her waist and said, 'I'm so glad you like it. I'll place the painting in the vault and we can lock up and leave in a moment.'

George lay the signed note he'd obtained from Turner to prove the painting's authenticity and the legal purchase, in the vault next to the painting which he'd slipped back into the paper casing for protection. He cast one more glance into the vault and then closed the door firmly and slotted the key into the lock and turned it. There was a satisfying snap as the key secured the vault. He tested the door to double check it was locked and then slipped the key into the pocket of his waistcoat and retrieved his hat from the table.

'Shall we go, my love?' George offered Cara his arm, and they exited the room.

The clerk locked the door and escorted them back to the reception desk. George signed the vault register, and the clerk handed him a receipt.

'Keep the receipt as a precaution, but the key is your absolute proof and a necessity for opening your vault.'

'What happens if we lose it?' asked George.

'I advise you to ensure that doesn't happen—the vaults are designed to be passed down through generations and the key is mandatory to gain access. If any change is made to the security system, we'll notify you by mail, so you can make the necessary adjustments.'

George inclined his head in agreement.

'Until whichever time you or someone on your behalf returns, your vault will remain untouched. You can rest assured there is no safer place in the world than the Bank of England,' continued the clerk.

They left the building and as if by magic, the royal carriage drew up in front of the bank and George assisted Cara up the steps and they settled into their seats. Cara looked out of the window as the bright London afternoon passed by and they weaved through the streets back towards Buckingham Palace.

George extracted the key from his waistcoat pocket and turned it over in his hands, enjoying the weight of the cold metal. He thought about Cara in York and how excited she would be to hear that he'd managed to store the painting in the vault and they could retrieve it and move forward with buying Willow Manor.

Part one of their plan was complete, and he was relieved he'd got the masterpiece into the vault, but he wondered when he would return to the future and be able to set part two of their exciting plan in motion.

Cara noticed his furrowed brow and the troubled expression in his eyes.

'What troubles you, my love? I thought you would be pleased to have put the painting somewhere safe like you've been meaning to do for a while.'

He popped the key back into his pocket and attempted to pull himself into the present. 'I am pleased. Shall we go home and have tea?' He smiled into the adoring eyes of his nineteenth-century wife but was frustrated at himself for wishing he was in present-day York. He envied the future version of himself, and he felt trapped by his lack of control.

And worse still—how could Cara ever understand he yearned to be somewhere else with someone else?

That night he dreamt of a life which was doomed to be always just out of reach and he awoke at dawn feeling bereft, his body coated in cold, clammy sweat. How he missed his normal life. He willed himself back to sleep, to dull the sharp pain of loss for a few merciful hours.

CHAPTER 21

Willow Manor, York, 1536 - Tudorville

Cara knocked sharply on the schoolroom door, turned the handle, and walked inside before Edward could respond.

'Mother! Mother!' shouted May, throwing her book down on the desk in reckless abandon as she shot up from the hard, wooden chair and covered the distance between them.

Thomas rose and bowed to his mother, always the more restrained of the two children. Cara saw a joyful smile light up his youthfully handsome face and she beckoned to him to join them. May clung to her, and Cara hugged her daughter's small body against her chest.

'What a surprise,' said Edward, his eyes searching Cara's, wondering what news she brought.

'Hello, dear Edward. It's quite wonderful to see you all. I didn't have time to send word ahead that I was on my way, so apologies for the unexpected disturbance.'

'Please don't apologise. It's always a pleasure to have you

back with us, Lady Cavendish. The children were asking only yesterday when they might see you again.'

Cara beamed at each of them and continued to hug the children, who were overcome by her sudden return.

'My, you have grown,' she said, holding May's shoulders at a distance so she could see her better. 'You are going to be a tall young lady—that much is clear. And Thomas, my boy, you have filled out and are growing into a fine young man. I have missed you both.'

'We've missed you too, Mother,' said Thomas, polite and earnest. 'Pray tell us what news is there of Father?'

'Father is on a mission for the king and I intend to continue on to join him shortly, but first I had to see you.'

The children had lost whatever concentration they had before her entrance, and Edward suggested they break for a while and go out to take some air in the grounds.

They made no complaints, and May chattered to her mother all the way down the stairs and clutched her hand as though she would never release her.

Seeing their little faces aglow at the sight of her, she felt guilty, as she so often did, that she didn't live at Willow Manor like before she was summoned to court. But this was their duty and as long as she and George enjoyed royal favour, they would spend a great deal of time in London at the various palaces. It was the way of things and there was no point regretting what couldn't be. The children were well cared for by Edward and their grandparents, and it was safer for them here at Willow Manor, far from poisonous court intrigue.

Cara contemplated what would happen if the timeline had reset. The year, 1537, flashed before her eyes—again.

'I've been hoping you would come, but I doubted you would gain permission to leave the queen,' said Edward, as they ambled through the gardens.

'Fortunately, the queen is sympathetic to our situation and gave me her blessing to travel to locate George.'

'She knows you're a time traveller and left Windsor disguised as a boy?'

Cara smiled and shook her head. 'Can you imagine? No—I explained only that I'm heartsick for George's safety and wish to see him. I couldn't stay in Windsor any longer, fearing for his life.'

'You look exhausted, my lady—you should rest.'

'I am rather, but I will rest later. First, we must talk.'

'All right. The last I heard, George was to go ahead of the Duke of Norfolk to help broker a peace deal on behalf of the king,' said Edward, offering Cara his arm.

'Yes, but the king has had no news of him and I suspect he's been captured by the rebels and is being held as some kind of bargaining chip.'

'Look, Mother,' called May. 'This is the den Thomas and I made the other day when we had fine weather.'

Cara approached and stooped to peer into the den which was constructed from an assortment of sawn-off tree boughs, branches, and foliage. A thick blanket covered the hard ground of the interior. 'My, it is grand, and very private, indeed.' Her heart melted at the proud expressions on her children's faces. She tousled Thomas' locks and clasped May's hand and dropped a kiss onto her palm before they both scampered off ahead of them down the windy track with Cornelius scampering alongside.

'Ten more minutes,' Cara called after them. 'I think it will rain soon.'

She turned to face Edward. 'You look well,' she said. 'It's so good to see you, again. It's difficult being in Tudorville without you by my side to talk things through.'

Edward assured her he was fully at her disposal. 'Go on, please continue about George.'

'Well, I have no more details but there's something much worse I must tell you.'

Edward's eyes scanned her face, his expression grave and his large nose bobbing up and down as she explained what she had seen at The National Archives.

'Oh dear. It sounds as though we have a deadly quantum time loop on our hands, rewriting history, just as I predicted. You did right to get here as soon as possible—we must save George from digging in any deeper.'

'I'm so scared for him,' said Cara.

Edward tapped her arm gently with his hand. 'Don't worry. Two heads are better than one—you're not alone anymore and we will figure out what to do.'

'Thank you, Edward. I can't tell you how good it is to be back.'

'We are warriors of time, you and I, and we must do all we can to reverse the situation so that George doesn't disappear in 1537. Otherwise, who knows what changes you will both encounter when you return to the present day? Anything could happen if we don't get a grip on reversing the quantum time loop.'

A shadow crossed Cara's face. 'I was afraid you might say something like that. I intend to visit Sylvia just as soon as I can, to see whether she is able to locate George. No one has reported seeing him at Pontefract in recent days, and you know the king has eyes everywhere.'

'I see,' he said, frowning.

'Edward,' she said.

'Yes?'

'There's something else I think may be significant, which I haven't told you yet.'

'You're freezing, my lady. Let us turn around and go inside to warm ourselves and ask Mrs Talbot to bring you something to eat and drink. Once you've rested and regained your strength, you can tell me the rest and we will decide what to do.'

Edward whistled to Cornelius and waved to the children. They all came bounding back towards them along the track, and Cara bent down to stroke Cornelius, who daubed a big wet lick across her freezing pink cheeks.

She was home. If only George were with them, it would be the perfect reunion.

City Centre, York - Present day

The morning after they returned from their trip to Richmond, they parked the car in the city and crossed through the cobbled streets, which gleamed like precious gems from the recent downpour.

'It's a bit of a walk to Sylvia's, but it's turned into a lovely day, hasn't it? We must have just missed the rain. It's good to feel the warmth on my skin,' said Cara, tilting her face skywards in search of the pale sun's rays.

They walked hand in hand in peaceful silence admiring the city's ancient beauty until George said, 'What's the latest from Tudorville?'

'I made it to Willow Manor after nearly freezing to death on the Great North Road. Sorry, I thought I told you yesterday.'

'No, no, you didn't. That's good you arrived. How are Thomas and May?'

'They're in fine form—they were surprised to see me, and the very first thing Thomas asked was for news of you. I daresay he's heard mutterings of the uprising.'

'It's strange—but from that one brief period I was aware I was in Tudorville, I recall just about enough to miss them, but not enough to have much in the way of anything to hold onto. I hope at some point I'll be able to remember more of our lives together. It's a shame to have such beautiful children and not to know more about them.'

Cara saw the pain on his face and her heart lurched.

'You do spend time with them whenever possible. You're a brilliant father and they adore you. Even if we weren't buzzing back and forth between timelines, we wouldn't be with them as much as we would like, given our positions at court.'

'That's some consolation, I suppose.'

'I will tell you more about what's going on. I forget how odd it must be for you. Talking of children, I wanted to ask you something.'

He looked at her expectantly.

'Is there any particular reason you know of that we didn't have any in Victoriana? It occurred to me that in those days it must have been much more unusual than it would be nowadays.'

He shrugged his shoulders. 'Um, perhaps we do go on to have children. I don't know, but we're still quite young.'

'Yes, but you said it's now 1848, which means we've been married for around eight years. That seems like an awfully long time not to have children if we wanted them, doesn't it?'

'When you put it like that, I suppose it does,' he replied, and then deftly changed the subject.

Still curious, Cara sensed there was more to it and decided she would ask Eddie what he knew about their childless state when she got the chance. George avoided telling her anything he thought would upset her. He did it to protect her. When they first met in the present day, his behaviour was the source of much tension between them because he would regularly withhold details which she would later somehow discover, and they would plunge headlong into a brutal battle of wills.

Cara was relieved there was no longer any need for complex layers of secrets between them.

'Here we are,' said Cara as they approached Sylvia's office. 'Would you like to go in first?'

George pulled a face. 'Can't we go in together? I feel naked with her knowing so much about me. I've never even met her before.'

Cara laughed at his panicked expression. 'Yes, I suppose we could. Don't worry—I'm sure she's used to knowing some very odd things about all kinds of people. This is what she does for a living.'

They entered the building and sat down in the waiting room for a few minutes before Sylvia opened the door to her office wearing a big, welcoming smile.

'Sylvia, I hope it's all right, but we thought we'd come in together,' said Cara.

'Ah, what a pleasure to finally meet you,' Sylvia said, her cat-like eyes sparkling as she gazed at George. 'You look exactly as I saw you in my visions.'

Despite the startling nature of her words, there was something about Sylvia that immediately put people at ease, and within a few minutes they were all chatting and laughing like lifelong friends.

'Okay, so what may I do for you both?' said Sylvia once they were seated. 'On the phone you said something unusual had happened.'

Cara coughed and cleared her throat, suddenly nervous. 'So much has happened—I don't even know where to begin. And it's never anything but unusual.'

Cara told Sylvia about the Pilgrimage of Grace, and her visit to The National Archives.

'I'm afraid if we don't course correct, George will die with the rebels next year, and who knows what awful consequences for the timeline there will be. Do you recall on my last visit I told you that Eddie said we're in danger of creating a quantum time loop because we're making too many changes to the past?'

Sylvia nodded. 'Shall we start with what's on the cards for George? That should be interesting because we've only ever seen his journey through your cards.'

Now it was George's turn to look nervous again.

'I won't pretend not to be a little wary of the dark arts,' he said. 'But okay, go ahead, you two mistresses of magic. I agreed to come so there's no point holding back, is there?'

'Don't worry, Sylvia doesn't deal in the dark arts. She's what's known as a lightworker—she uses her considerable gifts to help heal the consciousness of the world,' said Cara.

'Forgive me,' said George, looking at Sylvia. 'I didn't mean to offend.'

Sylvia said, 'Believe me, I've been accused of a lot worse than dealing in the dark arts. Besides, the cards have revealed to me repeatedly that you and Cara are Twin Flames. Please take solace we are connected for the greater good and it's your time to step into the light of understanding so you may fulfil your destiny together.'

Sylvia shuffled her cards as George looked on, fascinated, despite his reservations.

'What would you like to ask first?' she said, glancing from George to Cara. George looked at Cara.

'We need to know his whereabouts in Tudorville. Last thing I heard, he was invited to stay at Pontefract Castle with an old friend of the family, Lord Darcy. But I'm concerned that the rebels have taken control of the castle and he's gone missing.'

Sylvia laid the cards down on the table in front of them. 'Okay, so I'm using a mixed deck of cards—there are some

Tarot and some others from my Angel decks. Are you ready to begin?'

'Yes,' they chimed together, and Cara touched George's hand and flashed a reassuring smile in his direction.

'As I deal the cards, George, please tell me when to stop. There's no particular way to do it. Just prompt me when it feels right and keep the question about where you are in Tudorville, in your mind.'

Sylvia looked at Cara. 'Hold the question in your mind as well, Cara, and then we will transmit the power of three.'

'Stop,' said George after several seconds.

Sylvia flipped the Tarot card over to reveal a glossy image of a skeleton riding a white horse through a field of bodies. Cara gasped, and George said, 'Um—I'm not sure I like this game.'

'The death card is not inherently bad; particularly when it's upright like this one. I think you may have had it in previous readings,' she said, raising her head to look at Cara.

'Yes, and it terrified me then too. But, what do you think it means for our question of George's location?' Cara asked.

'I don't know yet. I usually get a better picture once we see it in the context of several more cards, but let's start with the possible meanings.'

'Go on, I'm bracing myself,' said George, trying to lighten the mood.

'Well, the upright divination is one of an ending: transformation, renewal and rebirth—that kind of positive death as opposed to a physical loss of life.'

'That's encouraging,' he said, and returned Cara's squeeze of his hand.

'If the card were reversed it could signify disaster, revolution and perhaps political change, which seems apt for the situation, so you must tread lightly, all the same.'

'Look at the banner with the emblem of the rose. I've

never noticed that before. It's not red like the Tudor rose, but it seems spookily significant,' said Cara.

'The upright death card also symbolises reincarnation and transformation, so it's a perfect card for you, George.'

'What do you think it means in this situation?' he asked.

'Let's continue,' said Sylvia as she continued to deal the cards.

George raised his hand and Sylvia paused once more, revealing a vividly coloured card. 'Ah, this is the Hermit card —we seem to be skipping the Angel cards today and are firmly on the Tarot track.'

'Is that a bad thing?' asked Cara.

'No, none of it is bad. It's simply the path George is on.'

'Somehow that doesn't put my mind at rest,' said George.

'The Hermit signifies silence, divine guidance and a teacher. Please keep your question in your minds because something is coming to me now.'

The room grew warmer and Cara removed her scarf as she watched Sylvia begin to sway gently and slip into a trance. Cara looked at George and smiled. She had grown used to readings with Sylvia, but this was an unfamiliar experience for him.

'George sits alone by a window in a room, overlooking a wild garden. I see monks all around and they are afraid for their lives.'

'Is George's life in danger?' asked Cara.

'Not at this moment, but it will be when he comes for him.'

'Who is he?' Cara prompted.

'Not all the rebels are good men. There is one man who wishes him harm. His excuse is to use George as leverage with the king, but he has his own sinister motives. He is a man of secrets.'

'It's as I feared. They've taken you,' said Cara, staring into George's brown eyes.

He reached for her hand again. They could see that Sylvia was now in a deeper state.

'Where is this room? Is it in Yorkshire?' Cara asked.

'George is imprisoned in some kind of monastery. His friend tried to stop them taking him but the man with the deep blue eyes insisted he would be safer there.'

Cara shuddered at the mention of blue eyes, and the image of the man who had been staring at her in The National Archives popped into her mind. 'I didn't tell Sylvia about the man,' she whispered to George.

'What more can you tell us of this man with the blue eyes?' Cara asked.

'He travels through time and he wishes George dead, so that he may have you again,' replied Sylvia.

'Have me? But who on earth is he?'

Sylvia shook her head from side to side and her eyes flickered open. 'I'm sorry. My connection broke without warning. Did I transmit anything of use?'

'You just blew my mind,' said Cara. She held out her hands. 'I'm shaking.'

'Oh goodness. All I remember is a man with the bluest eyes I have ever seen,' said Sylvia.

'It's him. It must be him from the archives,' said Cara, looking from Sylvia to George.

'I wondered when this would happen,' Sylvia said.

'When what would happen? Every time I think this can't get any stranger, it does just that,' Cara replied.

Sylvia rose and walked across the room to pour them all water from a carafe on a small side table. She handed them both a glass.

'As you know, Twin Flames are challenged to make peace with their past, in their quest to reach what the mystics call *ascension*. In your case, you are multi-generational Twin Flames which naturally comes with a lot of baggage—much of which you won't consciously remember. In the spiritual world it's called *karma*,' said Sylvia between sips.

'I always thought that was just another artificial construct to frighten people into good behaviour—much like organised religion,' said George.

'I think your karma is haunting you,' said Sylvia. 'If you pass the test, you'll be one rung closer to ascension.'

'And if we fail? Also, what's the man with blue eyes got to do with it? He seemed familiar to me somehow, but I can't put my finger on where I've seen him,' Cara blurted out.

'I'm not entirely sure, but watch your backs—if my vision was right, he thinks you belong to him and he's coming for you... My inner-guidance tells me the outcome of your karmic battle will determine whether George lives past 1537, or whether history is permanently rewritten,' said Sylvia.

She left the room for a few minutes, and then returned. 'I'm sorry I wasn't able to bring you happier news. Readings can be difficult sometimes.'

As they left the building and stepped into the sunlit street, George remarked, 'Well, I am pleased we had that uplifting experience. I feel much better now.'

Cara laughed, despite her sombre mood. 'What the hell do we do next?' she said.

'Nothing. I think we've done quite enough for one day. Let's go home,' he said, slotting her arm through his.

CHAPTER 22

St. Mary's Abbey, York, 1536 - Tudorville

George stared out of the window at the wildflower garden, wondering how long being locked in this room was to be his fate. He knew Cara would be frantic with worry, and he had no way of letting her know he was alive, never mind where to find him.

He only hoped that the Duke of Norfolk would realise he'd gone missing and would notify the king. Perhaps the army would storm the abbey and rescue him, but it was unlikely they knew where he was. He could see two guards standing by the wall which surrounded the garden. Apparently, someone considered him to be of value.

There was a knock on the door and in walked the monk who had brought him bread and water on the previous day. The monk entered with a similar meagre offering in a wooden bowl and laid it down on the low table, along with a small cup of ale. St. Mary's was a wealthy establishment, but the room may as well have been a prison cell. It was cold and sparsely furnished; lacking any comfortable features.

'Thank you,' he said to the monk, nodding graciously. George thought it unlikely the monk had any say in the matter of his imprisonment. The rebels had probably threatened to kill him and his fellow monks if they didn't comply with their demands. So much for the pilgrims marching in protest against the Dissolution of the Monasteries. What an irony, George reflected; as was so often the case, people bent their morals to suit their will.

'Do you know what they mean to do with me?' George asked.

The monk who was dressed in a simple brown tunic, covered by a scapula which was draped artfully over his thin, bony shoulders, shook his head, and looked mournful as he pointed to his sealed lips.

As the monk turned to leave, George sighed and settled back onto the hard chair as he nibbled the coarse bread and sipped at the warm ale. He would savour his meal because it may be some time before the monk returned.

George stood, and his eyes strayed to the window and studied the grounds once again, seeking an escape route in case he could find a way to break out. As his eyes wandered around the garden; a tall, well-built man wearing a sumptuous cloak and fine riding boots entered through the gate and stood in the courtyard below the window holding the reins of a huge shiny black stallion. After some discussion with one of the rebel-guards, the man looked up at the window. His eyes clashed with George's like bolts of lightning. Undaunted, George held his hostile stare until the man turned away, an arrogant smile on his lips. George sensed he must show no weakness; no sign he was intimidated. Who was this force of nature with the bright blue eyes, and what did he want from him?

Rose Cottage, York - Present day

George thrashed around in bed, and Cara, unable to ignore his restlessness any longer, sat up and reached out to gently prod his arm.

'Darling! Are you okay?'

George's eyes peeled open. 'Yes, yes, I'm asleep.'

'Well, you could have fooled me. You're thrashing about all over the place...and muttering too.'

George sat up and rubbed his sleepy, bloodshot eyes. 'I was having some kind of nightmare about that bloody man with the bright blue eyes you keep talking about.'

'What did you see? Perhaps it can help us in some way. Sylvia says that dreams are often visions and can give people access to their past lives but they don't realise at the time and so they overlook their meaning.'

'I was in a cell-like room and a monk entered with a bowl and a cup of ale. I saw a wildflower walled garden and then this blue-eyed bigshot arrived and stared at me through the window, as though he despised me and wished me dead.'

'That's just like what Sylvia saw in her vision.'

'Exactly, which makes me think I'm probably just dreaming about what she told us. That reading was certainly disturbing enough to give me nightmares. I'm in no rush to go back to see her.'

Cara stroked George's arm. 'Think carefully, darling. Was there anything else you remember that might help us figure out where the rebels are holding you. We must get to you as soon as possible.'

George flicked his fingers across his dawn stubble and said, 'There was something.'

'Yes?'

'There was a Latin bible and one of the front pages was

inscribed with a name. I think I read it at night to pass the time a bit.'

'Gosh, you must have been bored to resort to reading Latin scriptures.'

'Quite, although if it really was a vision, I imagine I would have been somewhat more God fearing in those days. Perhaps I was praying for our lives.'

'What was the name in the bible?'

George screwed up his eyes. 'I'm trying to think. I can see the words but can't quite make out what they say.'

'Damn,' said Cara. 'That would have led us to exactly where you are, so Eddie and I can figure out a way to rescue you before it's too late.'

Cara yawned and stretched. 'I know this is an emergency, but I'm exhausted and can't think straight. Do you mind if I try to sleep for a few more hours? I'll be much more use in the morning.'

George eased himself out of bed, bent down to kiss her, and tucked her in. 'It was five-hundred years ago, so I dare say it can wait a couple more hours. You sleep, my darling. I'm wide awake now. I'll go downstairs for a cup of tea and come back up to check on you later.'

'Are you okay?' she said, yawning again.

'Yes, I'm fine. Just too wired to sleep. I'll read a bit and see what I can find out about the monasteries in the area at that time.'

Cara tried to fight the heavy wave of weariness, but her eyelids drooped. George switched off the bedside lamp and the cosy mattress seduced her into a deep sleep and she dreamed they were all together again at Willow Manor, walking through the cornfields with Cornelius, and enjoying the long, lazy golden days of a traditional York summer.

A couple of hours later, George strode up the stairs, balancing a freshly brewed cup of coffee in his hand.

'Wakey, wakey, sleeping beauty,' he said loudly.

Cara opened her eyes and peered at him in the pale morning light. 'There should be a law against being as cheerful as you in the morning. I feel as though I only just fell asleep.'

'You've been asleep for hours, my darling. I've got loads to tell you, and I can't wait any longer. I thought you'd never wake up.' He kissed her forehead.

'What did you find out?' she said, instantly intrigued, but still groggy from the unexpected, heavy, second-wave of sleep.

'Drink your coffee and I'll tell you about my startling discovery.'

Cara pushed herself up against the pillow and sipped the coffee. She slowly perked up as the caffeine flooded through her system. 'Go on, I can't wait to hear. And thanks for this coffee—it's hitting all the right spots. I slept so heavily I must have been almost unconscious,' she said.

'I researched orders of monks and monasteries in York that would have been around in 1536, and I found a couple of possibilities. But when I read more detail, I knew immediately what we're looking for must be St. Mary's, the ruined Benedictine Abbey.'

'St. Mary's—yes; I know of it. I went on a school trip there when I was a kid. They had an impressive library until the Dissolution of the Monasteries and then the place was stripped and fell into ruin,' Cara said, taking another sip of coffee. 'It sounds like it could be what we're looking for, but what makes you so certain that's where you're being held?'

'I wasn't sure. But then I thought about the Latin Bible from my dream. In my online searches, I stumbled upon a related post about a Latin Vulgate bible which was auctioned recently, and they said it was inscribed inside the front cover with the name *Brother Grayson*.'

'Right...and?'

'Brother Grayson was the exact name I saw in my dream. The minute I read it, I knew.'

'Oh my God! So, presuming your location is correct and isn't just some kind of jumbled mix of memories of Sylvia's reading, this means that you somehow directly connected to your past life while you slept.'

'Odd as it sounds; it would seem so.'

'Amazing. I've heard of people being regressed to their past lives, but I didn't think that would work for us. I must get back to Willow Manor to see Edward, so we can go and find you.

She took another sip of her coffee and looked at George, excited to hear more. But then she felt the harsh, cold air of the vortex swirl around her.

'I'm going,' she said, putting the coffee cup down and reaching for his hand.

'Well, hang on a minute. Where? Let's go together.'

'We can't. I mean, I'm going to Tudorville, now!'

The last thing she saw was his confused face, and then she was gone.

George blinked.

'That was surreal.'

'What was?' said Cara, looking at George.

'You just entered the vortex while we were talking.'

'Did I? Bloody hell, I didn't feel a thing.'

George shook his head, bemused. 'It's the strangest thing.'

'How did you know I was going?'

'You told me.'

'I think we must be getting better at this time travel business.'

'It was weird, knowing you were going but you're still here too.'

'Yes, I bet, although it's just as well I went. I hope I

remember what you discovered about St. Mary's, in time to find you and reverse the quantum time loop.'

Park Lane, London, 1848 - Victoriana

George was despondent, which was rare. He couldn't get back to present day and didn't know why. They had successfully placed the Turner painting in the Bank of England vault, but now he couldn't retrieve it on the other side.

He worried about the future, and he grew more irritated each day. Had he and Cara tried to implement their plan to withdraw the painting from the bank? Had they succeeded, somehow? How would he ever know if he was stuck in the past indefinitely?

The questions whirled around his head, and he panicked at the prospect of being permanently cut off from his normal life. It was one thing time travelling to another era; there were incredible benefits such as meeting Queen Victoria, but after the attempted attack on her life, he'd had enough. The idea that it was all his fault, plagued him, and he suspected the plot only occurred because he had created a quantum time loop. He thought of Swifty, and how he had stumbled upon him at the palace. It had seemed like a significant coincidence, as though it was meant to be, but now he was wary of doing anything in case he unwittingly made matters worse.

Unable to talk to Cara about what was going on, he felt isolated, and decided to see if Edward had any ideas on how to speed up his return to the future.

That afternoon, George walked to Edward's house, which was only a short distance from Grosvenor Square. As he approached the luxurious Park Lane residence, his spirits fizzed at the thought of seeing his dear friend. The maid showed him in and it wasn't long before Edward bounced into the room in the adorable manner, particular to him.

'I've been meaning to call in to check on you again,' he said, patting George on the shoulder, beaming.

'Sorry I missed you the other day. I was at the palace,' replied George.

'I heard about that nasty business and that you were badly injured. I had a brief conversation with Cara, and she assured me you're recovering nicely.'

'Yes, it was just a scrape really, but thank goodness the queen is safe.'

'And how are other things?' said Eddie, cryptically, casting a glance towards the door to check they were still alone.

'Ah, yes, *other things*, unfortunately, are not going quite as well,' he said with a wry smile, running his hand through his hair.

'How is it you stay conscious of all your timelines simultaneously?' George asked, keeping his voice low, not wanting to arouse suspicion among the staff. 'I can't seem to stay on top of things.'

'I wish I knew, dear boy,' said Edward. 'Perhaps it's more complex with you and Cara being Twin Flames, and I'm just a simple time traveller,' he said.

'I think we both know there's absolutely nothing simple about you,' said George.

Edward was the smartest man George knew, but he had an endearing habit of playing down his incredible intelligence. Tea was served and when they were alone again, Edward said, 'So, what's the problem? Last thing I recall, I was with you in present-day York and we talked about quantum time loops and how to move the Turner painting between timelines.'

George explained what he remembered. 'The major problem now is that I seem to be stuck here. I can't get back, or at least if I do go back, I have no memory of it. And of course, I can't talk to Cara because she's completely oblivious to the whole thing. I'm becoming quite despondent, Edward, so I must ask you; is there any way at all for us to speed up my return to the future?'

Edward's mouth turned downwards, and he waved his hands in the air. 'I'm afraid I've made no progress with the Time Travel System. It seems, we remain at the whim of the vortex. And I still don't know for certain what triggers its appearance.'

'It's becoming more and more difficult to handle. Do you think our time travel is completely random?' asked George.

'Honestly, I don't believe in random, but unfortunately I'm no closer to understanding how it works.'

They chatted and sipped their tea on the sunny window seat overlooking the leafy park. 'I must ask you a favour,' said George.

'Anything at all. I'm at your service for whatever I can do to help,' said Edward.

'That's so kind. I'd be eternally grateful if you would deliver a message to Cara in the present day. Tell her I'm stuck here and can't get back. Please tell her that if they haven't already, they should go to the Bank of England and try and retrieve the painting, or we're going to miss the window of opportunity to buy Willow Manor.'

Edward nodded. 'Okay, I will, just as soon as I can. Anything else?'

'Yes, please allow me to pick your superior brain—we must figure out how to get the vault key to her. How can we do that, given we can't take any possessions with us when we travel?'

'That's a tricky one,' said Edward, running his thumb across his mouth.

Carlos entered the room, and George rose to greet him with a bright smile. 'How wonderful to see you,' said George, and they shook hands enthusiastically.

'I can't stay more than a minute, but just wanted to say a quick hello. It's good to see you out and about. We must all get together for dinner again soon and please give my best to your lovely wife,' said Carlos.

'Does he still not know anything about the other timelines?' George asked after they heard the front door shut with a resounding slam and saw Carlos' upright figure striding down Park Lane.

Edward shook his head, slowly. 'No, nothing at all as far as I can tell.'

'How extraordinary. I suppose I would be best to take a leaf out of your book. How do you stay so calm about it all? Doesn't it bother you not being able to talk to him about your other lives?' George asked.

Edward continued staring out of the window as Carlos' back receded from view and he considered George's questions. 'I suppose I'm used to it. I've been handling it for quite a few years now, you know. You are reasonably new to the back-and-forth of it all, and I was terribly lonely in the early days. But now that you, Cara, and Carlos are with me so much of the time, it's much more fun.'

'I was doing all right until I got stuck here. But now I can't stop thinking what a terrible thing it is to be trapped in the wrong time,' said George.

Edward nodded. 'The only thing I can tell you is that this *is* your time. All the timelines are our lives but by some strange turn of the wheel we get to revisit them. I try to see time travel as a gift rather than a curse, otherwise I would probably have gone quite mad with all of this time-hopping.'

'A sense of doom creeps over me—it's as if I know a clock is ticking somewhere in the cosmos and I'm not doing what I should be doing. I'm running out of time,' said George.

'Time is but an illusion, my friend,' said Edward, sounding just like his twenty-first-century professor-self.

'It doesn't feel like it. I'm letting Cara down when she needs me most. I messed things up in Tudorville after she warned me. And the worst thing of all is I feel so lost without her,' said George, bowing his head.

Edward reached out and gently patted George's shoulder. 'I understand how difficult it is. Try not to worry about Cara; last I heard, you were both doing well, but I promise I will get your message to her. She's in a slightly easier position because future you knows you are both time travellers, unlike Victoriana Cara.'

'True. I detest being so down in the dumps—sorry for offloading this onto you. It's the sense of uselessness that's getting to me,' said George. 'How do I avoid getting other people into dangerous situations?'

'I don't have all the answers you seek—yet—but if there's one thing I do know, it's that nothing stays the same for long. It will all change in a flash. The best way I've learned to tilt the odds in our favour, is to stop fighting so hard against what is,' said Edward, sipping his tea.

George nodded.

'Mother time is more powerful than us and she will always have the final say, no matter what we do. I suggest you relax because there's absolutely no way of knowing how long you'll be here, so you may as well make the most of it,' said Edward.

'You have a point. But what about the dreaded quantum time loops?' asked George.

'They're not in our control, either. You can only do what's in front of you to the best of your ability, with the information you have. As long as you don't consciously try to change past events, the odds are we will all be okay. Things have a way of working out just as they are meant to. In that way, time is always on our side,' said Edward.

George looked into Edward's kind, wise eyes and it was as though an enormous weight slid off his metaphorical shoulders and for the first time in days he felt buoyant.

'Thanks for the reminder, Edward. You are a dear friend —I feel so much better for speaking to you. I'll let things unfold, just like Cara says. You're right—there's no point driving myself mad over things that are completely beyond my control.'

CHAPTER 23

Rose Cottage, York - Present day

Cara heard the insistent ringing of her phone over the radio playing in the kitchen and dashed across the room to answer it.

'Good morning, Mrs Cavendish. This is John from Exclusive York Property.'

'Oh hello. It's great to hear from you—is there news on Willow Manor?'

'Something's come through from an American investment company showing interest on behalf of their international hotel chain.'

'Thank you so much. Do you know when they intend to view?' Cara twirled a lock of her hair around her finger as she spoke.

'They haven't moved to that step yet, but you asked me to give you a heads up if there were any serious enquiries.'

'Have you any indication of their budget?' Cara asked.

'I got the impression money isn't the deciding factor, and as you know, it's on the market for offers around the twenty-million-pound mark. It's rare to have an estate of this quality come up for sale and when they do, in my experience they're snapped up in a heartbeat.'

'How long do we have to make an offer, to make sure we don't miss out, would you say?' Cara asked, staring out the kitchen window.

The agent replied, 'Don't you want to view the property first?'

'Um...yes, but we're familiar with it and are working on organising the funds. I hadn't got around to booking a viewing yet but maybe we'd better do that now.'

Cara called George after she ended the call with the agent. 'Hi darling. Are you nearly home?'

'Yes, I'll be there in five.'

'Great. Do you mind if we pop out again...right away?'

'No, course not; where do you want to go?'

'The agent just called about Willow Manor. They've received an enquiry from a hotel chain and he was giving us a heads up, so we can make an offer.'

'But we don't have the funding without the sale of the painting.'

'I know, but I think we should go for a viewing, see what needs doing, and show we are serious. I made an appointment with him for eleven this morning.'

'Okay. I'll be there in a minute—come out when you see me and let's leave immediately. The traffic's heavy today because of roadworks so it may take us longer than usual.'

A few minutes later, Cara jumped into the car and leaned over to kiss George.

'Hey beautiful. I missed you this morning,' he said.

'Missed you too, darling. I've grown used to you being here when I wake up. How was your meeting?'

'It was pretty good.'

'I still can't quite get my head around your career change,' said Cara, watching him move carefully through the gears as they drove along the winding country road.

'Me neither. The *Tudor Kings' Manuscript* is still in the family, but other than that, it's as if none of it ever happened. There's no trace of Cavendish Fine Manuscripts. It's extraordinary—sometimes I think I must have completely imagined my former life.'

'But you had a career in import-export...' Cara replied.

'Yes, although goodness knows how I fell into that. Ideally I'd like to get back into something more aligned with my skill set.'

'You're brilliant with people. I bet you could make a go of anything as long as people are involved.'

'Well, if we can pull off the acquisition of Willow Manor, there'll be plenty of options,' he said.

'I was thinking perhaps we could start something together, on the estate,' said Cara, examining his face to gauge his reaction.

George looked at her briefly before turning his eyes back to the road. 'That would be fantastic.'

After slow progress through numerous traffic jams, they joined the road which bore them to Willow Manor, and they soon arrived at the entrance. George cruised in and they admired the rows of willow trees blowing in the light breeze, lining both sides of the grand driveway.

'Can you imagine us living here?' George asked.

'Oh yes. There are so many memories and so much of our history wrapped up in this place; I feel happy just looking at it.'

'I wish I could remember it too. Now I don't know what's going on in Victoriana either.'

Cara stroked his hand.

He glanced at her. 'Seriously, if I don't get an update soon, we won't be able to buy this place.'

'It'll all work out, don't worry. I'm sure you'll be back with all the latest news,' said Cara.

Cara had been turning this quandary over in her mind for the past few days. They seemed to have reached a dead-end if George couldn't remember what he'd done with the painting in 1848. Even if he'd managed to get it into a vault in the Bank of England, they had no details of how to claim it. Presumably they would need a key or code to withdraw it.

'Something will come to us. I feel like this is our time, and it's meant to be. I did a bit of research, and as far as I could see, Willow Manor hasn't been on the market since your however-many-times removed, great-grandfather, lost it in a card game,' she said.

'You're joking—what a bloody fool.'

'I know—I only found out the other day.'

'You kept that close to your chest,' he said, raising one eyebrow.

'I thought you had enough on your mind. Do you remember when you asked Kate, she said that the family fortunes had dramatically declined at the hands of one of your ancestors who had been a bit of a black sheep: a drinker, womaniser and gambler?'

'Ah, yes, I'd forgotten about that.'

'Well, it must be him. And if we don't buy Willow Manor now, it'll go to a hotel chain.'

'I wonder why the current owners are selling it.'

'Cash flow I would imagine; it can't be cheap to maintain a historically listed building.'

'I think you're right about this being our opportunity to correct my ancestor's screw-up, but how can we get our hands on the painting?'

'Let's talk to Eddie and see if he's got any suggestions.'

Cara's phone buzzed. 'Hello Eddie,' she said. 'This is unbelievable. What perfect timing. We were just talking about calling you.'

Cara put the call on speaker, and they chatted for a few minutes. 'We've just arrived at Willow Manor for a viewing,' she told Eddie.

'And to think in 1536, you and I were just there trying to figure out how to rescue George from St. Mary's Abbey,' he said.

'Ah, that's good—it means I've arrived safely with my latest updates intact. But here's the thing Eddie, as urgent as that is, we need your help with something else.'

'Okay...'

'George is stuck in Victoriana and hasn't been able to get back to reveal the whereabouts of the Turner painting. Either that, or he's got timeline amnesia. We're hoping it's the former and he'll update soon, but for now we're in a time crunch to raise the money to make an offer on Willow Manor while it's still on the market.'

'That's why I was calling you, actually,' said Eddie.

'Oh?'

'I've got a message from George in Victoriana.'

Cara and George looked at each other. 'This is a first,' said Cara. 'How clever. Why didn't I think of asking you to be a messenger?'

'As much as I'd love to take credit for this simple yet ingenious idea, it was George who thought of it. He visited me and asked that I tell you he can't get back yet. We don't know why, but the vortex seems to be out of order. He said to let you know he's okay and that the painting is safely stored in a vault at the Bank of England. He wants you to try and get it out, so you can sell it and move forward with buying Willow Manor.'

'That's fantastic news!' Cara said, beaming at George, and reaching for his hand.

'How do we get the key or what do we need?'

'Ah. I'm afraid that's where we've run into a minor problem.'

'I thought it might be too good to be true to be that simple.' Cara rolled her eyes.

Eddie said, 'We have to come up with a way to move the key between timelines. We've not done anything like that before...'

Hyde Park, London, 1848 - Victoriana

George and Edward strolled along the winding footpath between the lush foliage and tall trees in Hyde Park.

'You could hide the key at Buckingham Palace,' said Edward. 'We know that's still there in the twenty-first century.'

A gleaming chestnut horse and carriage whisked by with a young lady and her companion taking some park air and nodding at them as they passed. George bowed and turned back towards Edward.

'The nineteenth century is really rather charming. I must appreciate it more.'

'Yes, there is a reassuring slowness to the speed of life here. Sometimes I enjoy it more than the future,' replied Edward.

'About Buckingham Palace—I considered that, but we no

longer have any link to the royal family, so it would be impossible to gain proper access in the present-day.'

'There might be another way. When I was on the phone with Cara, I had an idea,' said Edward.

'How is she?'

'She's fine—she sends her love and says not to worry.'

'Thank you, Edward. I appreciate you being our go-between-timelines. So, what's your idea?'

'I think the most obvious place to hide the key is Willow Manor.'

'But the estate isn't in our family at that time.'

'Even so, how about we find a way to hide it in the grounds and then it'll be easy enough for Cara, and the future you, to retrieve it. There should be some perfect opportunities when you discuss purchasing the property, don't you think?'

George stared at Edward. 'My good man, you really are a genius!'

'Was that ever in any doubt?' Edward pulled a mock-surprised face and held his palms upwards.

'It'll take a bit of manoeuvring, but it's possible we can pull it off,' said George.

They chatted through possible options and came up with a plan.

'I'll leave for York first thing in the morning,' said George.

Willow Manor, York, 1848 - Victoriana

After several days of monotonous travelling, with too many stops along the way, George was grateful to arrive at the village near Willow Manor. He wished he had his Porsche and could fly along the Great North Road without all the cumbersome delays of nineteenth-century travel.

A hotchpotch of images of his ancestral home flipped through his head. After resting a while in his room and dining on a light meal, he requested another carriage.

The innkeeper had been puzzled when he asked to be taken to Willow Manor.

'Nobody's lived at the big house since the fire,' he said.

'There was a fire?'

'Oh yes, my lord—the word is—if it weren't for someone returning in time to discover the fire, the estate would have burned to the ground, with the master inside. They say, he was driven quite mad with love for a young lass in his employ.'

Questions popped into George's mind about his ancestor's troubled past, but he didn't have time to get into the rumours with the innkeeper now, so instead he said, 'I had hoped to have a look at Willow Manor—I'm thinking of buying it, you see.'

The innkeeper tutted. 'Well, they say it was the finest house for miles in its day, but it's lain in ruins for years. It's been like that for as long as I can remember. I don't envy you the job of bringing it back to life, fine as it once was...it'll be a hell of a job. Aye, I'd think twice about that if I were you.'

George paid for his meal, slotted his arms into his dashing double-breasted frock coat, and pulled his top hat firmly down onto his head. As the carriage drew up in front of the inn and he was about to exit the building, the innkeeper called after him, 'Beware of the ghosts—rumour has it that the lovers haunt the old place. It's a famous legend in these parts.'

He turned back to look at the man. 'I will heed your words. Thank you for the warning.'

George, still weary from the long journey, sank down

into the seat as the horse and carriage pulled away. He thought about ghosts and wondered what had happened at Willow Manor to cause people to believe it was haunted. He allowed his head to bounce gently against the seat as it bumped along the pot-holed route. Visions of the tragic master and his doomed love hovered in his consciousness as he dozed to the uneven rhythm of the carriage wheels.

The carriage drew up in front of the tall iron gates of Willow Manor, and George noticed the peeling black paintwork. He roused himself and jumped out to talk to the driver. 'Would you be so kind as to take me up to the house itself?'

George noticed a tightness cross the man's mouth.

'We don't enter Willow Manor, Sir.'

'And why is that?'

'The gates are locked, and the place has been derelict since I was a boy. If you want to go in, you'll have to make your own way over the wall or around the back; the best I can do is wait for you here.'

'Right, I see, thank you,' said George, surprised. He'd presumed the innkeeper was a superstitious type and was over-reacting, which wasn't unusual in Victorian England.

The driver leaned closer to him. 'When I was a boy we used to sneak into the grounds and play, until one day, my friend wandered into the house to look for our ball that had slipped through a broken window, and he came out trembling—he was white as a sheet, swore he saw a ghost. The place is haunted, Sir. We stayed away after that and if you'd like me to turn around and take you back to the inn, there's no shame in it.'

George could see the man wouldn't be persuaded to drive any closer to the house, and they probably couldn't access the gate, anyway. 'Thank you. I appreciate the warning, but I will have a quick look. Please wait for me and I'll be as quick as possible. I just want to get an idea of the look of the place as I'm thinking of buying it.'

It wasn't a lie—he couldn't tell the driver he would buy the house two hundred years into the future—and he didn't want to arouse suspicion, with rumours of a visitor from London breaking in. He knew how fast gossip spread, and he wanted to keep his visit under the wire. The more low-key he kept his entry, the better.

He tried to push the gate open, but it was locked. There was a large rusty padlock which he didn't fancy his chances of unpicking, so he walked around the side of the property to scope out an easier way in. The surrounding grounds were overgrown and neglected, but he glimpsed the top floor of the house looming over the high walls. It looked eerie, as though it hadn't been lived in for years. The wall which surrounded the front of the estate was crumbling, and many of the stones appeared missing or loose.

He reached out to touch one section and it came apart beneath his hand; the stones and dust scattered and coated his shiny black shoes. He spent several minutes trying to locate a piece of the wall that looked sturdy enough to bear his substantial weight; there was no point risking breaking his neck in his effort to transport the key to the twenty-first century.

If he had another accident, he would risk messing up the timeline, and losing his one hope of returning to his present-day life. No—he must be methodical and take great care to keep the timeline exactly as it was supposed to be. He inspected the stones, section by section, until his persistence paid off and he spotted a part of the wall which had broken and was lower than the rest but seemed solid enough for him to climb over. He had purposely left his coat in the carriage, so it wouldn't catch on the jagged pieces of stone and hamper his progress as he climbed.

A few minutes later, after some precarious footwork where he slipped and had to reposition himself, he landed on the other side of the wall in a bed of tall weeds in what must have once been a handsome flower border. He was rewarded for his efforts with a view of the gloomy remains of Willow Manor standing forlorn and godforsaken before him. One wing was tinged with black and grey; presumably the remnants of the fire, and another side of the house had crumbled completely. He wondered if that was where the carriage driver's childhood friend had gone to seek his ball and experienced his close encounter with the ghost of his ancestor.

A heavy sadness descended upon George and for a few minutes he stood looking at the remains of his family home: the home he had been born in and lived many happy years with his parents and Cara and his children, in Tudorville. He knew, partly from memory, and partly from stories Cara had told him, that Willow Manor had been an impressive property in those days. His father, George Cavendish, had been the lord of the manor and was highly respected, long before George was independently created an earl by King Henry VIII, for his services to the Crown. He couldn't fathom why his father's descendant would throw it all away and permit the estate to fall into such disrepair.

The innkeeper's words kept ringing in his head: *he was driven quite mad with love.* Emotion ripped through him and he was surprised to find himself close to tears, as if he himself had experienced the trauma of losing everything.

He wondered why his ancestor tried to burn the house down. George shook his head, trying to clear his foggy brain. He reminded himself he was only here to hide the key and mustn't let his complicated karmic connection to Willow Manor stop him from executing his mission.

He wandered around the neglected grounds, and images

of the meticulously tended gardens of the present-day hotel flitted around his mind like an old movie. Whatever happened here was indeed a tragedy, and he realised he was shaking. He resolved to hurry and find somewhere to hide the key, so he could escape the oppressive gloom of this place and leave for London at once.

And then his eyes lit on the perfect hiding place...

CHAPTER 24

Rose Cottage, York - Present day

Cara's heart lightened as she saw Eddie's name flash up on her phone.

'I bring a message from the past,' he said, a lilt in his voice.

'Well, I can certainly do with one,' said Cara, flicking her hair out of her eyes, and perking up at the sound of Eddie's reassuring voice.

'George asked me to let you know he managed to hide the key in the grounds of Willow Manor, so you can go and look for it and then hopefully retrieve the painting from the Bank of England.'

'Oh brilliant! Where exactly do I find it?' she asked.

'He said that in 1848, Willow Manor was derelict following a fire some years previously, so he didn't want to risk hiding it inside the house. He had to find a spot in the grounds that would still be accessible after the hotel conversion.'

Cara said, 'How awful. I wonder what happened.'

'I don't know; that's all he told me.'

'So where did George stash the key?'

'There's a beautiful old stone fountain at the centre of the rose garden. He said you used to leave each other hidden love notes in Tudorville before you were married. He thinks it may be called the Lovers' Fountain...'

'Oh yes! We walked in the gardens and I told him all about it when we stayed at the hotel.'

'He said you would know where to find it.'

'Don't tell me. Let me guess.'

Eddie chuckled. 'You're so competitive.'

'I bet the key is on the hidden shelf beneath the bottom tier of the fountain,' said Cara, closing her eyes briefly.

'Bingo,' he said.

'I'll have to find a way to get into the grounds as soon as possible. The agent has had some interest and it sounds like it might be snapped up from under our noses if we don't get our act together.'

'Let's hope the key is still there then, two hundred years on.'

'Thanks Eddie. I don't know what we'd do without you.'

'I'm pleased I can help,' he said.

Cara stared out of the window at the blustery trees as she told him about the strange blue-eyed man watching her at The National Archives, and Sylvia's vision that George was being held prisoner by the same man at what they thought was St. Mary's Abbey.

'She said something about karma, and he's my lover from another life. She thinks he's coming after me. I'm scared for George. What if Sylvia's right?'

Eddie was silent for a moment.

'What is it?' said Cara. 'That's an ominous silence.'

'I might know who the blue-eyed man is.'

'Who? I've had the chills ever since I spotted him watching me...and the way he just vanished. It was spooky as hell.'

'I didn't want to scare you, but you know how I've been time travelling longer than you and George?'

'Yeah.'

'Well, there's an ancient group of time travellers which has been around for thousands of years; they're known as karmic warriors. And they are dangerous; extremely dangerous. They're an evil sect of souls whose mission it is to eradicate Twin Flames to prevent the rising consciousness of the planet.'

'They sound terrifying. What do they do, exactly?'

'They're sort of like the opposite of Twin Flames; instead of trying to reach ascension and guide the earth to peace, they seek revenge upon every soul who hurt them in a past life.'

Cara sat down on a kitchen chair and rubbed her eyes. 'So, you think this guy is after me for vengeance?'

'Possibly, but by the sounds of Sylvia's vision, the blue-eyed warrior is after both of you and may be attempting to eradicate George from the Tudorville timeline,' said Eddie.

'I was right to be terrified for his life, then.'

Eddie continued, 'Last thing I remember, you and I were together at Willow Manor figuring out how to break into St. Mary's. We'll see soon enough if my hunch is correct, and the karmic warrior is involved with the rebels.'

'I wish I could go back to living a normal life, without bloody karmic hoodlums,' Cara said.

'Me too. But you wouldn't be with George if you went back to your old life. And there is no going back anyway—this is all some kind of karmic test and we have to pass it together.'

'I know,' she said.

They agreed that being time travellers really sucked and then ended the call.

Willow Manor, York - Present day

Cara was too impatient to wait for George to return so she jumped in her car and headed over to Willow Manor. The tall iron gates stood open and as she neared the end of the driveway she drove through the busy car park at the front of the house and steered the nose of her black SUV around to the side car park, where there were several vacant spaces. Judging by the number of cars, the hotel was at full occupancy. She grabbed her phone, and as she emerged from the car a stray willow leaf blew towards her and rested on the shoulder of her jacket.

Cara pondered how she always felt instantly at home there, no matter the century. Finding a way to get Willow Manor back into the family was the right thing to do; she was guided by a sense of inner certainty and didn't doubt it for a second. No matter how big a project it would be, they would figure it out.

Cara knew the hotel layout well from when they stayed the night. She walked to the end of the car park, slid back the small bolt on the side gate and slipped through to the back of the estate. She thought there were enough guests dotted about in the various portions of the grounds to make her presence inconspicuous. Cara smiled at an elderly couple taking a leisurely post-breakfast stroll around the gardens and walking arm in arm towards her.

'Good morning,' she said, and they nodded pleasantly in return.

Cara increased her pace and headed towards the rose

garden which was quite a distance behind the main hotel building.

Damn it.

As she approached she noticed a man kneeling near the flower beds, pulling weeds. He looked up as she approached. 'Good morning. May I help you?' he said with a cheeky grin.

'Good morning. You must have your work cut out keeping these enormous gardens in such good shape.'

'Yes, it's quite a job, but I love it. I've been working here for years,' he said.

'Well I don't want to disturb you; I just came for a walk. I remembered the rose garden and the fountain.'

'The lovers' fountain is a grade two listed feature,' he said.

She hadn't expected anyone to know the place well enough to call the fountain by its original name. Cara thought the name must surely have been forgotten over the centuries. Surprise registered on her face and the gardener said, 'My family is from around these parts and I've always taken an interest in Willow Manor. It's got quite the chequered history, you know.'

'Yes, so I hear. Is it true there was a fire that burned part of the house down several hundred years ago?' Cara said.

'That's right. It's a tragic story which has become a bit of a romantic legend in the villages hereabouts. The tale goes that the master of the house fell in love with one of the servants, and he was so heartbroken that he gambled Willow Manor away in a card game and then tried to burn it down to the ground while he was inside.'

'Goodness that is a tragic tale,' said Cara.

'Don't quote me on it though. I've heard countless versions, so I may not have it exactly right. It was all the way back in the eighteenth century if I remember correctly.'

'Thank you. I'll look into it. I'm particularly interested

because my husband is a direct descendent of the original owners from Tudor times.'

'Is that so?' the gardener said. Now it was his turn to look surprised.

'Yes, in fact, we're planning to make an offer on the property, that's if we can get organised before someone else pips us to the post.'

'It would be lovely to have a descendant of the family as the new owner,' he said, rising up and dusting smatterings of soil off his cargo pants. I hope you succeed, and if you want a gardener, I'll be more than happy to stay on—my lodgings are here on the estate.'

Cara shook his hand and smiled. 'I think you'll have yourself a job,' she said. 'There's no way we'll be able to keep all of this in order without your green fingers. I'm Cara Cavendish, by the way.'

'So, you are an actual Cavendish! I'm honoured to meet you, I'm Julian Lightfoot, but you can call me, Swifty.'

'Hello Swifty, I'm honoured to meet you too. I think this must be synchronicity at its finest,' said Cara doing her best not to betray how excited she was to meet a member of her Tudorville team, so unexpectedly.

Swifty looked over in the direction of the shrubbery and whistled, and then whistled again. A few seconds later, a silky, lithe greyhound darted through the bushes, muscles flexed as he bounded over and then came to an abrupt stop at Swifty's side. 'There, there, good boy. This is Cornelius, my dog,' he said.

Cornelius padded over to Cara, his long graceful legs taking measured steps, and he sniffed her hand and emitted joyful whimpers of recognition. 'That's odd, he doesn't usually take to new people so quickly. He's acting as if he knows you.'

Cara stroked Cornelius' silky head, and said, 'What a

coincidence. My husband and I met him when we stayed at the hotel; he must remember me. Do you mind if I have a little look around?'

'Not at all, I need to empty my wheelbarrow, so I'll leave you to it. Take all the time you need.'

'Thank you, that's very kind. Please ask the current owners to pass your details to me if we're fortunate enough to purchase the hotel. Bye, bye, Cornelius,' she said, patting the dog's head once more. He turned to lick her hand and then wandered off after Swifty.

Cara went straight to the Lovers' Fountain, stooped down, and rested her knees on the damp concrete and looked upwards towards the bottom of the lower tier. She tentatively pushed her hand into the hidden shelf—she knew the shelf was still there because she'd shown it to George when they stayed at the hotel.

She groped about for a few seconds; the shelf was too small to be able to see inside, so she could only stick her hand in and hope for the best.

'Bingo,' she said aloud, using one of Eddie's expressions. After several moments of probing around in the tiny space, and her heart chugging like a steam engine, her fingers touched a small cold object. She withdrew her now grubby hand to reveal a rusty key in the centre of her palm.

Mission accomplished.

Cara examined the key for a minute, looked about to make sure no one had seen her extract it from the shelf, and then placed it carefully in her jacket pocket, her hand still cradling it as she walked back towards the gate. She didn't want to take any chances of it bouncing out of her pocket.

'May I help you?' asked a member of the hotel staff.

Cara, who was lost in a world of her own, thinking about the unexpected appearance of Swifty, and the discovery of the key, jumped. 'No, I'm fine, thank you. I was just enjoying a quick walk around your beautiful gardens and am now about to go out for the day and will be back in time for dinner.' She smiled her most charming smile, ducked out of the gate and jumped into her car before he could interrogate her any further.

She sped along Willow Manor's driveway, and then called George. His seductive deep voice reverberated throughout the car.

'There you are, darling. I was wondering where you'd gone,' he said.

'Sorry I shot off before you came home, but Eddie called. And guess what?'

'Umm. I've no idea,' he replied.

'I've got the key,' she said, not having the patience to make him guess.

'The key for the bank vault?'

'The very same. And there's other big news too. You won't believe it. I've just left Willow Manor and I'm on my way. I'll tell you more at home.'

'Great. I'll be waiting for you. You're a star,' he said.

'Love you, see you soon.'

Cara turned on the radio and sang along at the top of her voice. A surge of pure joy shot through her as she cruised through the beautiful York lanes on her way back to George. Home was wherever he was. Perhaps everything would work out, after all.

Willow Manor, York, 1536 - Tudorville

Cara tried to relax and make the most of being at home with the children, but her mind kept hopping about at a frantic pace as she thought of all that could go wrong the next day.

After dinner, when the children had gone upstairs, she sat in front of the fire with Edward, nursing a glass of whisky. As she sipped, the alcohol sent a jolt of adrenaline coursing through her veins. 'I'm not one for the strong stuff but this is very pleasant,' she said.

'I thought we could both do with it to steady our nerves a little, so we can get a good night's sleep,' Edward replied.

They had planned George's rescue as carefully as they could without going to St. Mary's by day, and risking alerting anyone to their presence. Cara had received a note from the queen, saying that they believed the rebels were about to march, and she hoped Cara and George had been reunited in York.

Cara bid Edward goodnight and they both went to bed ready for an early start. She struggled to relax enough to sleep properly, and as agreed, they met Swifty at the stables at four o'clock in the morning when all was silent and still, and the only sliver of light was from the moon glistening in the black velvet sky. Cara shivered and wrapped George's thick cloak tighter around her tired, aching body. The manly smell of him lingered on the material and evoked his nearness so that she yearned for him all the more. She sent up a silent prayer.

Please God, let him be safe and well, and let us bring him home today.

Cara had been relieved to hear that Swifty had arrived at Willow Manor a couple of days earlier, exhausted and starving after being released by the rebels.

'I heard them say they were taking him to a place called St. Mary's,' he told them, and Sylvia's vision and George's dream were confirmed.

They gathered as much information as they could about St. Mary's, and began to formulate their plan.

If the rebels marched and reached London, it was proof

that the timeline had reset as Cara suspected, and George would be destined to die in 1537. If they didn't rescue him, he would either die at the rebels' hands for being loyal to the king, or on the king's orders for showing loyalty to the rebels. Either way, they must get him out before they missed their narrow window of opportunity.

An image of the blue-eyed karmic warrior flashed into Cara's mind, and she shuddered.

As they set out from Willow Manor, each riding their own horse, Cara whispered to Swifty. 'Did you see a blue-eyed man amongst the rebels at Pontefract Castle?'

'No, my lady, not that I recall.'

They rode through the remainder of the night and Cara's muscles still ached with weariness from her gruelling journey from Windsor to York. The first hints of a golden dawn began to break on the horizon and Cara felt the crisp morning air on her face as they cantered along the track in the direction of the abbey. It was cold but invigorating and she inhaled copious amounts of fresh air, in an attempt to energise herself for the challenge ahead.

St. Mary's Abbey, York, 1536 - Tudorville

George opened his eyes after an unsatisfying and restless sleep. He knew something was happening and had caught smatterings of conversation from the garden below, as his rebel-guards discussed the possibility of their imminent march on London.

He didn't know anything about his other lives but he did remember Cara's stark warnings about 1537 and he had done his best to heed them while trying to protect his friends, Lord Darcy, and Robert Aske. He sensed his life was in danger. Again. He thought he had proved himself loyal to the Crown and had not taken any unnecessary risks; just as Cara had urged him. But the rebels were a different matter. There was the blue-eyed demon who had begun coming to his cell daily to quiz and taunt him.

He replayed their latest conversation in his mind to try and pass the time until daybreak, when he would enjoy the distraction of looking out the window, and he hoped the monk might bring his breakfast bowl.

'Why do you side with the king when you are a northern lord by birth?' the man asked.

'I don't know what you're talking about. I was sent as an emissary on behalf of the king to broker a peace deal. That is all I have done, and I have done it in good faith. I wish for nothing more than a peaceful resolution and for the Pilgrimage not to end in bloodshed. Don't you see that no matter how large your pilgrim army, the king's men will outnumber you when you reach London? Marching on London will be a declaration of war and you'll be writing the death warrant of all of your men.' George's voice cracked at the effort of talking so much with his dry, parched throat.

The blue-eyed man asked him more questions about his intentions and what he knew of the king's plans, and then he said, 'Where is your lady wife? Is she with the queen in London?'

George was stunned by the personal nature of the question and after a few seconds, rallied himself and said, 'Why do you wish to know about my wife?'

'Answer my questions, and I'll see to it you get some ale and better food today.'

George had refused to give him any information about Cara, and the man had kicked him; hard, in the groin, causing George's eyes to stream, before the man strode out, cussing.

Why was he asking about Cara?

George had drifted off into another restless doze and dreamed of Cara on horseback; searching for him, until he awoke so low and despondent that if he'd had the energy he would have cried out and begged for God's mercy. He yearned to hold her again. He stared at the ceiling which was now coated in pale golden rays from the reflection of the breaking dawn, and George raised his aching muscles from the lumpy mattress.

He moved towards the window and looked out at the grounds surrounding the abbey. Nothing looked any different from the previous mornings he had surveyed his surroundings, but his heart beat like a metronome, and like a caged wild animal on high alert, he sensed something was about to occur.

Was Cara coming for him or was he deluded in his exhaustion?

CHAPTER 25

St. Mary's Abbey, York, 1536 - Tudorville

Cara, Edward and Swifty approached the abbey; all kitted out like cat-burglars on horseback. Cara put her finger to her lips; the silence was so complete, she worried even a whisper would carry on the still morning air to alert the guards. One by one, they slipped down and tethered their horse to the giant oak trees, still quite some way from the abbey. Cara scooped out a handful of oats for each of the horses, from her satchel she'd hurriedly packed and thrown over her shoulder in preparation for the journey. After letting the horses graze from her palm, she passed around a flask of ale to her companions and they each took a few quick sips.

They knew what was required of them and sprung into motion. The abbey walls rose up like a mirage on the misty horizon, and memories of Cara's school visit to the museum, the abbey gardens, and ruins, flashed through her mind. In just a few years, the monks would be pensioned off during Henry's Dissolution of the Monasteries.

Edward was familiar with the lay-out of the abbey, and he'd drawn it out for them, so they knew what to expect. He'd also found an illustrated book about monasteries in the library at Willow Manor, which contained plans of the abbey. As they neared one of the gates to access the abbey grounds, they spotted a guard slumped on a chair, seemingly in a deep slumber. The uneventful monotonous night duty must have proved too much for his weary eyelids and he'd been transported far away on the wings of exhaustion.

The rescue team worked on the assumption that the abbey wasn't likely to be heavily guarded or held by thousands of men like Pontefract Castle. They gambled that the rebels had whisked George away as a possible bargaining chip, in case the castle was stormed by Norfolk's men.

Cara took a sharp intake of breath as the pale stone walls of the awe-inspiring abbey appeared immediately before her, bathed in the soft glow of first light. Once again, she was living an historian's dream and wished she had the time to wander around and enjoy the miracle. St. Mary's was one of the wealthiest and most famous Benedictine monasteries in England, positioned in the centre of York and mirroring the majestic York Minster Cathedral.

According to Sylvia's vision, George was being held in a cell overlooking the wildflower garden, and their rough plan hinged on finding him in the right spot. Edward knew the wild garden's location and he led the way, signalling to them as they entered cautiously through a gate on the other side of the grounds. They took tentative steps, careful not to crack any twigs or do anything that might alert the sleeping guard in the breaking dawn, with only the sounds of chirping birds on the dewy tree branches above his head, to mask any sound they made. Cara winced with every step she took, and at any second she feared she would hear the guard spring to life and alert the abbey to their presence and attempted break-in. They weren't equipped either in strength or weaponry, to win a fight with armed guards, so they were counting on their stealth and wits to get them through.

Edward touched the handle of the large wooden side door of the abbey. They heard a click and it swung open revealing a dimly lit entrance. He took a few steps, checked no one was about and indicated for them to follow. The three of them moved silently through the gloomy entrance and followed the faint glow of the oil lamps, positioned sporadically along the thick stone walls.

The moment was finally here. If they didn't reset the timeline, the odds were that George would die with the rebels in 1537. Cara didn't know what that would mean for the future, but she wasn't prepared to find out.

She prayed he was still being held in the abbey and hadn't been moved to another location. Eerie echoes of melodic Gregorian chanting filled the large hall, and Cara shivered and pulled George's cloak tightly around her to keep out the bone-cold chill of the damp abbey.

'They're in early morning mass just as we hoped,' whispered Edward, turning to face Cara and Swifty as they followed closely behind. 'This is our chance to get in and out without anyone intercepting us. According to the abbey plans, there are three rooms on the upper floor, which all overlook the wild garden.'

They were counting on George being in one of them, but they had no idea which. They climbed a steep and twisting staircase, Edward continued leading the way, with Cara in the middle, and Swifty bringing up the rear. There was a loud, thumping noise as Cara's foot slipped off the edge of one of the steps. 'Ouch,' she said, cursing under her breath.

Swifty caught her foot and helped her steady herself to regain her footing.

'Are you all right?' asked Edward, looking over his shoulder.

She nodded, terrified they would miss their narrow window of opportunity to rescue George. They had no choice other than to succeed or she would lose him; possibly forever.

1537, 1537, 1537, the year of the mass rebel executions ticked through her mind as it had been doing ever since her visit to the archives, now tormenting her as she climbed the steps. She pushed on, treading gingerly as sharp pains shot through her foot, and Edward reached the top of the staircase. This was no time for indulging pain; she knew she would have to mind-over-matter-it and was prepared to pay the price later. She would pay any price to get George back to the safety of their family and estate at Willow Manor.

They followed Edward out onto the upper floor, and stood in a huddle for a minute, listening keenly for any sounds of life. All was quiet and still, except for the distant echoes of the hypnotic chanting rising up from the spiritual heart of the abbey. Edward advanced towards the first door on the side of the building which overlooked the garden. He put his ear to the door, there was no sound of any movement. He signalled them to step back and stay out of the way, and he tentatively turned the door's handle.

It swung open, and Cara held her breath as she watched him stick his head around the door and then slowly enter the room. Her heart thumped wildly and sounded so loud to her ears she wouldn't have been surprised if Swifty could hear it.

Edward backed out into the hallway, shook his head, and held his palms upwards, before closing the door slowly behind him, and advancing with careful steps towards the second door. He repeated the process and was soon back out in the hallway again. He approached the third and final door in the row and clasped his hands together in a prayer symbol and shook them in Cara's direction.

She stared at him, too rigid with fear to acknowledge his gesture. If George wasn't in the next room, all was lost. She couldn't see how they could break him out of Pontefract Castle, if they were still holding him there as it was now the chief command centre for the *rebel-pilgrims* who were preparing for all-out war.

Cara gulped, and waited. A few seconds later, she heard murmurings, and unable to hold herself back any longer, she dashed towards the room and shot inside. As she appeared around the door, her eyes beheld the beloved face she yearned to see, and Cara flew into George's arms.

'You are here,' she said, trying to choke back the pent-up emotion in her tight throat, but failing as thick, heavy tears slid from her eyes.

Cara stared at George's blackened eyes and bruised face. He'd taken a serious beating.

What have they done to you?

'You came for me! I knew something was happening this morning. I dreamed of it,' George squeezed her against his chest and held her tightly in his arms. This wasn't the first time they had shared telepathic dreams; Sylvia explained that telepathy was an intrinsic part of the Twin Flame connection.

'Much as I hate to come between you two; we have no time for this. We must flee if we want to be gone before mass ends and the place is overrun with monks and possibly even rebels too,' said Edward.

Cara drew back and said, 'Yes, of course. Let us make haste.' She grabbed George's cold hand, and pulled him towards the door, but then he turned back into the room.

'Hold on, let's take a quick look out of the window and see how many guards there are out there.'

'Good idea,' said Edward.

'I've been watching them, waiting for my chance to try and get away, but there's always been someone out there,' said George.

George and Cara approached the window and peered out from a distance, so they could see but not be seen.

'Oh shit, he's here,' said Cara, forgetting her modest Tudorville manners she was mindful to display at court.

'Who's here?' asked George.

'That blue-eyed man,' she said.

'He came to interrogate me. He's a nasty character and asked lots of probing questions about you.'

'Was it him who beat you so?' asked Cara.

George didn't reply.

'We'll have to reach the horses via a different route. Come on, there's no time to waste. He could be up to look for George at any moment,' said Edward.

They checked the hallway and slipped out of the room, one by one, and George quietly closed the door behind him, relieved to be on his way to freedom after being imprisoned in the dank cell.

Edward beckoned to them to follow him, and they crossed over to the opposite side of the upper floor. He opened a door and prepared to make a dash for it but immediately came nose-to-nose with a monk dressed in a black robe.

'Oh shit,' said Cara again, this time under her breath.

Rose Cottage, York - Present day

George was waiting for Cara at the door and swooped her up in his arms and kissed her on the lips. 'Come in and tell me all of the news, my darling. I'm making us a fresh pot of coffee. Are you hungry?'

'Coffee will be lovely. I think I'm too excited to eat.'

Cara placed the rusty, once silver key onto the kitchen table and looked at George.

'You did it!' he said.

'We did it! You pulled it off in Victoriana.'

'I will take some of the credit then, even though I haven't a clue what I did.'

'Do you realise this is the first time we've witnessed an object travel through time? I must tell Eddie that our plan worked,' she said.

'It's fascinating; although it didn't strictly travel through time. It just remained where it was, didn't it?' asked George.

'Yes, that's true; but if you hadn't smuggled it into Willow Manor it wouldn't have been there. Brilliant idea to store it in the Lovers' Fountain, by the way.'

'That is a brilliant idea. If only I had thought of it,' he said.

Cara's heart contracted—she could feel his frustration even though he tried to make light of the situation. How she had wished their time travel would stop so they could live a normal life, but now she saw how it was affecting him, she was having second thoughts. Eddie had told her that Victoriana George was stuck and frustrated about not being able to return to present day. Poor George wasn't having a good time of it in any of the timelines.

'Ready for coffee?'

'Ooh, yes. You make the best coffee,' she said as he filled

the two china cups and added a splash of oat milk to hers, with a flourish.

She breathed in the rich aroma, savoured the smooth flavour of the coffee beans, and after a moment, she said, 'You'll never guess who I met at Willow Manor.'

'Um—the American investor?'

'Nope, not even close.'

'Not more guessing games. Go on, just tell me.'

'There was a gardener tending the rose garden when I arrived at the fountain.'

'Right, and?'

'You won't believe who it was.'

'I'm intrigued. Come on, spill the beans.'

'Okay...it was Swifty.'

'Noooooo,' he said, his eyes shone like swirls of rich, rippled chocolate. 'How did you know? Did he look like himself?'

'Well, that's just it. At first, he didn't, but once he introduced himself, I realised he reminded me of a mature version of young Swifty.'

'How extraordinary...so, our lad's either reincarnated as a descendent of Swifty, or he is time travelling like us.'

'He's the head gardener, by the sounds of it, but he's not a lad; I'd guess he's well into his thirties. He lives in the grounds and said he'll be happy to continue in his role if we buy the estate. And there's more.'

'Go on...'

'He has a greyhound called Cornelius! That's why he was at the hotel when we stayed there.'

George continued to stare at Cara as he digested her revelations. 'Well that can't be a mere coincidence. I thought he must have been some kind of spirit dog.'

'Me too, something like that anyway—I thought he was

an apparition, but he's real and he licked my hand and he even knew me. Swifty remarked on how strange it was.'

'Well, well. That's incredible; so, we also have a time travelling greyhound on our team,' he said smiling into her eyes.

George pulled her into his arms and hugged her.

'It was so weird. I don't think Swifty recognised me, but he was excited to hear we're related to the original Cavendish family, and he talked about the house burning down and some kind of tragedy in the eighteenth century. I didn't have a chance to get into it as much as I would have liked because I was anxious to look for the key before anyone else noticed me wandering uninvited around the grounds.'

'I didn't even ask. How did you manage to get in?'

'I just pretended I was a guest and walked in as if I belonged there.'

'And you do, my darling. It will be ours again soon.' George held onto her hand as she buzzed with excitement.

'So, what's next?' he said, his eyes returning to the rusty key on the table which, all going to plan, would unlock their future.

'We must go to the Bank of England and get the painting out of the vault.'

'Do you think this old key will work?' George pulled a face.

'It hasn't aged well, but fingers crossed, they'll accept it. I had a message from the agent to say that the American group is moving forward with due diligence, so there's no time to waste.'

'We'd better get cracking then; let's go to the bank as soon as possible.'

'It might be a good idea to check their opening hours first, though,' said Cara.

She searched on her phone and said, 'Okay, so they do

private audiences for vault-owners, but we need to book a time online.'

She booked the first slot available which was for the next day and they prepared to travel to London again, this time by train.

The following morning, Cara studied George surreptitiously from beneath her lashes as he handled the Porsche with smooth elegance. She marvelled how they never tired of each other. There was the occasional cross word, as any couple would expect; when one of them was in a low mood, but it passed quickly without any need to mention it again. They'd been together every day in the present-day timeline for over a year and their connection only deepened. But then, five hundred years was a long time, she mused. It made sense they wouldn't get fed up of each other in one year when they'd been together through centuries.

'I love you,' she said. 'I couldn't love you more.'

He turned to look at her as he drove. 'I love you, my darling.'

He gestured for her to hold his hand, and she gently rested her fingers on his hand all the way to the train station as he moved through the gears. Cara felt a wave of contentment wash over her—all of the heartache had been worth it. It was worth every second.

London - Present day

That afternoon, they made their way down Threadneedle Street towards the Bank of England.

'I don't think I've ever been here before,' said Cara. 'What a gorgeous building.'

'Yes, it's quite something isn't it? But we had better hope

we've been here before or the painting won't be waiting for us in the vault.'

The huge stone pillars which lined the entrance of the bank were awash with the pale sun which cast a welcoming yellow light, as they stepped inside the building.

'Mr and Mrs Cavendish. My name is Benjamin, and I'm so pleased to meet you. Thank you for scheduling, please come this way.'

They followed the immaculately booted-and-suited bank official who had been waiting to receive them, through a maze of corridors into a small room where he beckoned for them to have a seat. Neither of them remembered a previous visit to place the painting in the vault so it was like a first visit in every respect.

'I took the liberty of looking up your details before you arrived, to save you time. I was astonished to find you are custodians of one of the oldest vaults in the bank. Only the royal family and a small number of other families have held a vault as long as you; right back to Queen Victoria's reign.'

George nodded and said, 'We can trace the family all the way back to the time of King Henry VIII, but I don't think you had vaults then.'

'That's truly impressive,' said the clerk. 'We no longer offer vaults to new private clients, and even hundreds of years ago, it's my understanding you could only secure one by special invitation.'

'I see,' said George. 'Aren't we the fortunate ones, then.'

'I'll need your code please,' said the clerk.

George shifted from one foot to the other. 'Code? We only have a key; and a rusty one at that,' he replied.

The clerk coughed and scratched the side of his nose. 'In that case, I'm afraid we may have a small problem. I'm only authorised to allow someone to access a vault if they are able to provide the code which is validated upon entry by our triple-backed security-vault-system.'

George's eyes moved from Benjamin's to Cara's face. 'Any ideas?' he said.

Cara shook her head and also turned to look at the bank official. 'When exactly was this new code issued?'

'I couldn't tell you the exact date off the top of my head, Mrs Cavendish...we've had the coded system in place for quite a number of years—long before my arrival at the bank. All I can tell you is that the bank's old analogue systems were upgraded when it became obvious the keys were no longer a secure or modern way to protect the vaults, and many of them no longer worked anyway. We're phasing out the private client vaults, you see.'

Cara picked up the key and held it in the palm of her hand. 'We can prove our identity. As you see, the key is rusty and may not have worked anyway, but we don't have the code.'

The clerk looked troubled. 'I do not wish to seem unhelpful but without the code, my hands are tied. I'm not even authorised to discuss the vault with you any further.'

Cara looked at George. He shrugged his shoulders.

What now?

CHAPTER 26

Bank of England, London - Present day

Benjamin smoothed his shiny black hair with one hand, and his eyes flitted from Cara to George and back again.

Cara cleared her throat and said, 'I appreciate your predicament, and I'm sorry for the inconvenience but we've been moving around on business and we didn't receive the code. Would it be possible to give us the address to which the code was sent?'

The clerk pondered for several seconds before slowly rising from his chair, and saying, 'Please excuse me for a moment. I will liaise with my colleague as this situation is most unusual. I must obtain special permission.'

'I supposed it would have been too much to expect it would go off without a hitch,' said George, after the clerk left the room.

'The key is so rusty I didn't think it would work, but I imagined they would just validate it somehow,' said Cara.

'Things have moved on in two hundred years—even in an establishment steeped in tradition such as the Bank of England,' he replied.

'If we can't get them to give us access this way, we may have to get Eddie to ask Victoriana George to try again,' Cara said.

'If only the vortex would come for me, I could whiz back without bothering him.'

Cara checked her phone. There was a follow up message from John, the property agent, asking whether they wanted to move forward. Quantum time wasn't working in their favour.

She raised her head, and said, 'But what would you do differently? They gave you the key when you put the painting in the vault, so without being at the right address to receive the code, we'd be none the wiser, would we?'

Benjamin reappeared and said, 'Thanks for your patience. I'll need to see some current ID and then I'm permitted to release the address of where the code would have been sent.'

Cara exhaled. 'Thank you so much, Benjamin, you're a star.'

George had anticipated needing some form of identification in addition to the key and immediately produced his passport and driving license. As you can see, I bear the same name as the original holder of the vault. Family tradition.' He channelled the full blast of his irresistible charm at the official.

'Right, well this all seems to match up.' Benjamin scrolled through computer records on a hand-held device. 'Hopefully I can find the details of where the code was sent. I'll need a few more minutes, please.'

Cara guessed George was as clueless as her about what address would be on record. They were still trying to fill in the blanks of what had happened in the earlier years of the new version of George's present-day life.

Several minutes later, Benjamin said, 'I've found a note on your account saying that we switched from key to code towards the end of the nineties and we wrote to request that you return your key to us to be destroyed for security reasons.'

'Okay,' said George, nodding.

'There's no record of it being returned,' the clerk said, his speech slow as he scrolled.

Cara tried to rein in her impatience. 'We obviously didn't return it because we have it with us today.'

Cara and George waited, the tension in the small room was palpable as Benjamin continued to study the device in a mind-numbing meticulous fashion.

'I'm trying to find the address to which we sent the code. It's all so long ago,' he said, glancing at them briefly.

'How bizarre that it should be safe for centuries, but we can't access it now due to modern technology,' said Cara.

More minutes ticked by and Cara fidgeted with the contents of her bag.

'Ah, here we are. I think this is it,' he said, finally.

Two sets of eyes bore into the official's face, waiting for the big reveal. George was intrigued to discover where he'd lived in the nineties.

'What's the address?' prompted Cara, shifting about on the hard seat, unable to sit still any longer.

Benjamin read out the address of Casa Cavendish, Seville, which was the Spanish villa where they had spent several glorious years undercover on behalf of Queen Victoria. The same villa where they made love the previous year, and the same villa where Cara had located George after the timeline had reset and she thought he was lost to her forever.

Casa Cavendish was central to their interwoven histories and was one of their favourite places.

Cara and George looked at each other. It seemed obvious to them both now; it was the perfect location.

'That's good news. At least the villa is still in our family, so the code must have either gone astray in the post or not been passed onto me upon our return,' said George.

'Or perhaps you filed it away somewhere and didn't realise its significance,' said Cara. 'Would it be possible to send out a new notification of the code, please?' She was determined to move the situation along now.

'I don't see why not—but it would have to be to the registered address.'

'The Seville one?'

'Yes, Casa Cavendish is the only address we have on record; there haven't been any updates since...since...' His words trailed off as he tried to find a date. 'It's highly irregular; I can't find any date other than when we transferred the manual vault account to the computer records. This entry was logged as transferred from the original handwritten record. It's most peculiar—I've never seen one like this before.'

'If you would hit whatever button you need to hit to shoot off a new copy of the code to our mailing address, we'd appreciate that,' said Cara.

'Very good, Mrs Cavendish, I'll do that for you now.'

Cara said, 'Thank you. What sort of timeframe will it be for us to expect the letter to arrive to the address in Spain?'

'I'd say, allow around ten days, as these codes must all be manually printed, validated and then mailed out by our security team, and it will also take longer for international post. As you might appreciate, we can't have vault codes whizzing about willy-nilly.' He stood, squared his shoulders as if to emphasise the importance of his statement, and then smiled apologetically at George and Cara. 'I'm sorry it's such a damned nuisance, but there's no way around the security, I'm afraid.'

'We quite understand,' said George. 'Thank you for your assistance.'

The clerk led them out of the room and back through the maze of corridors towards reception.

'How bloody frustrating, I don't see how we're going to get the code to sell the painting in time,' said Cara, sighing. 'One thing determines the next, and the agent is chasing me for an offer. Maybe it's a sign we shouldn't reacquire Willow Manor, after all.'

George captured her hand in his as they exited the bank, 'Nooooo, don't say that. I know it's frustrating, but if people gave up at the first sign of difficulty, most amazing things would never come to fruition. We'll figure something out—we always do.'

'I had a dream last night; well, it was more of a nightmare actually,' she said.

'Oh no. Why didn't you mention it this morning?'

'I thought I'd forget all about it.'

'But, you clearly haven't.'

'No. That bloody blue-eyed man was chasing me, and I couldn't reach you. It sounds crazy, but I think he might really be tracking us through time.'

'Crazy? I think we've already whistled way past crazy,' said George. He wrapped his arm around Cara and pulled her tightly against him, tucking her snugly into his side, so she leaned on him slightly as they walked. He kissed her forehead, and said, 'Don't worry, I promise to protect you from this blue-eyed menace. Shall we go for a drink and decide what to do?'

'Great idea. I could do with a stiff drink after all that fuss.'

They made their way briskly back along Threadneedle

Street, and the cold wind bit into Cara's skin and turned her cheeks a rosy pink.

They found an old pub near Bank tube station and sat down in a cosy corner.

'I never realised that Bank tube station was named because of the Bank of England,' said Cara.

'No, I didn't either, to be honest. It never crossed my mind. What do you want to drink?'

'A glass of white wine would be lovely.'

'I thought you wanted a stiff drink.'

'That's about as stiff as I can handle, or I may keel over. I kept waking up in the night. I'm shattered.'

While George waited to be served at the bar, Cara rose from her seat to get a closer look at some of the pictures on the walls. A few minutes later she returned to her spot but immediately felt someone's presence behind her. She turned abruptly but there was no one there. Cara caught sight of someone's back slipping away behind an alcove and she knew who it was without glimpsing his face.

Why was this time travelling warrior stalking her?

Rose Cottage, York - Present day

'I think the letter you asked me to look out for, has arrived,' said George's sister, after a few minutes of chit-chat.

'That is fabulous news. I thought it might be another week yet,' George said.

'It arrived this morning and I called you as soon as I had a chance.' Kate waved a stiff-backed envelope on the video camera as she spoke.

'Thanks Kate, I appreciate it. Please go ahead and open it now.'

She tore open the envelope and a thin piece of paper dropped out. 'It looks as though it needs rubbing to reveal the code.' She grabbed a coin from a nearby dish and proceeded to rub the rectangle on the paper.

'It's hardly Bletchley Park, is it? The way the chap went on about the coding system at the Bank of England, you'd think it was going to arrive encased in a gold envelope,' said George.

'Well, I did have to sign for it. Okay, I've got it. The code is 118887,' she read aloud.

'Do me a favour, sis, and snap a photo of it and whiz it over to me.' He paused and continued, 'How are things at Casa Cavendish?'

'Pretty good. We love being here—this place is so relaxing.'

'Glad you're enjoying it. It would be good to see you both soon. Any plans to come over for a visit?'

'I miss you and Cara. When will you be moving into Willow Manor?'

'Oh, I see...you only want to stay in our best houses,' George teased.

'I can't wait to get into that old place. I've been intrigued by it ever since we first heard the stories as kids.'

'Cara's made a few interesting discoveries about our black sheep of an ancestor who you told us about. I'm sure she'd love to chat to you about that. And you could help us sort the place out if you like.'

'I might just take you up on that offer, big brother. As much as I love the Spanish sunshine, it does become a bit predictable after a while. I could do with a change.'

'Well, it's raining today, but we have had some beautiful crisp sunny days.'

'What's the next step for buying Willow Manor?'

'We have a competitor, so the sooner we can raise the

funds, the better. We have to find a buyer for the painting and that should give us enough money to move forward.'

'How did you come to have this hidden-away-vault with a mystery Turner painting stashed away?' she asked.

'It's a long story, and you probably won't believe me, but I'll tell you all about it when you come over. Right now, I'll have to love you and leave you, as we need to get to the Bank of England.'

'It's all very intriguing,' she said. 'Never a dull moment with you two, that's for sure. Give my love to your gorgeous wife and tell her I can't wait to see you both ensconced in our ancestral home. Will it be Lord and Lady Cavendish like our ancestors?'

George ended the call before Kate could ask more tricky questions. Fortunately, she wasn't the envious type, but he wouldn't be able to indefinitely avoid offering up some kind of explanation about the painting. It would take some explaining. Kate had no idea how close she was to the truth, and he had no idea how he would ever explain any of this to her; never mind to his parents.

George went to find Cara and tell her the wonderful news. They would leave for London immediately and arrange to access the vault.

The Bank of England, London - Present day

George made an appointment with the bank, and Benjamin showed them into the small room which housed the Cavendish family vault.

Benjamin stepped to one side and beckoned for George to key in the code. 'I'll leave you to it,' he said, and quietly closed the door.

George pulled his phone out of his trouser pocket and flicked through the album, searching for the photo of the vault code which Kate had sent to him. He then handed the phone to Cara.

'Please read it aloud to me. I don't want to cock it up now,' he said.

'I'm nervous,' she said.

'It's hard to believe it will actually be there after two hundred years,' said George.

'Okay, are you ready?'

He nodded.

'1 1 8 8 8 7.' She stressed each number before moving onto the next.

George carefully punched the digits into the keypad, and Cara waved her crossed fingers in the air. They heard the satisfying click of the vault unlocking and looked at each other. George reached out and pulled the door open to make sure it didn't lock again by mistake.

Cara looked at him, her eyes wide. 'Thank God. I can breathe again.'

'Me too.' George exhaled and then knelt down by the vault door. 'Ready to see what's inside?'

Cara dropped down next to him and he pulled the door wide, so they could both see the interior of the vault. The contents were brightly lit by an internal light which was activated when the door opened.

'That looks like it could be the painting,' said George. 'I still don't remember stashing it here.'

He extended his arm and touched the slim wrapped package. He held it gently, brought it out of the safe and then tentatively laid it on the table.

'My heart's beating like crazy,' said Cara. 'I can't stand the suspense. Please open it.'

George unwrapped the faded layers of paper to reveal the

top of a watercolour painting, and then eased it out. He sneezed as the dust from two centuries tickled his nostrils.

Cara gasped. 'It's actually worked. I can't believe we've done it!'

The picture was coated in a film of dust but seemed in otherwise perfect condition.

'I don't know much about art, but it's stunning,' Cara said.

George put his arm around her shoulders and they stepped back to view the painting. He whistled. 'Unbelievable. Two hundred years it's been sitting here, and we knew nothing about it until recently.'

Cara looked at him. 'Hmm.'

'What,' he said.

'Well, yes and no. It was only here for two hundred years in the latest version of events. You rewrote history when you stored the painting and hid the key.'

George looked at her, pondered, and then said, 'That's true. And it looks as though we got away with it.'

'I didn't want to distract you when you were keying in the code, but those numbers are curiously significant.'

George raised an eyebrow and looked at her.

'I remember the number eight from reading about numerology. It signifies infinity because it has no beginning or end. And I think three eights together like in the code, symbolise abundance,' she said.

'Woo! That's twenty-five million pounds worth of abundance, all going to plan. Just from a little trip to Chelsea one fine and sunny Victoriana morning.'

Cara kissed him. All was right with their world. 'Perhaps time travel isn't that bad, after all.'

London, Five days later – Present day

Cara and George sat at their solicitor's desk in his Aldgate office.

The door opened, and he said, 'Thank you for waiting. I've got the contract, please read it over and sign here. The painting was released in your name, so we only need your signature,' he said, indicating the space for George to sign.

'So much for women's rights,' said Cara, rolling her eyes.

'No such thing in Victorian times, where did we go wrong?' George replied.

Cara play-punched his arm, 'What's the old saying? "What's yours is mine and what's mine is mine",' she smiled sweetly and batted her eyelashes at him.

'Everything I have is yours; it's not worth anything without you, anyway,' he said, suddenly serious.

'How gallant,' observed the solicitor, dryly. 'I assure you that's not the attitude most of my clients adopt. Mind you; I'd be out of a job if they did.'

'Thank you for organising this so quickly. I meant to ask before; who is the buyer?' said Cara while George reviewed the contract.

'I'm afraid one of the terms of the quick cash sale is that I don't reveal the name of the buyer; the purchase is to remain completely confidential.'

'Isn't that rather clandestine?' Cara asked.

'A little unusual, but not altogether uncommon. There can be all manner of reasons for a collector not revealing their identity. There are many art collectors who opt to keep their acquisitions private.'

'Okay, well that's their prerogative, I suppose,' said Cara. 'As long as they're paying the agreed twenty-five million, we have no need to know.'

'It's extraordinary really, isn't it?' remarked George.

'What?' she asked, tilting her head closer to his as the solicitor rose from his chair again and busied himself copying the signed document.

'That anyone would pay so much money for a painting.'

'When you put it like that, it is, yes. I'm glad they did though,' she said.

They finished up their business and left the solicitor's office with a copy of the contract tucked inside George's vegan leather satchel that Cara had bought for him recently.

She broke into an excited skip on the pavement outside the office. 'I love it when you carry that man-bag. It's so sexy.'

'You really can be very silly, you know,' he said smiling at her infectious mood. 'Women's rights have come so far, and all we get is a man-bag. You could at least let me enjoy the small victory without making me feel like such a cock.'

They strode along the pavement, hand-in hand. 'You did it! Twenty-five million pounds courtesy of Victoriana. I can hardly believe we pulled it off. I'm so excited I could burst.'

George pulled on her hand, so she swung towards him and then he caught her in his arms. 'Me too. There's no-one in the world with whom I would rather buy a house.'

'Don't you mean a stately home? Or a hotel, actually?'

They were high on life and almost flew down the street.

'I feel like the luckiest woman in the world. Not only do I get to be with the love of my life, or I should say, *lives*, but we will now get to live at Willow Manor. I know it's a huge undertaking, but I couldn't be more thrilled.'

'It is incredible. If I was a religious man, I would say we're blessed.'

'We're blessed by time,' said Cara, her heart full.

'Kate was asking some questions on the phone. We're going to have to come up with some kind of cover story about the vault and the painting. I hate deceiving her, but I don't want her thinking we've cheated her out of the family spoils.'

'Kate trusts you implicitly,' she said.

'Which makes keeping the truth from her, all the more difficult, but we can't tell her what really happened. She'll think we're deranged.'

'It'll be okay. She's terrific; we're fortunate to have her.'

'Yes, and when you think she wouldn't be my sister at all, but for Eddie's failed time travel experiment,' said George.

'I know. And I might never have realised you were free if she hadn't called me and left that message.'

'Let's not think about that, my darling. It all worked out for the best and we have our whole life ahead of us. I can't wait to move into Willow Manor and have the family over,' he said, his excitement building as the prospect of their new reality kicked in.

Cara leaned over to kiss him as they walked towards the tube station. 'It's been so hectic lately we've barely had a quiet moment to be together,' she said.

'Ah, I know that tone. Are you lusting after my gorgeous body, again?'

'Always.'

'I love that,' he said.

'What?'

'How open you are about expressing your sexual appetite.'

'It's only with you,' she said.

'I should bloody well hope so!'

'Seriously, I've never fancied anyone in the way I do you,' she said.

'I suppose there must be some truth to this Twin Flame prophecy,' he said.

'All I know is; when we're together, life is wonderful, whatever we're doing. Let's keep it like this, forever George,' she said, fear clouding her eyes.

'Of course. And you know what, we already have the perfect life. I'm going to stop dwelling on Victoriana and focus on enjoying our life here.'

'I think that is one of the biggest lessons we're supposed to learn. When we live in the moment and are grateful for what we have, things have a way of working out.'

They reached Aldgate Tube Station and headed through the busy entrance into the bowels of the Underground.

'How's Jane?' said Cara.

'She's doing well and said she'll come and visit soon.'

Cara didn't know how she would have lived with herself if George had lost his daughter. Fortunately, she had appeared in his new life as if nothing had changed.

Sylvia explained that some places and some people were just meant to be in your life. No timeline reset could change that.

'Did you make the offer?' asked George.

Cara nodded. 'I texted from the solicitor's office.'

When do you think we'll hear if it's been accepted?'

'Not sure. I'll ping the agent and nudge him if we don't hear from him soon. There's no reason to delay now.'

'Do you want to stay over in London or shall we head home?'

Cara looked into his eyes and knew he wanted to return to York. 'Let's get the next train home.'

'Oh lovely. I'm shattered and can't wait to get back. Just as well we're both not great fans of bright lights and big city life,' he said.

They enjoyed the occasional trip to London but one day was enough, and they'd been back and forth more than usual lately.

'Twin Flames, my darling. Twin Flames,' she said, raising her face to his as they kissed before alighting from the tube at King's Cross.

Cara knew George was right. They must both live in the moment and seize the day instead of constantly thinking about the other timelines. She didn't want them to miss the wonderful life they had created. They settled into their seats and she looked forward to the relaxing train journey from London to York. She had to trust everything was working out in Tudorville because there was nothing more she could do from here. And there was nowhere she would rather be right now, than here with her husband.

An hour later she drifted off to sleep and dreamed of the day they would move into Willow Manor. Then she awoke in a panic. 'What happened to Willow Manor?' she said.

George glanced up from his book, 'Nothing, my love. Hush, you were dreaming, that's all. We're about halfway; go back to sleep. I'll wake you up when we're almost there.'

Cara's head rested against the seat as the train sped through the countryside. Something terrible had happened in her dream but she couldn't remember what. She felt an aching sense of emptiness, as she tried to fall asleep again. Her heart thudded.

It was only a dream. Or was it?

CHAPTER 27

York - Present day

They slept well that night and George awoke to the sound of the birds. He read for a while until Cara stirred.

'Good morning, darling. I'll make us some coffee shortly,' he said, leaning over to kiss her.

After breakfast they wrapped up warm and went for a walk by the river. The sharp wind whipped up the surface of the water into choppy waves and the sky was a dull grey.

'I can't get hold of the agent,' said Cara, running a hand through her windswept tangles.

'Have you tried his office?' asked George.

'I've tried loads of times; the office number just rings and rings, and his personal phone doesn't connect at all.'

'Maybe you mixed up your contacts?'

'I don't think so, but you can take a look when we get back,' she said.

. . .

Later that day, Cara pushed her phone across the coffee table to George, and he intercepted it with one smooth movement.

'What's the surname?'

'Hamilton.'

George checked her address book, typing in several options, before he raised his eyes. 'I can't find any John with that surname or anything like it. Is it J-o-h-n or J-o-n?'

'J-o-h-n, but I searched the other way too.'

'That's odd.'

'I can't see any calls to him in my call log either. Maybe I lost some contacts with my recent update.'

'Possibly.'

'I really think we need to make sure he submitted our offer as I only sent him a quick text. How about we pop over to Willow Manor and see if we can meet the owner? It might be faster that way, anyhow.'

George took a final sip of his tea, grabbed his car keys and said, 'Okay. Let's go.'

It was only two o'clock, but the rain had been lashing down since they hurried in from their walk, and the sky was a moody, purple-tinged grey, and threatened to turn black. Rain drops bounced onto the Porsche's windscreen relentlessly, and then trickled downwards in large pear-shaped droplets before being disrupted by the hectic paced windscreen wipers. Cara shivered and turned the dial up on the heating. The warm air and the motion of the car seduced her into a light doze. She jumped and opened her eyes as the car edged its nose towards the hotel driveway.

'The gates are closed,' said George. 'Didn't you say the hotel was open last time you visited?'

'Yes, and it was full, judging by the carpark and the number of people strolling around the gardens.'

'I'll nip out and see if there's an intercom we can buzz to open the gates,' said Cara, stretching her arms out in front of her. 'It's a shame I didn't think to bring an umbrella.' She pulled her coat on and dashed out of the car, without waiting for George to reply.

He turned on the radio and watched her approach the gates, as he hummed along to a haunting piece of music on the classical music channel.

After a few minutes, Cara turned, moved back towards him, and jumped back into the car. She shook her head; her hair was coated in a sheen of rain and her face was drenched.

'Someone buzzed us in,' she said, wiping the rain drops from her face with a tissue.

The gates swung open, and the sports car passed through the widening gap.

George blinked and stared ahead, frowning. 'Are you seeing what I'm seeing, or am I in a parallel universe?'

Cara looked up from scouring the contents of her handbag, and her eyes widened.

'What's happened to Willow Manor?' he murmured.

'Bloody hell,' she whispered, and turned to George. She swallowed. 'This can only mean one thing. The timeline has reset. It's just like when I went to your workshop last year and it didn't exist anymore...you had disappeared.'

'But, I'm here.'

'Yes—thank God for that. Let's turn around and get out of here,' said Cara, shaking inwardly as she contemplated the potential implications of the timeline reset. 'Let's go home.'

She cast one more glance at the modern complex of luxury apartments where Willow Manor should have been, before George turned the car around and they waited for the gates to open again.

He captured Cara's damp, cold hand in his, then raised it to his lips and planted a warm kiss onto her skin. 'You're right; let's go home.' He was equally shaken but doing his best to stay calm.

'What do you think is going on?' she said.

'I wish I knew.'

They were uncharacteristically quiet during the return journey. The rain strummed on the windows and the classical music hummed gently in the background as the car powered along the wet York roads, and the windscreen wipers swished valiantly back and forth. Cara held George's hand for most of the journey, unable to get a handle on her rising panic. The Porsche finally swung into the lane that led to the cottage. Cara's body tensed even more, and she closed her eyes as the car turned into the cottage entrance. She heard the wheels crunch onto the gravel and waited.

That's a good sign.

'You can open your eyes now. It's all okay, darling.'

Cara's eyes opened, and she let out a long, ragged breath when she saw their wonderful cottage just as they left it.

'Breathe,' said George.

'I don't think I've ever been so relieved to see it. I was scared it wouldn't be here; that it would have vanished just like Willow Manor.'

'I guessed that's what you were worried about.'

'I think we had better call Eddie, later,' she said, her voice tremulous. They ran through the heavy rain and George unlocked the front door.

'Come here,' said George. He held her tightly and she was instantly soothed by his calming proximity.

'I'm shocked about Willow Manor, but I'm grateful you're here. Ever since last year, I've been scared the timeline would reset and I'd lose you again, forever. And now it has, but we're still together,' she said.

They remained like that for a long time, swaying in the cocoon of each other's arms in the cottage hallway, neither of them wanting to break the spell.

. . .

They dined on their favourite supper of spaghetti and George's home-made tomato sauce, which he said was the perfect antidote for a trying day. They cleared up and then Cara called Eddie.

After a quick catch up, Eddie said, 'It's inevitable with all of that stuff going on in the various timelines. It would almost be stranger if nothing changed... Please run through it again; slowly this time, and let's see if we can identify which piece of the puzzle created the quantum time loop and caused Willow Manor to disappear.'

Cara said, 'In a way, I think you're enjoying this, aren't you?'

Eddie chuckled, 'Is it obvious?'

'Yes, it is. We're having a torrid time and you're geeking out on quantum time loops.'

'I'm sorry, my dear. I feel dreadful about what you're both going through. But, it is beneficial for all of us that we make headway with the time travel research. That way we'll be able to understand the cause and effect of our actions, in the future,' said Eddie, his voice loud and echoing around the kitchen.

'I'd love to be able to understand how it works. I feel as though I'm going crazy when I'm trapped in time,' said George.

'We will crack the time travel code, it's just a matter of time; pardon the pun,' said Eddie, peering back at them on video. My theory about the quantum time loops is that they are time's way of pushing back.

'What do you mean?' asked Cara.

'I recently read a novel by Stephen King: *11:22:63*, about time travel. He describes how time pushes back in a chaotic fashion when the characters try to change the timeline; which reminded me of what's been happening with you.'

'Oh, yes I've heard of that book,' said Cara.

'In simple terms, the timelines have unfolded in a certain way, and then there we go, showing up to re-live them and instigating new events with or without realising it,' said Eddie.

'Pass me your phone, please George, and I'll look up Willow Manor while we're on with Eddie. I couldn't face it before, but I feel like I've begun to digest what's happened.'

Cara began searching. 'Nothing's coming up for the hotel-nothing at all. It's as if it never existed.'

'It probably never did in this new sequence of events. The question is what do we need to fix to bring it back and is it worth it?' said Eddie.

'Worth bringing it back? It's our family estate; of course it's worth bringing back,' Cara exploded.

'But we must also consider the ramifications of changing what's already been done. We might lose something even more important, such as one of you.'

Cara stared mournfully at George, who reached out and touched her arm. 'I can't see anything online except some links about the original estate. Hang on, let me click through and see where they lead.'

Cara scanned the content for a few minutes, and then read aloud, "Willow Manor, a Tudor Estate, once owned by the Cavendish Family, and considered one of the most beautiful estates in Yorkshire, fell into disrepair in the eighteenth century."

'Stop there,' said Eddie. 'That's interesting.'

'What is?' said Cara and George in unison.

'That tells us that in this new reality, the Willow Manor estate survived beyond the Pilgrimage of Grace.'

'Okay, well that's promising. But what happened after that? It doesn't necessarily mean that George is out of danger, does it?'

'True and that's exactly why we must find out why the

timeline reset now and caused Willow Manor to suddenly disappear,' said Eddie.

'Wait a minute... Eddie?' said Cara.

'Oh, I know that face. Tell me what's just landed in that head of yours,' he said.

'I have a strong feeling that the timeline reset has something to do with Ralph.'

'Ralph! Who on earth is Ralph?' said George, looking at her, baffled.

Cara looked away from the phone and turned to face George. 'Ralph is the blue-eyed guy who's been following me through time. The one Eddie said must be a karmic warrior. His name just came to me... I can't explain how but I know it's to do with him.'

'Do you remember in which timeline you knew each other?' asked Eddie.

'No. Maybe it'll come to me. Sylvia said to watch our backs because he's coming for us.' Cara shivered.

'You're cold,' said George, reaching for her, and rubbing his warm hands up and down her cold, pale forearms. He unfolded a blanket from one of the chairs and draped it around her shoulders. I'd better light the fire.'

'A chill ran through me at the thought of him. It happened when we were in London too. I think there's a lot more to this story than I realised,' said Cara.

'We can only go on what we have now, but we mustn't drop the ball on saving George from the abbey. We must get him to safety in Tudorville; perhaps that will restore the timeline. My guess is it may be as simple as getting him out of the danger of being tangled up with the doomed rebels. Of course, we won't know for sure until we do it,' said Eddie.

'Simple?' said Cara. 'I don't think it'll be that simple. Just the three of us; unarmed, having to break George out from under the noses of a band of angry rebels in the midst of a busy working monastery full of Benedictine monks.'

'You have a point, but what choice do we have?' asked Eddie.

'None, as usual. It's out of our control anyway. I bet we're breaking him out as we speak,' said Cara.

After the call ended, George said, 'Living in the moment with all this stuff going on hundreds of years ago, isn't quite as easy as it sounds, is it?'

'It's a bloody nightmare,' said Cara, moving her head from side to side. 'I'm terrified we're going to mess everything up again.' She drew closer to the fire, still shaking.

George poured them both a drink. 'Here,' he said, pressing a crystal glass filled with a generous shot of golden-brown whisky into her hand. 'You're in shock, drink that; it'll do you good.'

CHAPTER 28

St. Mary's Abbey, York, 1536 - Tudorville

Cara saw the astonished, pale-faced monk with a ring of hair encircling his smooth, gleaming bald head.

My God: it's a real-life Tudor Benedictine monk.

Her historian's fascination took over and she gaped at him.

'What's going on?' The monk whispered as he scanned the faces of George's rescue team, his vow of silence forgotten as he closed the door behind him.

George stepped forwards as he spoke. 'You treated me well in my short time here, and I'd like to thank you.'

'You're a good man, my lord; I was sorry to see you imprisoned like a common criminal. But if you are to escape you must hurry.'

'Thank you,' said Cara, finding her voice.

The monk smiled at her and she thought he had the

kindest eyes she'd ever seen. The man was a good soul, that much was evident.

She took a deep breath and tried to steady her racing heart. 'Brother Grayson is there another way out of here?'

A look of surprise at the sound of his name played over the monk's plain features.

'I saw one of the ringleaders arrive on horseback, you must avoid him at all cost, I don't want blood on my hands. Come, follow me...we must hurry before he comes to look for Lord Cavendish. On his last visit, he said he was planning on moving him today.'

They hurried, silently and in single file after Brother Grayson who opened the door to one of the rooms on the opposite side of the building. He signalled them to follow him into the room and then to close the door. Once inside, they watched him expertly move a section of the carpet aside and tap on the floor, looking for a certain spot. After a few minutes, he found what he was looking for and the wooden floorboard swung open, revealing a black hole.

They heard conversation and movement, and Cara's heart skipped from a fast, dull thud back into a rapid staccato beat which shook her chest as thoughts of what would happen if they were caught by the blue-eyed rebel, flooded her mind. 'Hurry, hurry,' she said. 'Someone's coming,' the words sounded strangled in her fear-constricted throat.

'This is a secret passage we dug out a few years ago. Hurry now—all of you—jump down as quickly as you can. He mustn't see you or we'll all hang for it.'

'Where will we come out?' asked Edward.

'Follow the path, and when you reach the end, look for a small tunnel—you'll have to crawl through and it will take you to the outskirts of the abbey and into the forest. You should be able to see enough with the light from above ground to be able to find your way. Be careful when you come out in case they realise you escaped.'

Swifty's sturdy frame flitted into the hole and his head disappeared down the ladder. Cara went next, looking anxiously at George and Edward as the black hole swallowed her up, and then Edward followed.

George turned to Brother Grayson and grasped his hand, 'Thank you, Brother. I know the risks you are taking by helping us like this. I'm forever in your debt. If there's ever anything you need you will always be welcome at Willow Manor,' he whispered.

'Thank you, my lord. Please hurry before we are caught, I will try and distract them from discovering your absence.' Brother Grayson blessed him with the sign of the cross, before George slipped into the hole to join the others. George moved his feet slowly down the rungs of the narrow ladder and saw the slit of light from above vanish as the monk concealed the hole. He reached the others waiting for him at the bottom. He could make out Cara's form in the thin shard of pale morning light and he reached for her and pulled her gently towards him.

There was a lump in her throat as she clung to him. 'Thank God we found you. I've been going out of my mind since we lost contact. Are you all right? How badly are you hurt?'

'Hush, my love, I'm all right now you're here,' he said, holding her tightly against him and smoothing her hair away from her eyes and kissing her forehead. 'We must make haste,' he said in a louder voice so that Edward and Swifty would hear.

They set off through the freezing underground passage, and Cara felt George shiver. 'You are weak and cold, here take your cloak.'

'My cloak?'

'Yes, I had to disguise myself for the journey. It's a long story. I wore it to keep me warm on my journey from Windsor to Willow Manor.'

'I wondered how you got here but there was a part of me that knew you were on your way; I can always sense when you're near. You wear it, my love. It's freezing down here.' He pulled the fur-trimmed hood over her head and touched her cheek. 'My page boy wife,' he said, his voice catching.

They moved quickly through the dimly lit passage; there was nowhere to go but forward.

'How clever of the monks to connect that room up with a passage to jump down for a quick escape. The poor things must have been living in terror since the beginning of the Dissolution of the Monasteries,' said Cara.

'Where did you leave the horses?' asked George.

'We tethered them in a hidden clearing by the river to disguise their noise in case they should become restless,' Cara whispered.

Even a loud whisper echoed around the underground tunnel and she was wary of their chatter being overheard. She estimated they must already be out from beneath the abbey and on their way into the forest.

Several minutes passed as they walked through an unlit portion of the passage, Cara stumbled and felt George's hands steady her from behind. He was slow bringing up the rear and she kept turning to check on him. 'Are you all right?' she asked.

He reached for her hand and squeezed it as he said, 'I'm fine. I'm overjoyed to be getting away though.'

Swifty turned and whispered, 'I think we're nearing the end of the passage. Here's the door.'

'Brother Grayson said there's some kind of secret tunnel we need to crawl through,' said Edward.

They fumbled around searching for the hidden exit until

Edward said, 'I think this is it. We'll need to get on our knees to enter by the looks of it.'

One-by-one, Edward leading, Swifty behind him and Cara and George following, they entered the confined space and began crawling through it.

Cara held back a scream, and let out a low whimper, as something brushed against her ankle.

'All right?' whispered George near Cara's ear.

'I think a rat just ran over my ankle.'

'Let's go as quickly as we can, and we'll soon be out of here,' he said.

A few minutes later, they saw a stream of light drifting into the gloomy, damp tunnel, and Edward whispered, 'Right, we're near the exit point. Are you ready to make a run for it through the forest?'

Cara longed to be back in the fresh air, but she stiffened as they heard voices.

A commanding voice said, 'You go that way, and I'll look around here. He can't have gone far.'

'Yes, Sir.'

George whispered, 'Sounds like they don't know the rest of us are here, so Brother Grayson must have managed to get back downstairs without giving us away.'

'What shall we do?' asked Edward.

'I think we'd better wait for him to check the area and move on.' George raised his finger to his lips, and they huddled in the cramped space.

'There's not much air,' said Cara. 'We need to get out of here soon.'

George reached for her hand. 'We will. Let's give him a few minutes and then we'll make a run for it.'

Cara's heartbeat still raced erratically, and she struggled to breathe as feelings of panic overcame her. She took some deep breaths of the thin cold air and rested her head against

George's shoulder and closed her eyes to try and calm herself.

The four of them were wedged beside one another, and they stopped talking and tried not to move. They didn't want to risk attracting attention now when they were so close to freedom.

The seconds and minutes felt like hours as they passed by, until George said, 'It's been quiet for a while. Let's make a dash for it; where's the exit?'

Swifty said, 'I can see it up there, there's some kind of covering we need to move. Shall I climb up and do it?'

'Thank you, Swifty, yes, please go carefully.'

Swifty manoeuvred his feet up the mud wall and scooted up to the top like a professional cat burglar. 'There are ledges to rest your feet on as you climb,' he whispered.

'You two go,' said George to Edward. 'We'll follow. If you see anyone just make a run for it towards the horses and get away if you can. Don't wait for us.'

One-by-one they crawled up the mud wall, Swifty had already emerged and was helping Edward out onto the damp forest bed.

'All clear,' he whispered.

Cara was next and crawled onto her knees and then jumped up and gulped huge breaths of the cold fresh forest air. 'Come on George,' she whispered, as he appeared.

Swifty who had lived on the streets for years and was alert to every noise, put his finger to his lips and made a hissing sound. They all stopped as they heard a loud voice in the distance.

'We can't let him get away. He must still be in the area. Let's continue searching.'

'We're out of time,' whispered George. 'Where are the horses?'

'That way to the river,' said Swifty. 'Let's go through the trees and we should come out in the clearing.'

They walked as fast as they could, trying to avoid crunching twigs and alerting their pursuers to their presence, deftly brushing through the tree branches.

Cara was soaked from the early morning dew on the leaves and reached for George's hand as she saw him slowing. 'You are badly hurt. You're limping,' she said.

'That bastard gave me a beating or two; my leg's a bit swollen,' he said quietly.

And then they heard the neighing of one of the horses, and the bubbling flow of the river.

'Here we are,' said Cara, feeling hopeful for the first time since they entered the monk's secret escape tunnel. 'I feel as though we've reached the Garden of Eden.' She offered up a silent prayer as she jumped onto her horse. George climbed up behind her, with a helping hand from Edward.

George said, 'Ride like the wind.'

Cara heard shouts and dug her heels into the horse's flanks, not looking back. She was too afraid she would see her blue-eyed nemesis.

'Hold on tight,' she said, her hair flying behind her as George grasped her waist and moved his head to rest lightly on her shoulder. A warm glow of optimism permeated his chest, and he kissed Cara's exposed neck as the wind ruffled his hair and he sank into the horse and leaned against her.

He was exhausted but free.

After a short time, George asked to swap over with Cara because he was in danger of falling asleep. When they set off again, he guided the horse carefully around the maze of tall boughs and across the leaf strewn forest floor.

Cara looked up and glimpsed the crisp blue sky through the web of emerald green tree tops, and thanked God for their lucky escape. 'I think we'll be out of the forest and on the road to Willow Manor, any minute,' she whispered, as she nestled into George's back.

'I can't wait to be at Willow Manor, again. Thank you for saving me from the abbey, my love. Isn't it supposed to be the other way around, with the knight in shining armour rescuing the princess from the tower?'

'Oh, that's so old fashioned. Things are going to be very different in years to come,' she said.

'Are you predicting the future again, my darling?'

'Something like that.' She hugged him. 'I'm just so grateful to have you back in my arms. I was terrified the rebels would drag you on their pilgrim's march.'

'It was all very strange, I must say, I am relieved to be out of that madness. I daresay the king won't be pleased about me returning without a signed peace agreement, but I'll have to hope Norfolk gets the job done.'

'What happened exactly? I heard from the king that you hadn't been in touch and they were concerned you were being used as some kind of pawn. And then, the queen warned me that Cromwell suspected you had gone over to the rebels and she heard him planting the seed of doubt in the king's mind.'

'What? That's preposterous. As you know, I went there in good faith by order of the king, but I found I was too late to persuade Robert and Darcy away from the cause. They'd already taken the Pilgrims' Oath and the rebels were holding Pontefract Castle as their command centre with Darcy's blessing. I am afraid the king will not judge him kindly.'

'Yes, we heard as much. I was scared you'd be named a traitor because of your friendship with them, and your allegiance to the north. That's why I knew I must come and find you at any cost. The king's loyalty flip flops faster than a jellied eel so we mustn't leave our fate in his hands.'

George chuckled. 'You do come out with the strangest

expressions, my love. What on earth is a jellied eel? Damn,' he winced.

'You poor thing, you're in a bad way.'

'I'm all right, my ribs are a bit sore, that's all.'

'I shall take care not to amuse you any further then, my lord,' said Cara.

'That man had the most piercing blue eyes I've ever seen. I swear they drilled right into my soul, and unfortunately blue-eyes didn't much care for what he saw there and didn't care much for me at all. He took great pleasure in kicking me in the ribs and anywhere else his expensive toecap landed,' said George.

'My poor love; we must be wary of him. He's an evil bastard.'

'Do you know of him, then? He kept asking questions about you as if he knew you. I suspected there must be a tie of which I was unaware.'

'I don't know much, but remember how before you left, I warned you about the future and how you must take extra care with the rebels because it wouldn't go well for them?'

George nodded. 'Did I mess things up? I tried to follow your advice, but tension was at boiling point at the castle.'

'You didn't mess anything up. It's not your fault. This man has got it in for both of us. Let's just say he's an enemy from another time—I'll explain more later. Tell me, was it him who kidnapped you from the castle and held you hostage at St. Mary's?'

'I believe it was on his instruction. He seems to have a senior commanding position within a faction of the rebels, although I've never heard of him before. Lord Darcy didn't speak highly of him and I doubt he was aware they took me. The man's name is Ralph Knight; I heard one of the guards at the abbey, talking about him in the garden beneath the window.'

'It's just as I feared. We'll go to Willow Manor, so you can rest for a day or two, and see the children, but then we must hurry back to court.'

George steered the horse around a ditch and Cara clung on to stay steady in her seat.

'And what of my parents? Are they well?' George asked.

'I'm sorry to say you're not going to see them this time because they are away. The quicker we get back to Windsor Castle, the better. If there's anywhere we'll be safe from the rebels and this blue-eyed madman, it's there. They're fortifying London better than Fort Knox.'

'What?' said George.

'Never mind,' said Cara. 'It's a silly expression I picked up. I know it will be hard to leave the children, but it's too dangerous for us in York, now, and we'll only put the family in harm's way if we stay. We must be under the protection of the king and give Cromwell no grounds to accuse you of sympathising with the rebels.'

They rode a while longer and then George reined the horse to a stop and asked Cara to pass the flask from her saddlebag. They rested against each other on the horse and took a few sips of the ale, looking around the peaceful forest.

Birds chirped in the trees; the branches rustling in the gentle breeze, and Cara breathed a sigh of relief. They had put quite a bit of distance between themselves and the abbey.

She returned the flask to the saddlebag and they prepared to resume their journey.

'I don't think he knows about Fort Knox, Lady Cara,' boomed the loud, commanding voice from behind them.

Cara screamed.

'There's a musket in my back,' she said, a few seconds later.

'What?' George turned, and his eyes clashed with a pair of piercing blue ones. 'You—what the hell do you want with us?'

'Listen carefully; follow my instructions and no one will get hurt,' he said. His voice was resonant and hypnotic, and weirdly familiar to Cara's ears.

'What do you want us to do?' said George, his velvety deep voice, low and reasoned.

'Get off the horse and join your friends. Instruct them you will all go on ahead without the lady. If you try and interfere I will kill you all. Believe me when I tell you so.'

Cara stared at George. 'Please do as he says, my love. I will be all right and will come to you soon.'

'I'm not leaving you with this fiend,' said George. 'If you want her, you will have to take me too,' he challenged.

'You seem to think there's room for negotiation. You're mistaken, and if you don't do as I instruct, I will kill her now, right in front of you,' said the blue-eyed karmic warrior.

George whistled to catch Edward and Swifty's attention, who had charged ahead on the forest trail. He called out his instructions as they trotted back towards them. They stopped and stayed in the same spot, waiting.

'Ride on and leave us. We have some business here,' said George.

Cara said, 'No, please wait; Lord Cavendish is coming with you.'

'I'm not leaving,' said George, his voice gritty.

Knight pushed the cold metal muzzle hard against Cara's temple. 'You always were a pompous arse, with your fancy title and estate. But this time, it's my turn to call the shots. Leave now or one of the shots will be straight into her head.'

'Be a man; let her go and take me instead,' said George.

'No, I'm not here for you. She's mine. You stole her and now I've come to reclaim my property. You've led me on quite a chase as it is.'

'Are you quite mad, Sir? We don't even know you. She's

my wife, how can she be your property? This must be a classic case of mistaken identity,' said George.

'The only mistake is the one you're making. I'll give you one more chance. Go with your friends here or watch her die. Now.'

George held up his hands.

'All right, all right, please stop pointing that thing at her. I'll leave as you instruct, but what do you want in return for her release?'

'George, I'll be fine. Please go with the others. The gentleman and I appear to have unfinished business. It's too complicated to explain now, but I'll follow you soon.'

Knight grasped Cara tightly by the arm, the musket still pressed firmly into her temple, forming a dent in her pale flesh. 'It's time to let her go, my lord.' He spat out the noble form of address.

George touched Cara's waist as a silent gesture of allegiance and helped her to dismount the horse.

'Go now, or I'll shoot her,' said Knight, his patience at an end.

George urged the horse on reluctantly and turned to look back at Cara, his expression, desolate. The karmic warrior pulled her up behind him and George watched them gallop away into the distance on the beautiful black stallion he had seen at the abbey.

His heart shook; the loss of her was a physical blow which ripped unchecked through his body and senses. He jumped off his horse, clutched his sides and retched violently, as Edward and Swifty looked on, helpless.

George slumped down on to a fallen bough of a tree, his head resting in his hands.

What kind of sap am I to just let her leave with him like that?

CHAPTER 29

The forest, York, 1536 - Tudorville

George and Edward stood in a clearing in the forest, reeling from the events of the morning. Edward had sent Swifty down to the river with the horses, so he and George had the chance to talk alone.

'You did the right thing, my lord. I believed him when he said he would shoot her if you didn't let her go with him.'

George shook his head, 'That may be so, but we must get her back. God knows what he means to do to her. Who is this fellow?'

'I must tell you something that will likely sound just as crazy as what that man did, perhaps even more so...but I ask you to trust me,' said Edward.

'I trust you with my life, Edward; and the lives of my family. If you know something that will help us to save Cara, then I'm willing to go along with just about anything. Pray tell me what's on your mind.'

'My lord, I ask you to suspend all disbelief as I tell you something that will sound so fantastical and outrageous that you may think me quite delusional.'

George looked at Edward, he felt as though his heart was breaking apart, and every muscle in his aching body throbbed. 'Let's rest here a moment while you tell me, and we await Swifty's return.'

And just like that, Edward told George how they were alive together in the twenty-first century, and that's how Cara knew the fate of the rebels, and why she had repeatedly tried to warn him they were doomed to execution in 1537.

'Let's say I have suspended all disbelief, for that's surely what it takes to believe this magnificent account. What of this man, Knight? What is his connection to Cara?' George asked, shaking his head.

'We have a problem; as I explained, we live in other timelines, but we don't necessarily remember everything that happens. In this timeline, you and Swifty are both sleeper travellers—neither of you remember our other lives together, whereas Lady Cara and I are conscious of at least two other timelines,' said Edward.

'So Swifty is involved in the time travelling, too? By God's bones,' said George as he clawed at scraps of reason in the midst of the whirling mayhem which gripped his skull. 'But this still doesn't explain why he took Cara.'

'The thing is, my lord, this man has been following you both for a while now, and at first, Lady Cara didn't know who he was, but a friend of ours who has special powers, saw in a vision that he is someone from another life. You and Lady Cara were together in yet a different timeline; we think it must have been during the eighteenth century. We don't know the details, but this man and Cara were childhood sweethearts, and when you and Cara met, you naturally fell madly in love because you're what's known as Twin Flames.

You are soul mates, destined to always reunite on your spiritual journey, and in your case, a journey of five centuries or perhaps even more.'

George looked stunned. 'This is an extraordinary tale. So, if I've understood correctly, you're talking about a time that's not even happened yet. A time still to come...the eighteenth century, you say? Assuming all of this is true, why is this man hunting her down here in 1536?'

'I'm afraid the tale grows ever more complex, my lord.'

George ran his hands through his dishevelled hair. 'Go on...'

'I believe this man; Ralph Knight, I think is his name, belongs to a group of souls known as Karmic Warriors. I had heard about them but don't know him personally. It seems he has the ability to travel through time as we do, perhaps even backwards and forwards on demand. Judging by what he said, he believes you stole Cara from him, and it looks as though he's been biding his time and now means to exact his revenge.'

'Time travelling—Twin Flames and karmic warriors. My head is spinning,' said George.

Swifty approached. 'Best we don't complicate matters further by trying to explain this to the lad, just now. His moment of truth will come. For now, it's safest to keep the circle of information as small as possible. I don't need to tell you we could all be burned for even speaking of such things.'

'Yes, quite so,' replied George. 'But we can't leave Lady Cara in the hands of this brute.'

George's hand was pressed to his side and he looked like he may pass out.

'Agreed, but you're in no state to rescue her now, and we have no weapons. We don't know where he's taken her and you're far too weak to launch a counterattack. You must rest, and we must bind your ribs. Let us go home to Willow Manor, and return later with weapons and reinforcements,' said Edward. If we go after her now when he expects us, we would likely put her in even greater danger.'

Cara's heart pounded, and she clung onto Ralph as he pushed the black stallion relentlessly onwards, and the distance between her and George grew. She was reluctant to touch him but would fall off if she didn't.

'Where are you taking me?' she said.

'You'll see soon enough,' he replied. His voice sliced through the air like a poison arrow.

Cara trembled at the thought of what he meant to do to her, and she sensed George's spirit was as low as hers. Tears welled in her eyes and spilled silently down her face as they rode. She wouldn't give this man the satisfaction of hearing her cry. It was the thought of George, bereft, not understanding what was going on that overwhelmed her.

After what seemed like hours, Ralph brought the black stallion to an abrupt halt. 'Get down, and don't try anything foolish or you'll pay the price,' he said, his voice full of menace.

How is this man someone I loved?

'Ralph, I'm afraid there must be some mistake. You said something about us having been together, but I don't know you. This is all just a terrible misunderstanding.'

'I feared you wouldn't remember. After all, our time hasn't come yet, has it? But it will. And you will rewrite it for us, my love.' He softened for a second and brushed his fingers across her cheek, emotion shining in his manic blue eyes.

'I'm not your love,' said Cara, a chill rippled through her body and she pulled away from his touch.

'No, you're not. But you will be. You destroyed our love. You destroyed me; you heartless vixen. But now it will all be different, you'll see. The timeline will be rewritten, and the future will reset. Things between us will be wonderful again—like in the early days. You are the one who made a dreadful error, but now you have the chance to put it right and redeem yourself.'

'I have no idea what you're talking about, Sir. No idea, at all. My husband is Lord Cavendish whom you have had the pleasure of meeting, and we have been married for several years.'

Ralph growled, 'And what about two hundred years from now? Do you remember anything about what happened between us, then, my dear Caroline?'

'How on God's earth, am I to remember what happens in the future?' Cara said, purposely looking blank. During the long journey, she had decided the best way to handle him was to act as though she had no knowledge of the future. Perhaps he would leave her alone when he saw he'd got it all wrong.

'You are not getting off that easily, Lady Cara Cavendish,' he enunciated each syllable. 'You're a countess too, now, I understand.'

Cara snapped, 'That's right, and what business is it of yours, Sir?'

'You are destined to be my wife, not his. You will see.'

He spoke with such chilling certainty that Cara began to doubt herself. She knew they were connected, but she couldn't remember how.

'If what you say is true, why are we in 1536, and not in the future you speak of?' she asked.

'You killed our future. You were my Caroline; my dearest beloved, until you met him and forsook me. You broke my heart and I've been burning in karmic-hell ever since. But no more. It's our turn again now, and you owe it to me to put things right. Now I've found you once again, you are mine.'

Cara bent her head and retched on the carpet of green and gold leaves that lined the forest floor. She prayed she was dreaming, and she would awaken soon from this hellish nightmare. She longed to be in George's arms again.

But no such luck was to befall her; instead Ralph grabbed her arm and pulled her along behind him through an opening which revealed a small cave. He pushed her roughly towards a rock on the ground. 'Sit there while I make up a fire before we rewrite history.'

Cara could feel George's despair in her soul—they were always connected even when physically apart. She knew he was going out of his mind and would want to come for her. But how would he know where she was? She calculated they'd been weaving through the forest for at least an hour and she looked about her in the dimly lit cave. She saw some of her captor's belongings scattered about; it looked like he had brought her to his den. Cara hugged her knees into her chest and rocked back and forth on her makeshift rock-seat.

How did he think she would rewrite history? And why did he call her Caroline?

An image of George appeared in her mind, and she heard him say, 'I love you—we will be reunited soon.'

Exhausted, Cara drifted off and then awoke with a jolt to the sound of her captor's voice.

'Caroline, warm yourself at the fire and I'll heat up something for you to eat,' he said. A gentleness she hadn't heard before permeated his tone.

She warmed her hands next to the blazing orange flames of the fire, grateful for the unexpected comfort. She heard Ralph moving about behind her in the depths of the cave.

While she slept he had scattered lamps about which cast an eerie glow around his den.

He handed her a bowl of warm pottage, and Cara hungrily drank the thick broth and nibbled at a hunk of hard, dry bread. The broth warmed her from within and she began to feel stronger. When they finished eating, he cleared away and then came to sit next to her. 'We're about to begin. First, drink some of this to soothe your nerves.'

She sniffed the contents of the cup; it was whisky, and she took a few sips.

'Drink a bit more; it will help you enter into a receptive state of mind,' he said.

'A receptive state of mind for what?' Cara asked.

A flash of irritation crossed his handsome features and he said, 'I told you we are going to rewrite history. If I could do it without you, I would have already done so. I need you to do your bit which is why you're here.'

He laid his hand on her shoulder and she shuddered and pulled away.

'I don't know who you think I am, but I don't have the bloody power to rewrite history,' she said.

He made a tut-tut sound. 'And yet, you talk like a woman not from this time. How do you explain that, my darling Caroline?'

'Who the hell is Caroline?'

'My goodness, we are going to have to do something about your vile tongue, my love. You talk like a village whore, not like the sweet, innocent girl I fell in love with, or the fine lady you became,' he said.

Cara shook her head and said, 'Look, Master Knight.'

'Call me Ralph, that's what you used to call me,' he said, reaching for her hand.

'Look Ralph, I'm deeply sorry for any pain I inadvertently caused you, but you have to believe me, I have no idea who you are, and this has been an awful mistake. You can let me go and I will see to it that my husband doesn't pursue justice.' She withdrew her hand slowly; as if hoping he wouldn't notice.

'Oh, I see, will you now? How very noble of you,' a thunderous shadow crossed his handsome face and she saw she had wounded him.

'You really don't remember me?' he asked.

'No, I really don't. I'm sorry. Release me and I will find my own way back through the forest.'

He gripped her chin and stared into her eyes. 'Oh, my darling, Caroline, do you truly think that because you've had a momentary memory lapse, I'm just going to let you go, after all of my efforts? Don't you realise I've been tracking you through time for hundreds of years?'

A deep chill ran through her again. This was even more deadly than she had feared.

'All right, so what is it you want me to do, exactly? Let's get it over with,' she snapped.

'Sip some more of the whisky and we shall begin in a moment. Much like your friend, Sylvia; I too have powers, and I'm going to use them to hypnotise you, so together we will right the wrongs of the future, once and for all.'

He began recanting some strange unfamiliar words, and although she tried to resist, against her will she found herself slipping into a light trance.

'Don't fight it, my love. This is your fate; I'm taking us to our destiny. Once we are reunited you will be absolved of the karmic debt you carry, and I will be freed of my compulsion for revenge. I will be released from the karmic warriors and we will live in bliss, forever,' he said, his blue eyes fiery.

'You are quite unhinged,' said Cara, struggling against the trance-like drugged feeling. 'You don't have to do this. Let me go before it's too late. George will set the king's army on you if you do this.'

'What we share is far more important than anything the king's soldiers could ever do to me. Don't you see that by now, Caroline? Relax, don't fight your fate any longer, my darling one.'

Cara whimpered as the heaviness overcame her and she fell into a deep hypnotic trance.

'Now, don't be afraid, my love. Instead of regressing you to a past life, as is the common practice, we are going to travel together into the future. A future where we are in love, and all is beautiful in our world. We're walking hand in hand on my parents' farm, as we used to. Do you see us?'

'Yes, I see us,' she replied, after a few seconds.

'Good; that's very good, my sweet Caroline,' said Ralph, caressing her hand. 'Let's travel to the day when you told me about accepting the position at Willow Manor.'

He continued to walk her through the events of their eighteenth-century life and guided her into an even heavier state. She fell deeper and deeper under his power and she was no longer in the dirty, dim cave. She was walking in the sunshine across one of the village fields, behind the Knight family's farm. She was bubbling with excitement; almost skipping as she walked next to a young and dashing Ralph Knight.

Oh my God, it is him. He is my friend; no, he's my suitor, and my arm is tucked in his.

'Lady Margaret Cavendish summoned me this morning, we met and at the end of our talk, she offered me the position of live-in lady's companion and governess to her daughter, Olivia Cavendish. The daughter is a pretty little thing; I think you must have seen her passing through the village in her carriage,' said the nineteen-year-old, Caroline, in her high-pitched voice, swinging on Ralph's arm.

'But she's not much younger than you,' said Ralph, his tone flat and lifeless. 'Why would they want you to be her companion? I don't understand.'

A shadow crossed her face; and her glowing smile slipped. She could see he'd hurt her with his thoughtless comment.

'That's not the case. I'm quite a few years older than her, not that it matters. Lady Margaret wants me because she thinks me a suitable companion for her daughter, and I've had a good education under my father's tutorage, unlike most of the village girls left with little more than a command to find a husband,' said the young woman.

Cara watched Caroline; the eighteenth-century version of herself, undeterred by Ralph's obvious disapproval, bounce back in animated fashion and continue to regale him with plans of her future at Willow Manor.

Ralph Knight, his face sombre, sat next to Cara in the cave, and said, 'This is the moment you left me for him. I can see it clearly now; at the time I didn't know what was happening, although I sensed it. Do you see how you abandoned me for your new life? You said you loved me, and we were going to be married, but you left me, and from the minute you stepped into the Cavendish house, things were never the same between us again.'

Cara's eyes were closed, and she shook her head, 'No, Ralph. I never promised to marry you. You said we would marry; I said I wasn't ready to marry, and I must find a meaningful post to contribute to my dear father's income.'

Knight slammed his hand down on his muscular thigh. 'Damn it, Caroline, why must you say such hurtful things? I refuse to listen to any more of this. Now we're going to rewrite history and fix our future, so we will be together, forever.'

Cara was too lost in the vision to break the trance. Her

consciousness was filled with Caroline; she was Caroline. She could feel the young woman's feelings and she read her thoughts as she channelled her.

Caroline was overjoyed at the invitation to be lady's companion to Olivia, and to live at the grand house, Willow Manor.

Then Cara's soul filled with melancholy as she watched herself and Ralph argue, and he forbade her to take the position. Caroline was resolute, but Ralph was stubborn.

'You are to be my wife, not some Cavendish lady's companion, which is just a glorified maid, after all,' he shouted.

Her captor interrupted Cara's thoughts, and said, 'We are now going to rewrite this unpleasant scene in our lives, so it never happens. I made a mistake before—I thought I could fix it myself, but it was not to be. You must never meet him at all—it's too dangerous and you are too susceptible to his charms. You are under my power now, and you will do as I say, do you understand?'

'Yes,' said Cara, her voice faint; her mind was heavy, and she was unable to repel his command.

'You will tell Lady Margaret Cavendish, you have had a change of heart and you must remain at home to take care of your father. You cannot accept her offer.'

Cara's eyelids moved rapidly, but she was silent.

'Is that clear, Caroline?'

'Yes,' she said, nodding her head as waves of sadness consumed her, but she felt herself resign to his will.

'Do I have your word that you'll do as we have said, and you will marry only me, Ralph Arthur Knight, as you promised?'

'Yes, Ralph, I will marry you,' she nodded again, all power to resist had left her and she saw her future as Mrs Knight roll out before her.

Ralph smiled and nodded. He then guided her out of the trance counting slowly as he did so, snapped his thumb and finger together, and Cara's eyes shot open.

'What happened?' she said.

'Do you not remember?'

'You called me Caroline and I was very sad. I don't remember more than that,' she said, rubbing her weary eyes.

'That's good; you did well. It's not necessary for you to remember what happened, only that you will be mine again. Your romance with the lord of the manor has been erased.'

It was all too much for Cara, tears streamed from her eyes and down her face, and loud sobs wracked her body as she bent over, not wanting her nemesis to see he had destroyed her, but unable to control her despair. She had lost George forever.

Ralph reached for her and encircled her in his arms.

'There, there, my love, it will be wonderful, you'll see,' he patted her back.

Her body stiffened; the very touch of him made her nauseous and she feared she would retch again. Cara struggled free and rose swiftly. 'I'm leaving now. I don't know what you expected to happen here after your hypnotic curse but I'm not going to just suddenly love you. I don't even know you.'

The tears dried in her eyes as rage gripped her, and she stood straight-backed and looked him directly in the face. 'You can hypnotise me all you want, it won't make me love you,' she said, and she turned and ran towards the exit of the cave.

'Caroline, you can run but you cannot hide. We will be together again soon; so, go now my love. Go wherever you wish, for you cannot escape me; you cannot escape us. Take care, and I will see you again soon.'

Cara knew he believed every word.

What if he was right and she had no choice but to be with him?

She fled from the cave, looking back every few seconds to check he wasn't following her. His awful prediction confirmed he believed she was his even if she got away.

Cara ran through the forest for what seemed like hours until she could run no more; she collapsed on the ground, exhausted and unable to go any further.

She rested a while, and then raised her weary frame from the mossy forest floor and started walking. After some time, she heard a familiar noise as she approached the edge of a clearing.

And there was the horse she had ridden earlier that morning; waiting for her, tethered to a tree near the river in the same spot as before they went into the abbey to rescue George. She patted the horse as he nuzzled lovingly against her hand, and then she mounted quickly. George must have left her horse for her, hoping she would make it back.

She wondered how he had managed to get away; he would have had to ride with Edward or Swifty. It was just like him to think of her rather than take the horse. She prayed they had got him safely back to Willow Manor to tend to his injuries. Cara could stand anything as long as he was all right. She readied herself to leave and as she pressed her heels gently into the horse's flanks, something caught her eye. Carved in a patch of soil; a few steps to the left, in the bed of the clearing were some letters. She moved closer and read: WM-BTN

Cara smiled at the sight of their code. This proved George was still alive and Ralph's attempt to rewrite history hadn't erased him from this timeline. She jumped down to pick up a stick and stabbed the letters until they were no longer legible and had blended into the soil as though they had never existed.

Willow Manor: Burn this note, was George's secret code to

tell her where to find him and remind her to cover their tracks.

Cara guided her horse through the clearing, and out of the forest and joined the road to Willow Manor. They may not be together in the future but at least he was alive today.

CHAPTER 30

Rose Cottage, York - Present day

George placed a cup of coffee in front of Cara on the table as she sat reading, curled up on the sofa. 'Have you seen Cornelius?' he said.

She winked at George as he sat down next to her. 'Yes. We got you out of the abbey, but then I was kidnapped by that crazy karmic warrior.' She ran her hand over his cropped hair. 'Has Willow Manor reappeared?'

'Not last time I checked. I think we may have lost that piece of our past.'

'I'm worried about Thomas and May,' Cara said.

'I talked to Eddie. He doesn't think they're in danger.' George sipped his coffee and stretched his legs.

'The karmic warrior let me escape after he hypnotised me; he said it didn't matter because he'd rewritten the future anyway.'

'Eddie thinks that Willow Manor disappeared before we

realised it had happened because the time sequence isn't an exact replica across the timelines.'

Cara nodded. 'Makes sense. Sometimes weeks have gone by when it's only days, or even hours there, and vice-versa.'

They phoned Eddie. 'I've run through every scenario and everything points to Willow Manor disappearing after Ralph Knight hypnotised you. It could be too late,' said Edward.

'Too late for what?' asked George.

'Don't you see? If you two don't fall in love in the eighteenth century, perhaps you won't meet in Victoriana either. And we have no idea what the knock-on effects will be.'

After the call, Cara was exhausted and went to take a bath. Her senses were still on high alert. When she came back downstairs, she sat staring out of the window watching daylight steadily creep into night. She turned to George, and said, 'There's only one way to fix this.'

Sylvia's Office, York - Present day

Sylvia came out to meet George and Cara as soon as they stepped through the door. 'Here you are, my loves. You've been on my mind since our phone call.' They took a seat in Sylvia's office. 'So, tell me what happened,' she said.

Cara said, 'Willow Manor has disappeared. It's as if it never existed. We've got the funds lined up and we're ready to make an offer, but we can't because it's gone.'

'And you think it's to do with the man I saw in my vision during your last reading?'

'Yes, exactly,' said Cara. 'In Tudorville, he hypnotised me to rewrite our future so that I would marry him. George and I were in love in the eighteenth century too. What we want to know is whether you can reverse what he did.'

They talked a while longer as Sylvia quizzed them for more details, and then she said, 'Okay, there's no time to waste. If he's a karmic warrior, there are powerful, evil forces at work.'

'What can we do?' Cara asked.

'We will play him at his own game, but we must regress you, so you go back to the past; back to when you were Caroline.'

Cara's stomach churned. 'I didn't like being hypnotised — I was terrified.'

'Yes, it can feel scary, but do you trust me?'

'You know I do.'

'There's nothing to fear. In the worst scenario we won't manage to regress you enough to rewrite the timeline,' said Sylvia.

'That's what I'm most afraid of. I don't want to imagine a life where I bounce about from timeline to timeline, never knowing when I'm going to arrive in the eighteenth century where I'll be married to a karmic warrior who I detest,' Cara said.

George captured her hand, 'Coming here was the right thing to do. Sylvia is our best chance at reversing what he did.'

'You're right. I'm being so feeble—I've got a bad case of cold feet,' she said, squeezing his hand and mustering a weak smile.

'Are you ready to begin?' said Sylvia.

Cara nodded.

'Take several deep, slow breaths, and try and relax. I am going to count backwards as you enter the trance. We know you are receptive to hypnotism or he wouldn't have been able to put you in that state. Follow me, and we will restore the timeline and undo what he did,' said Sylvia.

George watched, fascinated as Cara fell into a hypnotic

trance and Sylvia guided her back to her eighteenth-century life. 'After a few moments, Sylvia asked, 'What's your name?'

'Caroline, my name is Caroline,' Cara replied, softly.

'Where do you live?'

'I live with my father in the village, but I'm soon to be married to my betrothed, Ralph Knight.'

Sylvia glanced over at George and they exchanged a meaningful look, as she said, 'Caroline, can you tell me what year it is?'

'Yes,' she giggled, touching her hair. George gasped. Cara was behaving like a giddy young girl.

'The year is 1729.'

'And how old are you, Caroline?'

'I'm nineteen.'

Sylvia continued to pull Cara ever deeper into the trance as she established a stronger connection with her hypnotic subject. George stared at them both, transfixed; unable to move.

'Are you listening carefully?' asked Sylvia.

She confirmed that she was, and Sylvia began the reversal.

'Ralph Knight is not the man you will marry. You are destined to fall in love with someone else. I don't know if you will marry him, but meet him and fall in love, you will. His name is Lord George Cavendish, and he is the master of Willow Manor.'

'Lord George Cavendish? I know of him. But, surely there must be some mistake. I'm to marry my childhood sweetheart, Ralph.'

'Listen, Caroline. It's critical you don't marry Ralph Knight. He is a dangerous man and is not the one for you. You must accept the position you will be offered at Willow Manor. You must do as I say. Do you understand?'

Sylvia continued to drum her instructions into the

hypnotised Cara's mind, before she turned back to George, and said, 'I've done all I can. I hope it will be enough.'

'How will we know if it's worked?' he asked.

'If what you believe is correct, the eighteenth-century timeline should have reset again, and your past will have been rewritten, which means that Willow Manor should be restored to the here and now. If it's not, then I confess I'm out of tricks,' said Sylvia.

Sylvia instructed Cara to snap out of the hypnotic state and walked her gently back to herself.

Cara opened her eyes, looked at George, and said, 'I don't remember a thing.'

George said, 'For a minute I thought I might be married to a nineteen-year-old giggly girl called Caroline.'

'Did it work?'

'We don't know yet,' he replied.

They stayed and chatted with Sylvia for a while so Cara had a chance to rest before heading back to the car.

Then they eased out of the busy car park and drove to Willow Manor, only exchanging the occasional word. Cara was exhausted. As the car hummed along the road which brought them towards the entrance of the grand estate, she said, 'I can hardly breathe.'

'Same here,' George replied.

'I'm going to close my eyes before we get there. I can't bear the suspense,' she said.

'Okay, well I'd better not close mine.' George swung the car into the entrance of what used to be Willow Manor. After a few seconds, the car came to a halt, and he said, 'You can open your eyes now.'

Cara heard the happy melodious notes in his deep voice, and her eyes flipped open and she saw the familiar open gates and the sandblasted Willow Manor Hotel sign, in front of her.

'Ahhhhh...' she said. Cara threw her arms around George's neck and clung onto him as he held her tightly. 'We've done it,' she said.

'It looks like it,' he said.

Their eyes danced.

George drove slowly along the willow tree lined driveway and they savoured the moment as their five-hundred-year home rose up to greet them like a beloved old friend.

He parked the car and turned to Cara. 'Ready to go in and make the offer?' he asked.

'Almost. I'm just double checking the bank account to make sure nothing weird has happened with the timelines.'

He leaned over towards her. 'Good idea. And?'

She held up the phone, so he could see the bank statement.

'Twenty-five million pounds,' he said, a lilt in his voice.

She kissed him several times, nodded and then they got out of the car and walked hand in hand into the Tudor style hotel.

About an hour later, they sat on the back terrace of the hotel, sipping complimentary coffee, and overlooking what would soon be their estate. The owner had accepted their offer on the spot, explaining that John, the agent who had been handling the sale of the property had advised him only the previous evening that the American investors had withdrawn their interest.

Cara said, 'I'm so relieved. It's as though all of the pent-up fear drained out of my body when I saw Willow Manor back where it belongs. It wasn't only about the house. If it wasn't restored, we might have lost each other forever.'

George reached for her hand, and said, 'I'm so excited. I can't wait for us to get the keys. I've got an idea that I didn't want to tell you about until we knew Willow Manor was ours again for sure.'

'Oh?' she said.

'How about we open a Tudor Heritage Centre? I've been thinking about it ever since the property first came on the market. It would be perfect for both of us, and also provide the solution to fund the property. You could do your consulting work from here if you want to, and I could get back into poking around in history. Either way, it would be brilliant for both our careers. We can even showcase the *Tudor Kings' Manuscript*.'

Her eyes sparkled. 'What an amazing idea. I love that! But first, look over there.' She pointed in the direction of a man and a dog crossing the manicured lawn. Cara rose from the table and caught George's hand. 'Let's go and say hello to Swifty and Cornelius,' she said, as they strolled out into the sunshine.

THE RUNNER (TWIN FLAMES 3)

Willow Manor, York - Present day

Cara and George walked hand in hand through the lush green gardens of the Willow Manor estate to check out the latest renovations in their new Tudor Heritage Centre.

'Sometimes I can't quite believe this is all ours and we're free to build our dream life,' she said.

George turned to face her and brushed a lock of chestnut hair away from her eyes. 'It's okay to be happy,' he said, pulling her closer and holding her in his arms. 'The struggle is behind us now, my darling. Let's allow ourselves to relax and enjoy it.'

He was right. She hugged him, and they spent a carefree afternoon making plans for the grand opening.

The next morning Cara rose early and went into the library to tackle some boxes of old books. This was her favourite room, and the place where she felt most at home in the old Tudor house. She withdrew one of the faded bound tomes and took a step back to survey the floor-to-ceiling oak shelves laden with books.

Cara blew the dust off the cover, which made her sneeze violently, and then she manoeuvred the heavy tome onto the shelf. Her weight pressed against the wooden frame and a portion of the bookshelf creaked and then swung open to reveal a hidden passage. . .

Continue the adventure with *The Runner* on Amazon

EXCLUSIVE BONUS PROLOGUE

The Forgotten Meeting

Get the exclusive bonus prologue, *The Forgotten Meeting,* and read how it all began for Cara and George.

This is a new chapter I wrote especially for readers who want to know what happened even *before* book one.

www.Rachelhenke.com/subscribe

TWIN FLAMES SERIES

Book 1: Twin Flames

Book 2: The Uprising

Book 3: The Runner

Book 4: The Covenant

ABOUT THE AUTHOR

Rachel dreamt of writing novels since she was a little girl. Always an avid reader of historical romance and fascinated by the mystical and spiritual realms, she discovered Plato's Twin Flame phenomenon, and was inspired to write the first novel in the much-loved time travel romance series: Twin Flames. Cara and George popped into her head and began telling their story of star-crossed soul mates in love for centuries.

If you enjoyed this book, please leave a quick review on Amazon or Goodreads. Thank you.

ACKNOWLEDGMENTS

Special thanks to Russell Cooper for being my brilliant editor and cheerleader. Writing books wouldn't be this much fun without you.

With thanks to Clare Marcus Levy and Iris Ben-Zvi for encouraging me in those memorable early days in the British Council library in Jerusalem.

Thank you to my wonderful Advance Reader Team: Greta Cooper, Anita Davis, Emily Mace, Clare Horrocks, Donna Peerce, Arnica Yuille, and my dear friend, Kim Kaase. You are simply the best.

With love and gratitude to my amazing family and friends.

Printed in Dunstable, United Kingdom

64454049R00201